Over My Live Body

OVER MY LIVE BODY

Susan Israel

THE
STORY PLANT

The Story Plant
Stamford, Connecticut

The Story Plant
Studio Digital CT, LLC
P.O. Box 4331
Stamford, CT 06907

Copyright © 2013 by Susan Israel
Jacket design by Barbara Aronica Buck

Print ISBN-13: 978-1-61188-118-9
E-book ISBN: 978-1-61188-119-6

Visit our website at www.TheStoryPlant.com

First Story Plant Printing: March 2014
Printed in the United States of America

0 9 8 7 6 5 4 3 2 1

ACKNOWLEDGEMENTS

I'd like to thank members of the NYPD for their gracious cooperation and generous assistance, without which I would have felt even more like a rookie describing their world. I'd also like to thank the New York Studio School as well as members of the Yale Police Department.

Special thanks to my editor and publisher Lou Aronica for your vision and suggestions.

Thank you to my family, Bob, Meri, Michael and David, who always have my back, and to my friends who believed in me and this book and kept propelling me forward.

And thank you, Mom, in whose memory I dedicate this novel.

1

IVAN IS USING THE *NEW YORK TIMES* AS A TABLECLOTH AGAIN. I NEVER get to read it anymore without seeing jelly stains, big blobs of coffee, and buttery fingerprints blotting out connecting words, smearing print.

"I wish you wouldn't do that," I tell him. "I have place mats."

"It's my paper." He turns the page and I see crumbs fall on the floor. I hear my mother's voice echo in the kitchen: *You're making more work for me. You never pick up after yourself.* It's my father she's yelling at. I feel like I've flipped back the pages in some history book. My father never responded. I bite my tongue. Ivan is too argumentative lately, too quick to respond and not just with words any more. Silence is better. At least when we're not at each other's throats I can still appreciate what attracted me to him: the looks, the *so-gorgeous-they-ought-to-charge-admission-for-this* looks, looks that could kill. I can't get off on this superficiality any longer; he scares me. The radio commentator droning in the background about some unidentified female homicide victim reminds me why I *should* be scared. I reach for the Metro section to see if there's any mention of it there. Ivan pushes my hand away. "Look at this," he points to something in Section D about bond trading. I scowl and open the refrigerator to get half-and-half for my coffee. The smell of it makes me wince and I pour it down the drain.

"I forgot to tell you," Ivan says. "Someone called you last night before you got home."

"Who?" I remember that I didn't bring my cell phone when I ran out to the store to buy marinara sauce, but Ivan wasn't home then and when I came back he was. A lot can happen in ten minutes.

"He didn't say." The 'he' hums around the room like a menacing insect.

"What did he say?"

Ivan smiles. "Expecting a call, Delilah?"

"What makes you think I am?"

"It's not the first time he's called."

"How am I supposed to know who it is? He didn't leave his name, you said so yourself. It could be anyone. Anyway, why didn't you tell me about this before? And why are you answering my cell phone? I don't answer yours."

"I figured it would all come out in a matter of time."

"What would all come out?"

"The identity of your secret admirer."

"Secret admirer? What are you talking about?" I sip at the black coffee and scowl at him. "You're crazy."

A siren screeches outside. Then another. Somebody downstairs screams. Wandering into whatever mayhem lurks outside would be preferable to dealing with the brutality of Ivan's polite innuendo. I haven't done anything to deserve this. I feel like screaming myself, but the last thing I need is the EMS people, not to mention the police, knocking down the door. *"Hey, lady, lady,"* they would holler, *"are you all right? What's wrong? Why'd you scream?"*

And I'd have to say something like, "Never mind, guys, I'm sorry, he's just shooting accusations at me and they're not even loaded. Too bad you weren't around the other night when he shoved me into the wall."

Yes, too damn bad.

The ringtone of my phone revives me. Shrill even when it's turned to low, it never fails to make me want to dance, but today it's not a happy dance. Ivan's eyebrows shoot up. "There he is now."

I throw a crumpled napkin at him. "Hello?"

There's a lot of static on the line, that and garbled voices in the distance, but no one jumping in to say, "Hi, Delilah." No one saying anything.

"Telemarketer," I announce cheerfully as I hang up.

"Sure." Ivan folds the paper sloppily and puts it to one side as he gets up. "Who'd he ask for?"

"*No* one. No one was on the line. Just a lot of noise. Must have been a bad connection or something like that."

"Yes, something like that."

A vehicle starts up outside, horn blaring, siren wailing, and then pulls away into the gridlock of downtown traffic, the general cacophony of other horns, other sirens. I'm still thinking about bad connections. Ivan gets ready to head out the door. "See you later," he says. I take it as a threat and nod. Let him think he will. If he just simply vanished like the screech of the sirens I wouldn't care; I'd be relieved. I have to be out all day and I've made up my mind that when he comes back tonight, he's not going to be able to get in. I could stay out all night; wouldn't he be surprised. No. He'd more likely suspect I'm with my 'secret admirer.' If I'm lucky, maybe he'll decide he's had enough and pack his things and go, but he's more than likely going to come back after work and lie in wait for me. The best thing for me to do is have a new lock put on the door, so I don't have to worry about that. But first I've got to go to work.

2

IT'S DAMN COLD IN THIS STUDIO. SOMEBODY MUST HAVE LEFT THE WINDOWS open for days to try to air out the smell of turps and they didn't succeed. The cyan fluorescent lighting doesn't warm things up any. I throw each item of clothing that I take off on a folding chair. I'm down to my bra and bikini and, as I undo the hook behind me, I feel another cold breeze waft by, caused by people rushing around getting supplies, cutting through the large studio to get to smaller ones. My nipples harden. I take off the bikini. More people scuttle past me. Then a dark-haired gnome of a man who I assume to be the instructor struts in and surveys the set-up, myself included. He moves a chair here, a piece of drapery there, then gestures to a spot where I should stand, where it feels even colder. "Will somebody please go get a space heater for our model?" he asks. I notice a hint of Eastern European accent in his nasal voice. He has had to notice quite a lot about me to prompt him to request a heater. Most instructors pay little attention. Some even refer to the model as "it." The students are too busy mixing media and trying to outdo each other to treat the model as anything other than a still-life prop; a peach, maybe, or a basket of eggs. This is the way it's supposed to be. I'm not real. This is what I always tell the men in my life.

My pain is real enough. Ten minutes into the pose and I'm hurting. There's a kink in my calf, my leg has fallen asleep, and there's a streak of vermilion on my foot. I rub at it, but it's there to stay, at least until I get home. The only thing that gets paint off skin safely and gently is baby oil, and I don't have any with me. There isn't anything I know of that gets it out of clothes, so I wear grunge going to and from a modeling stint and nothing on the job.

This is something I don't always tell the men in my life. At least not right away. Not until I know them better, get a feel for how they can handle it. Ivan has *never* handled it well. I'm used to it; this is something he also can't handle. I'm usually far more embarrassed by the dirt that sticks to the soles of my feet than by my undressed state.

But not today. This instructor extravagantly draws everyone's attention to me. "Make love to her with your brushes," he urges, his hands imitating a voluptuous sable caress that makes my skin prickle. In the process his hand brushes my bare hip, the bruised one, just a light swipe, but it startles me, this breach of protocol. People who have been wandering in and out stop and watch. Someone in the hall bellows, "Hey, you! You're not supposed to be there. What d'you think this is, a peep show? Get back to work!" I don't know who's being yelled at or who's doing the yelling, but I'm suddenly aware of every pore on my areolae, every pubic hair, every part of me I was brought up to believe should be hidden, and of eyes looking at me, hundreds of eyes, what with people who don't look like they belong here cutting through the place, people who are here to do a bit of carpentry work, perhaps, or fix the wiring, eyes of every color, every shape, sizing me up, thinking libidinous things. I can read them. I feel a sudden chill that doesn't come from the direction of any window. Up to now I've been a nude. Suddenly I'm naked.

During a break, I tiptoe over to my belongings and whip out my phone to check my messages.. All I hear is breathing. My calls-received log lists a number I don't recognize. If I call Ivan and accuse him of checking up on me, he can counter with another accusation that it's my 'secret admirer.'

All I know is during my next break, I'm looking up locksmiths.

3

I'VE GONE FROM POSING IN ONE STUDIO TO POSING IN ANOTHER IN LESS THAN an hour. Ordinarily I don't complain about the cold. I don't move before I'm told to. I try to be the model I've never had the good luck to hire. But today I feel like I'm lugging around a portfolio of hypersensitivity along with my usual artist supplies and it's not even justified; I'm among *friends*.

The instructor of this class has drawn a chalk outline of where I'm supposed to lie and indicates the pose she wants me to strike, that of a classic come-to-my-casbah odalisque. I feel my calf muscles tighten as I scrunch up into the framework of the drawing on the floor. There are no new faces in this class, no surprises; I'll be forgiven if I twitch or scratch an itch. Morgan, one of the best artists and my best friend, has brought poppy seed pound cake and stops what he's doing to tiptoe over and feed me morsels of it. "Should be grapes," the instructor says. Someone down the hall is playing Carmen on a boom box. "Should be Scheherezade," Morgan says, winking at me.

The wink isn't misunderstood, wouldn't be even if Morgan weren't gay.

We artists are like a cast ensemble in repertory. Many of us have seen each other nude in classes. I'm dressed in the part I'm playing. It's when I change locations, freelance in other schools, that I've felt uncomfortable, and I've tried not to do that too often. I try not to, but sometimes I need the money to buy extra supplies or pay off mounting bills and I have to do it, like I did last night. I sometimes say *never again!* What do I need this aggravation for? I feel smarmy; it makes me fight with Ivan more. Except, like a new enrollee in some 12-step program, I'm learning to recognize what I have and haven't the power to change, and ironically, now that I've decided to kick Ivan and his half of the rent money out, I'm going to have to pay more bills than ever, starting with the new lock I'm having installed.

"Delilah, you moved!"

I look down and see my arm and leg protruding from the smeared outline marking where they're supposed to be. "I'm sorry."

"Delilah rarely strays," Morgan says with a smile, holding a pencil up to me to gauge the span of my body stretched out in front of faded brocade. Another artist, Keith, moves in for a closer look, so close that I can smell the eucalyptus cough drop lodged in his cheek that I first thought was an abscess. The others take turns approaching me, walking around me, appraising me with the dispassionate curiosity they would exhibit while looking at a piece on display in a retrospective at the Museum of Modern Art. The instructor, their tour guide, calls attention to my posterior as the center of gravity upon which all else rests. She points to my right shoulder with a well-sharpened Conté crayon and lightly touches it, then moves on to the sole of my right foot. My toes curl. "Notice how the light is distributed here and here, how opalescent these areas seem compared to *this*." I feel the pencil glide along the base of my spine. "I want you to pay attention to these tonal differences in your drawings as if you were painting them, because you will be."

The door bangs open suddenly, unexpectedly; no one

casually walks in and out of this studio. "Phone call down-stairs for Delilah," someone hollers, retreating down the hall.

"She can't come to the phone right now," the instructor bellows back. "Take a message."

"Tell whoever it is I'll call back," I add, "unless it's Ivan." I know it's Ivan.

One of the graphic arts students backs into the studio and looks around furtively, like one more step and she'll be accused of breaking and entering. "He said he'd call back."

"Who was it?"

She shrugs. "Beats me. He didn't say."

"Another member of your burgeoning fan club, Delilah. Maybe someone who's seen your exhibits and wants to buy all your sculptures," Morgan suggests, smudging the charcoal on the page with the heel of his hand.

"I wish."

"Hey, you never know."

I know it was Ivan on the phone. He's the only person who has ever called me here. I can feel his heavy-breathing impatience wafting all the way up from Wall Street. He knows a call from him will unsettle me, make me put my clothes on to rush to the phone at the very least and not be able to get back into the right pose and the right mood afterwards. He gets off on this. I'm not taking any calls until I'm through for the day.

"Delilah!" someone else calls. "Telephone!"

"Jesus, again? Doesn't he take a hint?"

"It's okay, take a five minute break, you're marked," the instructor says as I scramble to my feet clumsily. I grab a blue-and-white pin-striped man's shirt from the back of Morgan's easel and throw it on and pad down the cold corridor and down the stairs, pulling the shirt closed around me, grumbling, steeling myself for what I have to say to him, and that is, "Leave me alone!"

"Is that any way to answer the phone?"

I look down at the way I'm dressed. Is that any way to answer the phone? "Who *is* this?" It's not Ivan's voice. He's the only person who has ever called me here, but it's not him. Someone he put up to calling me, though, I'm sure of it, one of his co-workers wearing an oxford shirt not unlike the one that I've got wrapped around me like a toga, only stiff, as if starched, and buttoned down. "Get him to come to the phone."

"You don't want to talk to anyone else," the voice declares. "It's *me* you want."

"No, I don't."

"Don't say that!" the voice snaps. "You do. At least you will."

The receiver nearly slips out of my hand. "Who *is* this?" I hear static in the background and several muffled voices and then nothing. I'm still holding the receiver when Morgan comes looking for me. "They want you back up there." He takes a good look at me. "Are you okay? Who was that?"

I shrug. "I don't know."

"You don't know if you're okay or you don't know who it was?"

"Both."

The instructor yells down the stairs, "Delilah, you're off the phone. Good. Hurry up, we want your body."

Morgan puts his hand on my shoulder. "Want a Snapple?" I nod. He retreats to the kitchen, to the well-stocked refrigerator. His lover is a gourmet Italian chef in an uptown trattoria. On a good day, my stomach might growl at the thought of the array of goodies meticulously stored in those labeled Tupperware containers, but right now I'm feeling slightly queasy. *Someone called you last night before you got home. It's not the first time he's called.* Morgan reappears with a raspberry iced tea. I chug-a-lug it. "Thanks," I say, handing him the nearly empty bottle. "I needed that."

"Guess you did. What's going on, exactly?"

"I'm not sure, exactly. That was a guy I don't even know telling me I want him. Ivan told me someone's called me and didn't leave a name. My bad for leaving my cell phone where he can get it. It's probably coincidence. Can't be the same person. Anyway, I'm not even sure if I can trust Ivan's account of things. He might have set someone up to make that call. I wouldn't put anything past him now."

"Threatening phone calls. There seems to be a lot of that going around."

"What do you mean?"

"Vittorio got a couple. Something to do with work conflicts. He changed his schedule so he could be free for our anniversary party Saturday night. Remember when you ate with us at the restaurant last week and he excused himself to talk to the manager? Well, someone apparently didn't like it, said he'd be sorry. Sounded like a scene from a Fellini film. You should've heard. *Mamma mia!* Anyway, he shrugged it off as nuisance calls." He finishes off the tea. "Yours don't seem like nuisance calls."

"It's just one phone call, Morgan."

"Did you report it?"

I shake my head. "Did Vittorio report his nuisance calls?"

"He talked to somebody in *Italiano.* I don't know who. Probably the head chef. I think you should be talking to the police. Especially after what Ivan did to you the other night. Did you report *that?*"

"It was just a little shove." I walk back upstairs to the studio. I'm starting to feel guilty for holding up the works.

"A little shove that made you look like you fell down a flight of stairs."

"It shoved me into action, Morgan, that's good enough. I'm changing the locks on him as of this afternoon. A locksmith's coming at four. Before he comes back from Wall Street. He won't hurt me," I lick my lips. "I don't think."

"What are you going to do if the locksmith doesn't show?"

Morgan frowns. "Go back there and act like nothing's wrong?"

"I'll call Sachi to see if I can crash on her couch. "

Morgan snorts. "Have you ever been able to reach Sachi when you need her?" *Noooo.* I shake my head. *"Cara,* if you're in a pinch, you can spend the night at *our* place."

"Thanks." I peel off the shirt and watch as everybody's attention focuses on The Bruise. Morgan winces. "Men!" he says, and rolls his eyes, "They're such beasts!"

4

"IF YOU WAS MY GIRLFRIEND, I'D WANT YOU TO HAVE THIS LOCK HERE."
The locksmith holds up a piece of unwieldy hardware with a
bar running through it that looks like a smaller version of the
bike lock I've seen linked on the fence in front of my building. For the last few days it's been minus the bike. The locksmith babbles on about the difference between vertical and
horizontal deadbolts, and I'm too tired to appreciate any of
the details until he gets to the prices.

"I'm not your girlfriend," I remind him, "and I can't afford
this lock here. Or that lock there, for that matter. What do
you have that's cheaper?"

"I thought you was worried about someone breaking in."

"I am," I say, "but I'm also practically broke. So what can
you do for me?"

"Well, I can put on another rim lock between the one you
got here and the chain. It's not going to cost you as much,
and it'll give you a little more security. Say I'm someone who
wants to break in and I see all these locks you got here. I'm
probably not gonna be able to take the time to figure which
one goes which way or want to make a lot of noise kicking
the door down. But then there's always someone who might.
You want it or what?"

"Yeah, sure," I yawn. "Put it on."

I take a quick tour of the apartment while the locksmith is yanking tools out of his box. It looks the way I left it earlier: the same chipped coffee cups are still in the sink, the newspaper with its buttery fingerprints folded sloppily on the chair. The bed looks like it was sat on since I left. Trust Ivan not to tidy up after himself. I give the coverlet a yank to make it smoother, as if that's all I have to do to remove evidence of him ever having been here. He's not here now; that's all that matters. I made sure he wouldn't be. I called his extension at work and hung up on him. Now I look at my cell phone. On cue the voice mail alert chimes.

"Well, are you gonna play that thing back or stare at it all day?"

I jump. "Are you going to install the lock or stare at me all day?"

"Touchy!" He throws a piece of hardware on the floor. "Hey, you never know who it could be. Could be Hollywood calling." He picks a hand drill out of his tool kit and starts to make holes in the wood under the chain lock. The drill almost but not quite drowns out my cell phone. I can't not answer it. What I really feel like doing is throwing it through the window. What does he want this time?

But it's not a he this time, it's a she, someone who introduces herself as Heidi Obermeyer calling from the place I worked this morning. "Ah know this is short notice. You came *hahly* recommended and ah wondered if you'd be free ta work for mah late afternoon class today. It starts in an hour."

The Southern drawl takes me back to a long-ago home and I find myself slipping into it, saying, "Sure ah...I will," without thinking about how much I hated yesterday's class, the letchy professor with the probing fingers, the beady-eyed students, the men who were at liberty to walk in and out of the room while they worked on overhead wiring. I hope that Heidi Obermeyer is teaching this class, not just doing the hiring for someone else. "*Mah* class meets at the *East* Side location," she adds, and gives me the exact address, immediately putting my fear to rest. Being a woman, being a *Southerner,* she'll insist on more decorum, making sure I feel at home. *Oh, the sun shines bright on my old Kentucky home.* The sound of her voice sure suckered me into taking this job. It even made me forget the hassle of getting an uptown bus on Third Avenue during rush hour and that it's going to be nearly dark when I get to my destination and a whole lot darker when it's time to go home.

But it's not like I can afford to blow off many jobs anyway. I've already rationalized that I can't. Not even the ones that are dangerous to get to and from. Not even the ones that I hate.

The locksmith shrugs and turns back to his work when he hears the click of the receiver. I wonder if he gets paid by the hour. He's been here half the day already, or maybe it just seems that way because I was up all night. Now he's on the other side of the door, holding it open with his foot, securing the lock plate, screwing it on tight. "I guess I don't have to tell you how this works, since you got another one just like it, but this one's new, it's gonna feel stiffer at first. Want to try it?"

"I will when you leave."

"That'll be fifty bucks."

"What? I thought you said…"

"Flat fifteen-dollar fee for the house call and labor included."

"You'll take a check, right?"

"Yeah. But I think I better warn you there's a twenty-five dollar surcharge for returned checks."

I scrawl out the amount hurriedly and slap the check in front of him. "No bounce, see?"

"I need your address and phone number under your name

there. And I've got to write your driver's license number too. That is, if you got a driver's license?"

I dig deep in my wallet for it and hand it over. "It's slightly expired. I don't live in Kentucky any more."

"How about a credit card. You got one that's not maxed out, by any chance?"

I dig deeper for my Visa. He laughs as he scribbles the information. He takes the check and almost forgets to hand back the license—I have to grab it from him. He gestures at his handiwork as he leaves. "Don't forget to lock the door."

5

Heidi Obermeyer may sound like a Southern belle on the phone, but in person she's pure punk. She greets me at the door wearing a skin-tight black velveteen dress that's shorter than the shortest shorts I've ever seen. She's from Texas, hasn't lived there in "oh-ah-can't-tell-you-*how*-long," and the accent resurfaced after she had her tongue pierced "because raght afterwards it hurt *sooo* much to talk lahk a Yankee." Her hair glows purple under the klieg lights she's set up in the classroom. She's hired another model too, a male who's off in the corner wearing a terry cloth robe, sipping espresso. I recognize him. I've used him as a model myself. I turn my back to the window and start to undress. A couple of students say "Hi." I don't know if they remember me from other classes or they're just being friendly. I say "Hi" back.

"What ah want the two of you to do is reenact some Bible scenes," Heidi suggests airily, fondling the crucifix dangling between her nascent breasts. "Be as inventive as you lahk. Ah lahk my students to have fun."

So for the next two hours I'm Eve being banished from the Garden of Eden, I'm the Virgin Mary receiving news from the angel Gabriel, I'm Lot's wife looking over her shoulder for all eternity—or what seems to be—because Heidi is not very good about giving us breaks on time. I've calmed down a lot since I walked into the studio; I'm not shaking any more, not even from the cold. The improvisations absorb me. I find myself getting into each incarnation more and more. So are the students. They're lapping up every minute of the blasphemy they're committing and grinning like Cheshire cats as they put the finishing whorls on their last drawing of the evening. And Heidi Obermeyer seems to be enjoying it most of all. She thanks me profusely after I've dressed, as I'm heading for the door, and asks me back for next week. She's a real work of art herself, the downtown variety. She fidgets a lot with her hair, her clothes, her jewelry. Right now she's running her fingers through her purple frosted hair, pulling it back and up, revealing her earrings—gold bullets with black tips that make them look like they've been dipped in dark chocolate.

6

"EXCUSE ME."

I look up, annoyed. There's no way I can be in anyone's way, scrunched up as I am in this seat near the back of the bus. There's hardly anyone on board now. I expect it to be some street beggar who's going to try to shake me down for spare change; they're everywhere now, even on mass transit. The mayor's pledge to clean up the streets has only made them pop up and multiply in other places, like random phantoms in a computer game gone amok.

I look up at him. He's staring at me. This is no street beggar, just some guy wearing a Grateful Dead T-shirt and indigo jeans splotched with white blobs that stand out much more than he does. "What do you want?"

"Oh...I'm sorry," he mumbles. "I thought you were somebody..."

I am somebody.

"...somebody I knew. You look familiar." He hoists a dirty green backpack and slings it over his shoulder, nearly hitting me with it. "Sorry."

"It's okay."

He sits splay-legged across from me and stares. I turn around and look out the window at the flash of brightly lit storefronts along Seventh Avenue. I must look familiar to quite a lot of people. I wonder how many people in this city have drawn or painted or sculpted me over the last two and a half years, uptown, downtown, all around the town. And across the river even. Hundreds. How many people have seen me nude, contorted this way or that, plus or minus five pounds, with and without a tan. Maybe this slightly strung-out looking guy is one of them; he could very easily be one of them. I'd never recognize him, but surely he would recognize me, especially if he'd seen all of me. How many guys who smile at me on the street are smiling knowingly or just because they'd like to know me?

I wonder if this guy has a sketch book in that grungy backpack, if there are pictures he's drawn of me in there. How many pictures of me *are* out there, and where are they? Are there some yellowed and curled, stored in the back of some struggling artist's newsprint pad with all the other sketches of all the other models he or she has ever drawn, or matted and framed and displayed in a hallway or study or bedroom?

That was Ivan's take on it. One man's 'fine art' is another man's jerk-off material.

I shrug it off. Ivan has made me paranoid. With just cause. *You're not going to brush me off that easily.* It's not like I wasn't warned a few nights ago.

The next stop is mine. I go down the three stairs at the exit and have to give the door a shove to make it open. The brisk air sends a chill up my spine. I turn down the corner at Waverly Place and go up the steps leading to my building, sidestepping the concrete flowerpot on the top stoop as I fumble for my keys. The minute I've unlocked the second door, the one with the beveled glass window you can't see through, and step inside, I know I'm in trouble. Someone vaults down the stairs two at a time and grabs my arm. Anyone in the building would recognize him immediately and not question what he was doing here, and he knows it. No one else would suspect what I might be in for. He looks so upstanding. He could have been waiting here for hours in his jeans and Brooks Brothers shirt and no one would think anything of it. He probably was. "I want *in*, Delilah." Ivan's voice is a deep guttural growl.

I try to pry his hand off me. "No!"

"Come on, I'm not going to hurt you. I just want my things."

"Where are you going to put all that stuff? Are you going to carry it? I don't think so."

"I've got my car parked a few blocks away. I'll go get it now so I can load the stuff in the trunk."

"I don't believe you."

He pokes the cleft in my chin with the tip of his index finger the way I poke cookie dough to see if it's done. "You're going to have to let me in when I get back, Delilah."

And then he turns around to go; miraculously he's gone without following me up the stairs, without trying to push his way into the apartment. I'm not used to the new lock. I drop my keys twice before I manage to get the door open and when I do, I slam it behind me. I don't even bother to turn on the lights. I dig my phone out of my bag and try to read the number of the local police precinct that I wrote in small block print on a message pad stuck on the refrigerator door. I press 7-4-1, then start fumbling. I get the wrong number twice. I press one number too many. I flick on the light and try again, poking each number with breathtaking accuracy.

"Sixth Precinct." The voice could be male or female, but couldn't be flatter. I wonder if it's on a machine recording. I wait a few seconds. No beep. "Hello? Is anyone there?" The voice sounds animated this time, animated and annoyed, and this isn't the best way to appeal for help.

I take a deep breath so I won't ramble. I already hear the downstairs door open again. *There's no way he could have got-*

ten his car that fast. "Could you send someone over to my place right away?" I tell where I am.

"What's the problem there?"

"Delilah, let me in, goddamn it!"

I pick up the phone and walk with it so that the banging on the door is audible to the NYPD android on the phone. "Someone's trying to get into my apartment."

"Do you know the party? Is he armed?"

"Yes, I *do* know him and no, I don't think he is, not the way you mean. But he has two arms, and I'm afraid of how he's going to use them if he gets in."

The voice repeats my address mechanically and I confirm it. "Please hurry." I implore. *"Please?"*

"Delilah, cut the crap and open this goddamn door now. I'm warning you. For your own good."

"Or else what?" I shout through the door. "What can you do to me if I don't let you in. Nothing. Whereas if I do..."

"Delilah, what you're doing is illegal. Some of my possessions are in there. I have a right to get them. If you don't let me in, you could be arrested for criminal lockout when the police get here."

"I could be what?"

"If I decided I wanted to press charges."

"You called the police?"

"But I really wouldn't want it to come to that. Come on now, let me in before they come so there won't be any trouble." The door rattles incessantly. The vibration of the chain lock makes good accompaniment for my jangled nerves. "Delilah, open the fucking door!"

"No! I don't want you in here. I don't want to be alone with you."

"Well then, you won't be. The police should be here any minute."

"I hope so," I shout. "That's what they told me too."

"What? *You* called the police?" The rattling finally stops.

"Well, they're here. Now will you please open the goddamn door before you get yourself in a shitload of trouble?"

"Not until I hear you let them in. Stop bullshitting me."

"I left the door open for them. I'm considerate. Look, Delilah, for the last time..."

I hear the muffled squawk of a two-way radio in the hall.

"Too late, Delilah. I tried."

My fingers slide the chain lock and fidget with the new rim lock and my hand sweats all over the doorknob as I turn it. There are two uniformed officers on the landing right below. Ivan speaks *sotto voce* to them and turns around to point up. They trudge up the eight stairs and suddenly I'm craning my neck to look up at them and feel on the defensive. "We received a complaint phoned in from this address," one of the officers says.

"Actually two complaints," adds the other.

"Yes, that's right," Ivan and I say, glaring at each other.

"You both called in complaints."

"Yes, probably at the..."

"Same time." Ivan takes a few steps closer, and I move to the right of the officer standing across from me.

The officers look at each other and then back at me. "This your boyfriend, Miss?"

"Not any more."

"He just told us he had some things in there that you wouldn't give him access to. Were you two cohabiting?"

"Did you give him a set of keys so that he had free access to the building?"

"Sir, do you receive any mail at this address?"

"Excuse me," I rap on the door jamb behind me. "But aren't either of you going to ask why I wouldn't let him in?"

"We had a lover's quarrel a few nights ago," Ivan says with a shrug. "No big deal."

"Aces. And I still have the bruise to show for it."

"She jumped backward and tripped."

"He pushed me into the wall. Hard."

The taller of the two officers turns his back on Ivan and gestures for me to follow him down the stairs. He stops me halfway. "Sit down. Relax. I just want to ask you a couple of questions." He sits two steps up from me and smiles a tired smile, like he already knows my answers will be the same ones he's heard a hundred times before. I glance down at the name tag pinned on his pocket. VINSON. I recite it silently and think of a word that sounds like it so I'll remember it if I ever need to call the police again. "Did you call us to file a complaint about the other night?"

"No."

"Did you tell him to get out then?"

"No."

"So when *did* you tell him to *vamoose*?"

"I had the lock changed just today."

"Did you tell him you were going to do this so he could clear out?"

"I was afraid to tell him. I didn't think he'd leave if I told him beforehand. As it was, I had enough of a time scheduling the lock change for when he wouldn't be here. He was here around lunchtime. I called to check my messages and he picked up. Wouldn't say anything, but..."

"Delilah, what are you talking about?"

"Why didn't you say anything when I called earlier?"

"Because I couldn't. I wasn't here. I haven't been since this morning. I just got here about a half hour before you did and waited on the stairs."

"Liar," I snarl at him.

"Must have been another of your bad connections," he says with a shrug.

"Look," Officer Vinson appeals to me, "you're going to have to let him in to get his things. Officer Coolidge and I will be right here and make sure he just goes about his business and then leaves; nothing will happen to you, all right?"

I shrug. "I won't be alone with him?"

"We'll be right here."

"You heard that?" I glare at Ivan as I open the door.

"Loud and clear. I've got to go move my car so I can put the stuff in my trunk. Okay if I double-park out there?"

"We're not going to ticket you, but there's no guarantee someone else won't."

"Well, can one of you watch my car while I'm packing stuff in here?"

I feel a chill go up my spine.

"Absolutely not," Officer Vinson snaps at him. "Where do you think you are, the Water Club having a five course meal? We're not providing valet service. Just hurry it up and leave."

Officer Coolidge mumbles something about a "clothes job" into the radio mike clipped to the lapel of his jacket. I step aside to let the two officers in, but they stay by the door. Officer Coolidge keeps looking over his shoulder anticipating Ivan's return. Officer Vinson looks at the array of locks on the door, then at me. "This the first time you've changed the locks on him?"

"First and last," I say. "He's not getting in here again."

His grimace tells me he's not buying it; he's seen this program rerun so many times he knows all the lines by heart. When I hear the front door crash against the back stop, I flinch. Someone gallops up the stairs, and judging from the gait it's not my next-door neighbor Mrs. Davidoff. Ivan barges past the two policemen carrying a corrugated cardboard box and drops it at my feet, then sets to work gathering his things. He darts from closet to closet to CD tree. Watching his choreography is dizzying. Just as he comes back from the bedroom, my voice mail chimes, an audible exclamation mark. "Looks like we're all going to hear your messages, whether you want us to or not," he says with a smirk. He looks over my shoulder at the two policemen. "She's a popular girl."

"I have nothing to hide," I retort. "I'm putting this on speaker phone."

"Hey, Delilah," Sachi's voice echoes through the room. "Did you kick the bastard out yet? I *hope* so. I've left Parsons for the day. Call me later if you need me."

Ivan stops in his tracks and leers at me.

Beep.

The second call is a click. Ivan chuckles.

I back up to where Officer Vinson is standing. "I've been getting a lot of hang-ups lately," I explain.

"You've become an expert on hang-ups, Delilah," Ivan says, stretching his arm behind the desk to unplug the stereo.

Beep.

The third call is a click.

The *fourth* call is a click.

Beep.

Officer Vinson shifts the gum he's been chewing from one side of his mouth to the other with an audible snap.

"You look good without your clothes on," a male voice suddenly snarls. It's muffled, but sounds familiar. So does the screech of static that follows. I gasp and back into Officer Vinson. He gently shoves me aside. The two officers approach my cell phone tentatively like they expect a suspect to pop out of it, but only a voice does. "You look good with them on too, but not half as good as you do naked. And I like the way you look at me when you're doing that slow strip of yours, like you're doing it just for me. One of these days, you will be, Delilah. Now that you finally dumped that tightass, it'll be sooner than you think. I can't wait."

Beep.

Ivan's face turns the color of the plaster I cast figures in. "Delilah, who *is* that?"

"I...I don't know," I stammer.

"That's not the first time he's called." Ivan says. "I've heard that voice before. I'm pretty sure he's the one who called your cell phone." Ivan gives me a you-know-what-I-mean look, then looks over my shoulder at the officers and his face gets all crinkly with concern. This is his big chance to prove to them he's not the bad guy. "I told her to report these calls and she didn't take me seriously. Maybe now she will."

"You spoke with him when he called?"

"Several times over the last week or so."

"Why were you answering my phone," I interject.

"What did he say?" Vinson asks, ignoring me.

"I began to get the sense that they...he and Delilah...were maybe more than casual acquaintances. Nothing he said, per se. But he sounded...urgent. Yeah, urgent, like it was of paramount importance that he speak with her. When I told her someone called, I teased her, said it was a secret admirer and she went into her big denial act, so I assumed it was more likely a *not*-so-secret admirer."

Officer Coolidge alternately taps his knuckles on the metal back of a kitchen chair and looks at his watch. I turn to Officer Vinson and clear my throat. "I think he called me at work early this afternoon. I got a weird call. I thought it was *him* at first because he's the only one who's ever called me there." I point to Ivan. "But it turned out not to be."

"You don't know who it was?"

I shake my head vehemently.

"Well, he knows who *you* are," Officer Vinson says. "He knows your name and where you can be reached. This fellow here who you're so terrified of is telling us this guy called you at home before; now you're saying you *think* he called you at work. That, and he's maybe the same one who's been calling and hanging up on you in between. Did you report any of this to us?

"No."

Officer Vinson looks skyward. "Well, if it happens again, I suggest you do. It helps to establish a paper trail of incidents like this just in case."

"Just in case of what?" Officer Vinson is starting to scare me more than the phone calls.

But not as much as Ivan. He edges closer and closer and suddenly drapes his arm around me. "I think you should have someone stay with you for a couple of days," Ivan suggests huskily. "Make sure this nut doesn't get any closer."

I shake him off with a well-placed elbow jab to the ribs. "It sure as hell won't be you."

"Hey," Officer Vinson taps his shoulder. "Keep your distance from her, okay?"

Ivan brushes him off. "Maybe Sachi will," he suggests. "Call her."

"I will."

"Now. I don't like the idea of you staying alone while this is going on."

"When you leave."

The two policemen are taking this all in, drinking it up like their evening coffee served light with lots of sugar. "Are you almost through over there?" Officer Vinson gestures toward the half-filled box near the stereo. Ivan turns around and looks surprised to see it, then smiles ruefully. "I just have a few more things to throw in," he says. "You guys must have more important things to do than to stand around and watch me pack." He turns back to me. "She'll call you if she needs you. I think we'll be all right now."

Oh no, we won't.

"We'll stay until you're through," Officer Vinson says, "and hurry it up." He gives me a look though that makes me feel like I've been shot. *You're worried about this guy? He could be one of us, a member of New York's finest.* Both officers look bored. Officer Coolidge yawns and wipes a tear away from the corner of his eye. Officer Vinson turns to me again. "Just a word of advice. You ought to think about pulling the shades if you're parading around naked in here. You never know who can see in. You don't want the whole world to see you in your birthday suit, do you?"

Ivan burns me with one of his smart-ass stares. *If they only knew.* All he says is, "That's the last of it, I think."

I wheel around defensively as he approaches me, the box tucked under his arm. A lavender sleeve hangs out of it. "You think! Take another look around while you've got the chance."

He puts the box down and steps toward me. "Delilah..."

Officer Vinson deftly moves forward, ready to yank Ivan by the collar if he gets any closer. He immediately retreats and smiles sheepishly. *See what a good guy I am?* His face hardens again as he turns back to me. "If you get any more calls or messages like that..."

"I'll call them." I gesture to the two officers.

"And if you *do* get any messages like that again, save them," Officer Vinson adds tersely.

The three men go down the stairs talking so amiably that I half-expect that when they get outside they'll keep it up, maybe even over doughnuts. I watch from the window. Ivan pulls something out from under his windshield wiper. The two officers haven't left yet; they loiter beside the cruiser a few minutes waiting for Ivan to pull out ahead of them before getting in and taking off. The minute they're gone, the minute the street is quiet and dark, the first thing I do is pull the shades. Then my phone rings.

7

"SOMEONE'S WATCHING YOU."

"That's what the police think," I tell Sachi. I don't want to think about someone watching me.

What I expect from Sachi next is a lot of tell-me-everything questions. She likes to be in the know. What I'd like to know is how could she set me up for more trouble by leaving a voice mail message like that without knowing what's going on. But I don't get to say any more because what *she* says is, "They're on the second shelf, next to the whipped cream."

"Huh?" I suddenly realize she's not alone. I hear a male voice in the background. This is a new development. When she left for the Cape last weekend, she was groaning about the dearth of men in her life. I haven't been able to reach her since, not until now. *No wonder.* I can't make out what he's saying in the background, but what this is saying to me is that this isn't a very good time to suggest a pajama party. Chances are that they're not wearing any. "Anyway, Ivan's got all his stuff out of here now, so *he* shouldn't be bothering me any more, and I'm not sure *what* the phone call business is all about, but it's just phone calls, you know?" Sachi doesn't say anything, and I wonder if it's because she's contemplating what I'm saying or her lips are sealed, as in *with a kiss.* "I'm going to work in my studio tomorrow," I tell her. "Tomorrow's Saturday, right? I'll probably be there around ten. I'll call you sometime after that."

"I gotta go. You be sure to call me if you need me," she gasps before abruptly hanging up.

I'll be sure to get no answer if I do.

I turn off the light. Even with the shades drawn, someone might be able to see my silhouette as I strip off my clothes, not slowly either, not tonight. I climb into bed and pat down the rumpled sheets. There's still an indentation in the bed marking the last time Ivan slept here, and I can smell him. I'm lying here aching from the sudden shock of physical withdrawal, and my lower body is screeching *I-want-him, oh God, how-I-want-him*. It's only his extremities I really want, his fingers rambling all over me, his legs entangled with mine as he thrusts deep inside me at first slowly, then fast, then faster. I crave the feeling of him on top of me, under me, side by side, the false sense of security that only a male body would provide right now and only to get me through the night. Great sex is the glue that bonds some people who would be better off being separate pieces. The only thing that's going to put out my lights tonight is great sex, damn it, and the only way I'm going to have any is with what my college friends and I used to obliquely refer to when we were horny and boyfriendless as "Mr. Hand." My fingers slide down between my thighs. Then the cell phone rings. I don't answer.

8

PUMMELING COOL CLAY FLESH ONTO A TWISTED METAL SKELETON RELEASES
my pent up frustration better than anything else I've ever
tried. I don't even want to stop long enough to take a sip of
lukewarm coffee. Nobody else is here yet, no one except for
Louise, the front desk receptionist, who looked at me funny
when I strutted in and said, "Boy, you're early." The armatures lined up like soldiers in the studio border a new front
facing the wall, behind which are winding alleys and tiny
backyards. Sometimes I'm envious of painters like Morgan
who have upstairs studios with windows that look out on
the multicolor town houses that make MacDougal Alley look
like a row of petits fours. But I know I would find it distract-
ing day after day, particularly on bad days when the work
isn't going well. "Makes you feel like jumping out," Morgan
once told me, and I believe him. I have nothing to show for
my efforts yet except terra cotta stains on my hands from
kneading clay into the metal grooves of the armature. It looks
like dried blood. I wipe them off on an old shirt and look at
my watch.

There were several messages tacked to the bulletin board
behind the coffee stand when I came in and I grabbed the
ones with my name on them and put them on the work table.

I notice that there's a wad of notes there, clipped together like dollar bills. I spread them out in front of me. There's a work assignment for Monday just a few blocks from here, another one Tuesday night in Brooklyn, there's a message from Morgan that he wrote out himself reminding me *again* that I'm invited to his loft later this evening for a dinner Vittorio is preparing for their anniversary, and then there's the one I've been waiting for, the biggie, confirming the December 1 date for my exhibition on Lafayette Street. My stomach feels like it's fallen into a sinkhole. I can't believe how far behind I am in my work. I glance at the other messages. Nothing from Sachi. There are two from Ivan telling me I can call him if I need him, if I get any more of 'those calls,' as if he knows I will. My palms start to sweat. At the bottom of the pile are four memos informing me only that a big question mark telephoned and will call again later. *He won't leave his name,* the receptionist scrawled in bold black ink.

I yank a clump of clay from the armature and knead it in my hands until it takes on the form of a misshapen head. I shoot at it with a neon-green water pistol and throw it on the floor and stomp on it, pick it up, throw it down, stomp on it again.

"Yeeeeeow!"

I grab a razor knife from the work table behind me and whirl around. Morgan shakes his head at me. "Hey, Delilah, I thought you swore off the high octane stuff and switched to decaf."

I throw the knife on the floor too. "What I *need* is one-hundred proof!"

"In that case, I guess we can count on you to bring the booze tonight. You *are* coming, aren't you?"

"Vittorio straightened out his work conflict?"

"He'll be there with us, cara. He assured me in his own inimitable way. This will be a feast to die for."

I show Morgan the most important message in the pile.

"Look at this. My 'Rome in One Day' exhibit's been moved *up*. I'm going to have to work more than seven days to finish it. More like forty days and forty nights"

"Starting tomorrow. You've simply *got* to come to our dinner party, Delilah."

"Okay," I agree. My stomach, when it crawls out of that sinkhole, will still need to be filled. "I might be a little late..."

"Don't be *too* late. The food might be more than a little gone."

"You want red wine or white?"

"Something that snaps, crackles, and pops and I don't mean cereal. It's our anniversary."

I bend down to pick up the knife I dropped. Morgan pauses at the doorway and points at it. "Why'd you grab *that* when I came in?"

"I thought I was alone in here. I got scared."

"I scared you? Poor baby." Morgan comes over and wraps his long skinny arms around me and gives me a quick hug. It feels good but makes me want the kind of comforting I'd never get from Morgan. I flush when I think of last night, when I think of how I fantasized about Ivan being with me only after I knew he was gone and I was 'safe.' *As if the devil I know is safer than the devil I don't.*

"I'm okay now," I say. If I say it enough, maybe I really will be okay. Morgan seems convinced. He gives me a quick kiss and a wave. "See you at eightish," he says, and he's off. I'm left picking up the head of what's going to be a Vestal Virgin and reshaping it. The clay feels cool and is more malleable. I get the same pleasure out of molding it that a Kentucky farm wife would from kneading dough to make high-rise bread. And hopefully from this exhibit I'll get some recognition—that and, of course, a few bucks. That would please me immeasurably. The school isn't pressuring me to accomplish this at breakneck speed; I'm on my own autobahn here. I asked for this, now I've got to deliver. And it's not like I can suddenly quit modeling so that I can concentrate solely on this. I can't afford to.

I hear the thumps of footsteps as more and more people start drifting in to do a morning of independent work. A couple of other sculptors come into the central work area and skitter around me to gather work supplies. They're acting like dogs sniffing the scene out and trying to decide if I'm friendly or likely to bite their heads off if they come too close. One of them is dragging along scraps of sheet metal. The other, a gangly blond girl, is carrying a big black boom box. The sight of it makes me cringe. The school prides itself on breeding cooperation between artists. It doesn't always work out that way. I force a smile at these two and they nod in response and set up a distance away from me and each other at the other end of the studio. The blond suddenly bends down and hits the play button on the boom box. The 'music' that blasts out of the speakers sounds like the muffled screams of a person put through the wash cycle.

There is no way I can listen to this and work. There is no way I'd ever want to listen to this, period.

"Excuse me," I shout loud enough, hopefully, to be heard. "I really can't concentrate with *that* going. Don't you have an iPod?"

"I did, but it was stolen," the girl shrugs. "So I have this. Is that a problem?"

"Yes!"

The two girls look at each other. I know what they're thinking. *We got a real bitch here, sister.* "Here, I'll turn it down," the blond grumbles.

"Turn it *off.*"

"That's better," the blond says after barely touching the volume dial.

I throw a new lump of clay on the floor, strut over to the other end of the room, lean over and click the on/off switch. "*That's* better," I say.

The music stays off for about five seconds. No sooner am I back at my work table picking up clay than the CD is turned back on to spin and dry.

I need some air.

The vestibule between the two entrance doors leading into the building is where most students and instructors go to have a cigarette. The small area is empty right now, but the concentration of smoke would make a person who's not in the know yell, "Fire!" I open the door. I'm about to step out onto the sidewalk when what feels like a wall suddenly walks into me. He must have been standing just to the right and about to come in when I opened the door. He's rock solid. I still feel the impact after stepping back and looking him over. "Can I see stuff on exhibit here?" he asks.

"There's a student show," I tell him, pointing behind me. "You go up the stairs and it's hung in rooms to your left and right. But you can't go anywhere else in the building."

"Are *you* on display?"

"No, none of my stuff is here. I'm having my own show...uh, later." This guy is staring at me from under the brim of a dirty blue baseball cap. His eyes are grubby blue too; the shadow from the brim makes his irises look like they're flecked with soot. He waves a crumpled newspaper in his hand, folded to the Arts and Leisure section. Probably a wannabe. Practically everyone I've met visiting student exhibits are students, their families and significant others and wannabes. He's looking at me the way the guy on the bus did last night. I turn away from him to unlock the door. *How many people have seen me nude?* I'm getting too paranoid.

"Is it going to be written up? I look in the paper for announcements of art exhibits all the time. I'll look for an announcement of your show."

"Well, actually it's not going to be here. It'll be down in a loft in Soho. You're more likely to see fliers than write-ups."

"I'd still like to see it. I'm Curt," he says, and he's not kidding; the name suits him to an oversized tee. "That's short for Curtis." He extends his hand and I give it a quick shake and let go, wiping my hand on my coverall.

He leans in closer, waiting for me to reciprocate, tell him *my* name. I back away "Curtis what?"

He ignores that part. As I turn and go back in, he follows me up the small circular staircase past a sculpture that looks like a shrunken head. "This guy's here to see the exhibit," I say to the receptionist.

"You can just go in these rooms here," I hear her tell him. I walk over to the coffee station to pour myself a cup to steel myself for another confrontation with the shrews and have to sidestep Curtis no-last-name to head back to the clay room. He's looking all around and not just at the paintings.

"Could you, uh, go out for coffee with me and talk?"

"You mean, now? No, I can't. I'm way behind in my work. And besides," I hold up the cup I'm holding onto for dear life, "I've already got coffee." *And it's sloshing over the rim and burning me. Get lost, jerk.* "Sorry." I force a smile and turn my back to him.

The desk receptionist is watching him. "A fan?"

"A follower of the arts." I shrug and close the door to the clay studio behind me. There is no sign of the babes with the boom box; I figure that while I was gone they must have moved on to the welding room to listen to and play with heavy metal in more appropriate surroundings. I pick up the lump of clay I dropped on the floor, shoot more water at it to make it softer, and poke it around the clay I've already mashed around the armature's metal skull with a wooden spatula. No sooner do I build than I subtract. Sculpture is as much the art of what is taken away as what remains. All I need to represent is what is basic, what is essential. Little gobs of clay pelt the floor around my feet one after the other, making it seem like it's raining terra cotta. I'm beginning to see something slowly spring to life here. My heart races. I pick out more clay with the sharp edge of my tool and hold my breath. Then I use the flat edge to smooth out the plane of what is shaping up to look not so much like a vigilant keeper of the flame but rather a mask of horror dating back well over a thousand years.

I take a step back. *Yeah, I'm getting somewhere.* But not nearly far enough or fast enough. I've got to quit for now. I'm hungry and anyway I can't do too much in one session. The quality of the work might suffer. I pick up the water pistol and blast the entire figure—what I've done of it so far—until it's fully saturated and glistening under the fluorescent light, then I mummify it with damp cheese cloth and bag it with black plastic that I knot at the base of the modeling board. Then I wheel the stand to the far corner of the room to keep company with the other bagged figures of various proportions lined up there.

After lunch, maybe I'll work on it some more if it's not too crowded in here by then. If the girls with the boom box don't come back.

Maybe.

I check the message board one more time and I notice something with my name on it that wasn't written on the standard memo pad. I take it down. It's printed in block letters on a sheet torn from a yellow legal pad. Every letter is legible. Whoever left this wanted to make sure I had no problem deciphering it. Whoever left this already knows my name:

> For Delilah Price,
>
> You can see now how much I like you. You'll like me too when you give me a chance. I'm going to make sure you get that chance. You'll be sorry if you don't. You're the only real work of art I've seen. I can come find you any time I want to. You won't have to wait very long.

9

THERE'S SOMEONE NEW WITH WHITE HAIR SITTING AT THE RECEPTION DESK, his face hidden behind an open book. "How long have you been here? I ask him.

He puts his technothriller face down, looks up at me, then down at his watch. "About twenty minutes."

"Did anyone call and leave this message for me since you've been here?" I dangle the message in front of him like a malodorous fish.

He squints at it and hands it back to me. "Where was this?"

"On the message board. I just got it. It wasn't here a couple of hours ago." I stash the note in my jeans pocket. "There hasn't been anyone else covering, has there?"

"Not that I know of. You'll have to ask Louise when she gets back from lunch. That should be around two." He frowns and shakes his head. "I can't imagine who would leave you a note like that, honey."

I can imagine. A heavy-set guy wearing a dirty blue base-ball cap. He knows my phone number. He knows where I work. Now he's shown up where I work. It's got to be him. This has to be more than a coincidence. I can't have that many people calling me, following me, leaving me messages. I've seen him now. I can attach a Pillsbury Doughboy face to that disembodied voice that's been leaving messages for me. A *name*, even.

Knowledge is power. The next time he makes one of those heavy breathy, static, chomping at the bit calls, I'm going to yank the reins. Hard. The prospect of stopping him in his tracks is comforting. I may be looking over my shoulder as I'm walking to get my falafel on pita sandwich, but at least I know who I'm on the lookout for. I'm sure I'd spot him if he were out here on the street stalking me. He's nondescript. I may have seen him dozens of times before he made his presence known to me, but now that he has, I could single him out by body type even if he changed his clothes, even if he took off the baseball cap.

Anyway he's not around. And there are lots of people out on the street, hanging out in the park. There's safety in numbers.

Even when one turns out to be a hot number I just broke up with. I hear Ivan calling my name even before I see him, and all of a sudden there he is in the middle of MacDougal Street stopping traffic. Then he stops me. I look around to reassure myself that there's no lack of potential witnesses.

Excluding Curtis.

"You didn't return my calls."

"I was working."

"I was worried about you."

"Is that why you're hanging around, breathing down my neck, almost like you're stalking me? Because you're *worried* about me?" I laugh nervously. "That's very sweet, but you really don't have to. Being stalked by one guy is quite enough. Oh, yeah, I found out who's been calling me." I smile, trying to be reassuring, mostly to myself. "Turns out it's some guy I don't think I ever saw before in my life. I didn't recognize him, anyway. He came in the school this morning to look at the exhibit and was asking me to go out with him, then he left me a note." I pat my pocket and hear paper crumple.

"Let me see it."

I dig it out, scraping my knuckle in the process, and hand it to Ivan.

"The guy even introduced himself to me. Said his name was Curt. Short for Curtis."

"Well, *that* certainly narrows the field. Curtis what?"

"I asked him. He didn't say."

"Hold on to this," he hands the note back to me. "Have you gotten more calls since last night?"

"When I got in, there were a few messages with no name on them. Louise even wrote that he wouldn't leave his name. Just the usual 'will call back' checked off."

"You talked to him. Did it sound like the same voice you heard on the phone?"

I shrug. "Less muffled. I'm not sure."

He squeezes my arm as if to say "mine!" to Curtis or any-one *else* who might be hounding me. A guide dog leading his master is the only passer-by now, and even he's not looking our way. "I don't like this, Delilah."

"You think *I'm* crazy about it?"

"I'm sorry if I didn't take this seriously before. I don't know what got into me." His grip eases, but he doesn't let go. "*Who-ever* is doing this is a sick bastard. I want you to be careful."

"I *intend* to be careful."

"Don't isolate yourself. Make sure someone knows where and how you can be reached, wherever you are. Maybe you shouldn't model until this blows over..."

"I *have* to model. I need money to *live* on. And for sup-plies."

"You're just setting yourself up for trouble. This guy, Cur-tis or whoever the hell it is, saw you naked. He said so on that message he left you last night. Of course *you're* not going to remember, you've posed for so goddamn many people..."

"This conversation, it seems, is turning out to have more to do with my modeling than my safety. We've been through this before. You can't tell me what to do. You have no claim on me."

His grip tightens again. "If this keeps up, if, God forbid, this gets worse, you're going to have to go to the police. They're going to ask you things like, where do you work, what do you do? What are you going to tell them?"

"The truth."

"Look, Delilah, one of the cops who was in your apartment last night was chewing you out just for not having your shades pulled down. Do you really expect that they're going to be terribly sympathetic to your plight after you tell them you make a living posing bare-assed all over the city?" He chortles. "They'll probably just want a piece."

"I may not even have to go to the police. I have a pretty strong suspicion who's behind all this now. Once he knows that I know who he is and that I'm not interested, he'll probably move on to other prey. Someone new who he figures he has a better chance with..."

"Or he may try a *lot* harder to get close to you."

"I don't want to think about that."

"You'd better think about that, Delilah. You'd better think a *lot* about that, about what you're going to do to protect yourself *now*. Last night you called the police on *me*. Like I would ever hurt you..."

"You did."

Ivan groans. "Maybe you should have shown the good officers this infamous bruise of yours. Everyone else has seen it, what's two more voyeurs. That tall one you were batting your eyelashes at probably would have been more than happy to kiss it and make it better."

"You just said a few minutes ago you don't know what got into you. Sounds to me like it's never gotten *out* of you." I begin to walk away from him. He reels me in like a fish, his last desperate catch of the day.

"If you don't let go of my arm, I'm going to flag down the next cruiser I see"

"And I'll tell whoever is driving it that we're having a lovers' spat and he'll let it go." He looks around. "Do you see anyone paying any attention? Do you see anyone reacting with concern for your welfare?"

"No, and that includes you." I'm looking up and down the block for an NYPD cruiser to come to my rescue. They must be in the park making drug busts. All I see are yellow cabs.

"What are you talking about?" He mutters under his breath. "I *love* you."

This kind of love I don't need. I can feel the painful pressure of each of his fingers through the down-filled sleeve of my anorak. Even his stare bruises me. He mumbles on about wanting me to come back to his place, where I'd be safe, where he'd protect me. My mouth goes dry and my throat constricts. I'm cursing every cab that cruises by for not being a police car, for not being driven by someone carrying a badge and a gun, a cop who would see a distressed female in the company of a very good-looking, well-dressed guy and probably assume we'd had our car stolen or towed, a cop whose presence would defuse the situation just long enough for me to get away.

At least *this* time.

I don't want to think about how many other times a scene like this may be in store for me.

Or Curt. I definitely don't want to think about Curt. Curt is the least of my concerns right now. Until the next time he calls or shows up. Then I'll get rid of him.

The devil I don't know is safer than the devil I do.

A blue-and-white pulls up at the light on West 4th Street, and after I look around to make sure there are no cabbies around to confuse, I tentatively raise my hand to summon the car over to the curb. Ivan releases me promptly. I walk in front of the cruiser and over to the driver's side. The window is already open. "Hi." The officer places the cheeseburger he just took a big bite of back on its greasy wrapper on the passenger seat by his side. I wait for him to finish chewing. "Anything wrong?" I turn to point at Ivan. He's not there.

10

"So I tell him 'everything,' I tell him everything that's happened and that I want a writ to keep Ivan away. Otherwise I don't think he's going to leave me alone, and this officer says *very politely* that there really isn't much I can do because I didn't call the police on him when he *allegedly* hurt me. And anyway where *is* this guy? He left me alone just *now*, didn't he; he took off, just like that. If he hurts me again or threatens to, I can have him arrested. He'd have to go to court and I could get an order of protection then. But not before, because I have no proof. Isn't that great?" This isn't exactly my idea of party talk. I take another sip of brandy and sink deeper into Morgan's cushiony white leather sofa. His loft gives new meaning to the word sparse; there are more paintings than pieces of furniture in the living area. It's the room that gets the least use, he once explained, taking me on a tour of the place after he and Vittorio moved in. The kitchen area is a lavish exhibition of every sort of apparatus anyone could ever want to have, including some I've never seen before. Pans of every size and shape hang from the wall and ceiling, pasta-making and pastry-making and cappuccino machines line the mosaic counter. His sleeping quarters consists of a king-size wrought iron bed. He's got everything he needs here, including peace of mind and a partner who cares about him. More people are coming into the loft now, and I pull myself out of my near-fetal position. Me lying around looking catatonic isn't likely to put many people in a convivial mood. I don't want to spoil Morgan's party.

"I 'm still going to see if I can take civil action," I say, holding out my brandy snifter for more. "That's my only hope unless something *else*... develops." I shudder. "But I can't do anything about it until Monday when the courts are in session. And it's basically my word against his. I'm a sculptor of slender body and slenderer means who has to pose nude in order to make any extra living money. Ivan works for a fat cat investment firm. Who's the judge going to believe?"

"Get a good lawyer."

"With what? My looks?"

"Seems like they'd suffice to *me*."

This is one of those times I damn God for not making Morgan straight. I take another sip of brandy, then another. The paintings on the wall start to look even more abstract to me. If I have one more drink, the room, like my life, will start to spin out of control. And I'll lose my appetite. I can't afford to lose my appetite. This is a *dinner* party. I'm not likely to be able to feed myself this well for months. The aroma radiating from the kitchen is enough to make my stomach growl and make me think about something *other* than who's going to be waiting for me when I go home tonight. I owe it to myself not to face potential danger on an empty stomach. I think of how participants in marathons eat platefuls of pasta the night before the run. My circumstances are probably going to require a whole lot more than carbo loading, but it'll do for now.

"Tagliatelle en brodo," Vittorio announces with the beaming pride of a parent delivering his own offspring.

"Dinner is served," Morgan interprets cheerfully.

Morgan seats me to his left. He passes me a soup bowl and

fills it to the brim. He passes me a basket filled with loaves of pannetone and focaccia squares, after which he passes the lasagna pan for people to help themselves. Next come the plates of veal piccata. I'm eating so much that I'm afraid I'm going to pass out. I can't remember what I did with my brandy snifter. Every time Vittorio and Morgan look at each other, they glow brighter than the candles in the centerpiece. I can't remember the last time anyone made me glow like that.

Vittorio uncorks the champagne I brought and sighs, "Ecco fatto!" as foam spews over the rim of the bottle like lava from Mount Etna. Morgan holds out long-stemmed glasses, two at a time, to be filled.

"I'd like to propose a toast." Gary, one of Morgan's friends, stands up behind his lover Abel's chair and puts one hand on his shoulder caressingly.

He raises his glass of champagne with the other. "To Morgan and Vittorio. May they stay happy and healthy together for a very long time. May they be an inspiration to their friends here, gay *and* straight."

"May no harm touch these two," another friend says.

"May I find someone who looks and cooks like Vittorio."

I take a sip from my glass. I wonder if I'm going to have room for whatever's going to be for dessert. I wonder if a diced and sliced me is somebody's idea of a just dessert. A person I don't even know. Or somebody I know all too well. The sudden wail of an alarm outside coincides with the ringing of the phone and makes me jump. I feel the champagne bubbles go up my nose. Morgan pats my hand and refills my glass. Vittorio mutters "Scusi" and pulls his chair out with a screech. Morgan stiffens as Vittorio picks up the phone and babbles into it in broken English. He stretches the phone cord to the limit as his voice rises.

"I wonder who *that* could be," Morgan says. "How can they

have the nerve to call him *here, tonight.* What do they expect, him to drop everything and..."

I put my hand on his wrist. "He's here with us, not there."

The call doesn't take long. Vittorio waves his hands at Morgan.

"Mangia, mangia," he insists. "Is nothing. Bad connection. Wrong number."

"He's bullshitting me to make me feel better."

Vittorio blows Morgan a kiss across the table. "*Later* I make you feel better."

11

IT'S A COUPLE OF HOURS LATER AND *I'M* NOT FEELING BETTER AT *ALL*.

"I'm going to call you a cab," Morgan insists as I hesitate at his door on my way out.

"Yes, I'm a cab all right, fast and reckless, careening toward trouble."

And yellow. Very, very yellow. I kiss his cheek. "Thanks for the dinner. It was great. I'll remember it for the rest of my life."

I'm not sure how long that might be.

"You've had *way* too much to drink to be able to get home okay. Wait here. Vittorio's going to wait outside. He'll buzz to let us know when the cab comes."

"What time is it?"

"Ten after eleven."

"I better check my messages." I turn on my cell phone and encounter a dark screen. I forgot to charge it. "Uh, maybe I don't want to check my messages. Honest, Morgan, I can walk a couple of blocks and grab an uptown bus. It's not that late. I'll be okay."

"*No*," he protests. "I won't have you doing that, Delilah. I don't want anything to happen to you. I feel responsible. You're bombed. Anyone could tell. Never mind Ivan the Terrible, you could be mugged by some street criminal or worse. You're an easy hit."

"Thanks a lot," I mumble, "I guess."

A staccato buzz behind me makes me jump.

"Your cab, ma'am," Morgan pats my hand. "You'll be okay?"

I squeeze his hand. "Happy anniversary," I say for the twentieth time tonight and take the service elevator down to the street level. Vittorio nods and says, "Ciao." I kiss his cheek too and smile my thanks tentatively, at a loss for what else to say as I crawl into the cab. Vittorio speaks very little English and the only Italian I know is ripped off from memorized menus. Morgan and Vittorio seem to get around the barrier just fine; the thing they have going has a language of its own.

"Where to," the cabbie grumbles.

"Corner of Seventh and Christopher," I tell him. He thrusts the cab into gear. I think of places where I could use the phone, where I'd be safe, one per each tick of the meter. Sachi lives on Prince Street. I could always backtrack to Prince Street if I absolutely had to.

Nobody would probably answer the buzzer if I did.

"Keep the change," I tell the cabby after he drops me off and I've handed him a bill that Morgan slipped to me on my way out of his place.

The cabby unfurls the bill and blasts the horn at me before I've had time to step onto the curb. "Hey, girlie, this ain't enough."

"It's all I have."

"You owe me two more bucks. Plus the tip." He gestures wildly at the leather pouch slung over my shoulder. "Big bag like that, you gotta have more than booze and condoms in there. You're not gonna stiff me. Try looking."

"What did I give you?" I turn to slam the door. Instead I lean back into the cab, a move he didn't expect, and I recognize Alexander Hamilton's face before it disappears into the cabby's grimy pocket. "Like I said, keep the change. And I hope you *do* get stiffed before you're through for the night!" I yell over my shoulder. I most definitely am not as drunk as I thought. The buzz has forced me to be more on guard than ever. I bump into two people in Sheridan Square and mumble, "Excuse me," then realize they're statues and back away. I cross over to Christopher Street and head for shelter in a bar I was taken to once by a guy I dated when I first came to the city, before I began to model, before I met Ivan. I'm tipsy and I'm elbowing my way through a Saturday night crowd in a bar, looking for a pay phone. Do they even exist any more? Most of the clients here probably have portables in their pockets, along with their little black books. Most are gay.

"What will you have?"

I clear my throat. "A telephone."

A guy to the right of me laughs. "That's a new one on me. How do you make that? Vodka? Vermouth? Tell Chuckie here, he can mix just about anything."

I ignore him. "I need to use your phone," I tell the bartender.

"You going to order something?"

"I've already had more than enough."

"You can't just walk off the street smelling of booze you didn't get here and expect me to hand over the phone to you."

I lick my lips. "Please. I think I might be in trouble."

"I'll get you a drink," the guy to my right says, "not a telephone. No one here knows how to produce that. How about a scotch and soda?" He leans in closer. "Nah, you're more the sweet liqueur type. I can practically taste it on your lips."

The bartender scowls and slams a big black phone on the faux-marble bar. "Keep it short," he snaps. I start to press buttons but my hand freezes on the fourth digit as I see Ivan walk by outside. Someone who looks a lot like Ivan, anyway. Maybe I *am* as drunk as I thought. I slam the receiver down and duck, pushing away from the bar. Someone laughs behind my back. "Guess she expected a *princess* phone."

I go outside and look to my left. Then my right. I don't feel safe using a payphone out here, even if I could find one. I don't dare go in any other place to try to call home. Better to *be* home. I see someone in a uniform in a doorway a few feet behind me. A cop. What a relief. Who says they're not there when you need them? I step off the curb so he can see me, so he can see if anyone steps out of the shadows and grabs me. I head east up Christopher Street, weaving around other pedestrians, mostly males, most of them with other men. I cross West Fourth Street. I'm almost there. Every time I hear footsteps gaining on me, I spin around. No one I know. I don't even see the cop any more, just every exhaled breath in front of me. It smells like Cointreau. If someone lit a match, I'd probably ignite. I run the last two blocks and grab the railing leading up to where I live. My fingernails knock off a chunk of peeling brown paint, exposing a layer of still darker brown paint and rust. I fumble with the key. Dampness makes the door stick; a really good shove unglues it. The door slams against the backstop, the beveled glass window rattles in its frame.

As I weave up the stairs, I hear a door open. My next-door neighbor Mrs. Davidoff looms above me in a quilted blue bathrobe and fuzzy scuffs. As I come closer, she takes a tissue out from under her sleeve and dabs at her nose, then stuffs it back out of view. She's looking me over good and her expression is telling me I haven't been good at all. Like the times she's stared me down in the hallway the mornings after Ivan and I had sex. For a woman well into her eighties, she hears everything. And sees and smells pretty efficiently too.

"I wonder, Miss Price, if you could ask your friends to please refrain from banging on your door…"

"I'm sorry about last night, Mrs. Davidoff, I'm really terribly sorry…"

"I'm not talking about last night, dear. I'm talking about tonight," she sniffs.

"Tonight?"

"About nine o'clock. I know it was nine because I was just starting to watch Real Housewives when I heard him."

"Him?"

"Your young man. Well, one of them, anyway, the one you're usually with. You should maybe tell him if you're not going to be home, so he doesn't come here knocking on doors and kicking and yelling. I'm an old woman. It's not good for me, all this excitement. At first I didn't know who it was. It went on for so long that it frightened me, I had to call the police."

"You called...the police?" I feel like bending down and kissing her.

"To make whoever it was stop. I looked through the peephole and saw it was him, so I opened the door a crack to *tell* him he'd better go or he'd probably be arrested for disturbing the peace. Which I didn't want to see happen because he seems like such a *nice* young man."

"Yes, very nice, Mrs. Davidoff," I gulp. "And then..."

"He left. That is, after he asked me if I'd seen you. I said you hadn't been around all day."

"What happened when the police came, Mrs. Davidoff?"

She shrugs. "I called back and told them not to bother, I had made a mountain out of a molehill, they have enough to deal with in this city without this *mishegoss*. They came anyway, but by then he was gone." Mrs. Davidoff sniffs and shakes her head. "Tell your friends that maybe next time I won't be so considerate and maybe I'll have something to say to the landlord too, if this continues. It's no good, disturbances like this. It's no good."

My heart races. It was too good to be true, the thought of Ivan being hauled off in handcuffs for disturbing the peace while I was safely tucked away in Morgan's TriBeCa loft. It would have solidified my case against him. I could have gotten a protective order that much more easily. My only meager hope is that a warning warbled by an old woman who thinks he's *such a nice young man* is going to be enough to deter him from making any more visits in the future. At least I got in the building unscathed. *That's* something.

"Mrs. Davidoff," I sigh, "I really appreciate you being so concerned."

She looks at me warily.

"When I first moved to the city, I was told nobody looks out for anybody here. That you could be stabbed or shot and nobody would lift a finger to help you. I'm glad I was misinformed." I grin. "It's good to know that I have neighbors who worry about my welfare. So much so that they call the police if they think something's wrong. Just as I would if I thought someone was bothering *you*."

Mrs. Davidoff clutches her robe closed and steps backward toward her open apartment door as I open mine. "Yes, well, I hope there's no more trouble here."

"I hope not too, Mrs. Davidoff."

And just before I close the door, I hiccup, an ill-timed hiccup for sure.

Mrs. Davidoff shakes her head and slams her door behind her. I lean against mine and secure the first of the deadbolts, the middle one, and sigh as I hear the tumbler click, sealing me in for the night. I fasten the rest of the locks from bottom to top. And then I plug in the cell phone charger. The second it gets juice, my phone rings.

"You're home," the male voice says. "It's about time."

It's not Ivan.

"Who is this?" I ask, though I have a damn good idea who it is. The number that shows up on my screen is unfamiliar. Probably a prepaid phone.

I hear voices in the background, the old familiar static. Whoever this nut case is, he should invest in a better model.

He probably can't hear me any more clearly than I can hear him. "Curtis? This is Curtis, isn't it?"

I hear muffled breathing. Then I shout so he'll get the message, "Leave me alone!" and press the end-call key.

The phone rings again.

"Talk to me," he commands.

I disconnect.

The phone rings again. "Look, you've got to stop calling..."

"I want you."

"And you've got to stop leaving me notes and messages..."

"I didn't leave messages this time. I'm tired of one-way conversations. I waited until you got home."

"What made you think I was out?"

"I saw you. I knew you were out. Couldn't have been anything special. You would have had a better time if you were out with me."

"What makes you think it wasn't special?"

"You weren't dressed up for anything like that." He goes on to tell me what I'm wearing and I look up. The shades are still drawn from last night. He's not learning anything new from looking in here from a nearby building, that's for sure.

But he was out there tonight, watching, waiting for me to come home.

"Oh, but it *was* special. Very. I didn't have time to change during the day, that's all."

I hear him breathing on the other end, waiting for me to say more. *Are you ready for this?* I'm still feeling the effects of all the brandy and champagne I drank. Even after all that food. I unbutton my coverall and step out of it. *Too bad you can't see me now, asshole!* "And it didn't really matter since I wasn't going to keep my clothes on very long anyhow."

Silence.

"You're wasting your time on me," I say, unbuttoning the cotton Henley jersey. "I've already found the somebody I want."

"That tight-ass stockbroker…"

"No, not him. It's over between me and him. There's somebody else."

"You work fast, don't you? Why won't you even give me a chance?"

"Maybe if you keep looking you'll find someone who wants *you*." I hear his breathing quicken. "You've got to stop calling. I've already reported this to the police. If you keep calling, they'll go after you. Do you want that?"

"I don't think *you* want that. And I've already told you what I want. You."

"And I'm telling you for the last time you can't have it…uh, me."

"We'll see," he hisses.

I hang up and pound the play button for my voice mail. The ensuing chimes keep pace with my frantic heartbeats. Following the last long beep is a string of messages asking if I'm available to work a couple of classes next week. I jot down the phone numbers of the callers so that I can get back to them tomorrow at a reasonable time. My hand is shaking so bad that the numbers look like hieroglyphics.

That's it, that's all the messages.

So maybe Mrs. Davidoff was a little slow getting around to canceling her complaint; maybe she waited for a commercial break to pick up the phone and say "Maybe you shouldn't bother coming after all, everything's quiet here now." Maybe the police stopped Ivan on the way down the stairs or lurking across the street looking up at my windows. But I know they didn't because I saw him walking down Christopher Street when I was in that bar using the phone. Too bad. Too bad the cops didn't come across Curtis too. A New York City marathon eve two-for-one special. Everyone running to my rescue, rounding up the bad guys.

I leave my clothes in a heap on the floor where they fell as I shed them and plop on the bed face-down. The screeching sirens in the distance are a Manhattan lullaby.

12

THE RINGTONE OF MY PHONE IS A WAKE-UP CALL. I LOOK AT MY ALARM clock. I haven't even been asleep two hours yet.

The voice on the other end just says, "Delilah, it's me." I'm groggy and my body is confused. My heartbeat accelerates and I feel warm wetness between my legs. I am so used to this voice waking me in the middle of the night, wanting something. I can practically feel him down there, entering me, and my hand reaches out as if to coax him, guide him.

I'm more awake all of a sudden, and it enters my mind that this is the last thing I want.

"I came over tonight. Your buttinsky neighbor said you weren't home."

"That's right," I mumble, "I wasn't."

"I saw someone following you back to the school this afternoon," Ivan says. "He came out of the park after you finished talking to that cop and followed you practically right up to the front door."

"Did he go in?"

"No."

"And where were you all this time?"

"Following you," he confesses. "He looked like a bouncer. Big hulk of a guy, he was wearing a baseball cap..."

I hoist myself up on my elbows. "Blue baseball cap."

"This the same guy who came in the school and left you the note?" Ivan pauses. "I brushed by him, bumped into him. I thought maybe he'd say something and I'd recognize his voice from the phone calls."

"Did he? Did you?"

"No. Delilah, this guy's stalking you."

"So are you."

"I'm worried about you. This guy thinks he's got a grasp on you. He's crazy."

"You had a good grasp on me earlier today. I have bruises on my arm where you grabbed me..."

"You're pretty thin-skinned. I wasn't holding you that hard."

"The cop you saw me talking to seemed to think you were when I showed him." I look down at my unblemished arms wondering if, like Pinocchio, telling a lie will alter me and make an indelible bruise materialize.

"What was the point of that? You've got this guy chasing after you, calling at all hours, leaving you notes..."

"Like you're *not?*"

"...who's nuttier than a pint of Ben and Jerry's Chunky Monkey and you're complaining to the cops about *me?*"

"*You're* the one whose imprint I've got under my skin. Damn it, Ivan," I'm trying hard to keep the tears out of my voice, "*you're* the one I'm getting a protective order against."

"You don't want to do that."

"Why wouldn't I?"

"It's just a piece of paper, Delilah. If I did mean to do you harm, which I don't, a piece of paper wouldn't keep me away or anyone else who wanted to hurt you. A loaded gun might, but I'm not saying that's the way to go either. Not in *this* city. Remember that subway vigilante guy," he pauses. "And remember if you do go out and get an order of protection against me and you have me picked up if I violate it, I won't be around to keep an eye on you if this other guy comes after you. What are you going to do about that? Get another protective order? You know how that's going to look, Delilah? Flaky, very flaky."

"I didn't ask you to keep a constant vigil over me. I didn't ask for this. You're not my bodyguard."

"If you're going to go down to Centre Street, make it worth your while is what I'm saying. Get an order against this other guy who's following you. You don't know *what he's* capable of."

"But I thought you just said it's just a piece of paper. How's it going to keep him away," I gulp, "when I don't even really know who it is?"

"Okay, so make police complaints every time he establishes contact. That should come as second nature to you. Save all the tapes with his messages, notify the cops if he shows up in person, have something to show for it. But *don't* screw up your credibility by going down there and whining to the prosecutor about *me.*"

"That wouldn't look good down on Wall Street, would it?"

"Delilah, ever hear of the boy who cried wolf?"

"Yes," I say wearily, "And as I see it, it's just a question of which wolf has the sharper fangs."

Or of staying out of the forest, I think as I press the disconnect button like I'm squashing a bug.

13

IT'S A BEAUTIFUL MARATHON SUNDAY. THE FIRST VOICE I HEAR IS THAT of the weather guy on the all-news radio station, extolling the couldn't-be-more-perfect-for-a-Marathon weather, like he deserves all the credit. I turn on the TV instead. Shot from above, the people cramming the Verrazano Narrows Bridge look like a swarm of ants. "It's a beautiful Marathon Sunday," one commentator after the other says. I turn down the sound and watch as the throng pushes forward, seeming to move slower than ants until the ground-level camera takes over and focuses on thousands of muscular legs pounding the pavement as they begin to cross into Brooklyn. The part I want to see, the runners crossing into Manhattan, won't be for a while yet. Last night Morgan told me he and Vittorio were going and asked if I wanted to join them, but I declined. I thought maybe I'd get a glimpse of them cheering the runners on along First Avenue, but that's clearly not going to be for a while and I want to get an early start on my work today. If you can call ten forty-five early. It's going to be even later than that by the time I get to the studio.

It's a beautiful Marathon Sunday. Nobody is lying in wait for me as I leave the building and head east, stopping for a cup of coffee on the way. Even more beautiful is the fact that the clay room is empty when I get there. I have it all to myself. I unbag and unwrap the head I was working on yesterday and shoot water at it and start working the clay with my hands and my paddle and my sculpting tools. I lose track of time as the head takes shape. My fingers gouge into the clay, making deep eye sockets. Muffled voices behind the closed doors suddenly make me glance at my watch. *Hours* have passed. Nothing could be more beautiful.

Morgan sticks his head in the door. "Hey, you're back." I'm still smiling at the molded clay. "How was the Marathon?"

"All right, what I could see of it."

Morgan doesn't look like the happy camper he was last night. He must be hung over. He and Vittorio probably celebrated long after all the guests left. I back further away from the head I've been working on and take a better look at Morgan. He looks like *his* head needs to be worked on. His eyes are red-rimmed and glazed. His jaw is tight. "Morgan, what's wrong?"

He shakes his head and mutters, "Vittorio." He picks up one of my sculpting tools from the work table and turns it over and over in his hand. "Everything was *so perfect* last night. Today he turned on me. He was testy even before we left to go to the Marathon and wouldn't let on what was wrong. Once we found a place on First Avenue, he said he was cold and didn't want to stay, so he took off on me."

"Oh, Morgan, I'm sorry," I hug him.

"He's never acted this way before."

"Maybe he was just hung over and didn't feel so good," I suggest. Allowances have to be made for bad behavior in the course of any relationship, at least once in a while. Morgan and Vittorio have just had it too good. They've been cruising down the avenue of love without hitting any potholes. They're both spoiled.

"Maybe." He sounds less than convinced.

"Or maybe it has something to do with that business at work."

"Somebody called again late last night. He said it was a wrong number. But he was okay *then*. I mean, *really* okay." I know what he means. I'm not going to push it; he feels and looks bad enough already. I give him a last perfunctory squeeze and let go. He's not ready to let go. "But I wonder if..."

"What?"

"If there's somebody else. No, that's crazy of me, forget I ever said that. You *saw* how we were *last* night. Anyway, I don't want to distract you," he says. "It looks like you're on a roll here."

"You really think so?"

"Are you kidding? It's *beautiful*." He hands me my sculpting tool and manages a forced smile. "I dropped off some left-overs for you earlier. They're in the refrigerator whenever you feel like eating. Now get back to work."

The next time I look at my watch, it's midnight and there's a knock on the door; the night guard is kicking everyone out of the building. I finish draping the head with damp cheese-cloth and bag it and wheel the stand against the wall. I've done a marathon and it *feels* beautiful.

There's another more impatient knock on the door. I open it a crack. The night guard scowls. "You Delilah Price?"

"Yes."

"You've got a phone call," he points to the front desk. "You don't need to go back in there for anything, do you? I'm going to lock up."

I steel myself for this. Curt or Ivan? Ivan or Curt? Who's it going to be this time?

I lean against the front desk for support, calculating how many blocks I've got to go to get home. It's not *that* far from here. I managed okay last night. Better a phone call than to have whoever it is waiting for me outside. Whoever is making this call could be waiting for me outside, right down the street on the corner of Fifth Avenue. I open my mouth, but nothing comes out. I feel like I've got lockjaw. I clear my throat and say, "Hello?" It sounds like the death rattle coming from the throat of someone being strangled.

"Delilah, you're still there, thank God."

"*Morgan!*" *What a relief.* "That food you left me was out of this world. Mmmm. Even cold."

"I didn't know if you'd still be there. I tried calling your cell, but there was no answer."

"I've been here since late this morning," I remind him, not adding that I turned off my phone. "I told you I was going to stay." I did tell him, *didn't* I? I've been so absorbed in my work that I only vaguely remember his brief visit this afternoon. *There's something funny about this call.* Usually Morgan works in his studio almost as late as I do, and he knows me well enough to know *my* work habits. *Something's not quite right.* Morgan has never called me this late or sounded so desperate to talk to me before. Or has he? He sounds like he's choking on something. "Morgan, what is it?" I ask him. "Did Vittorio not come back?" There's a long pause and I hear male voices in the background talking to and over each other. I wonder if he's in a bar. Sunday isn't a night for cruising bars and I've never known Morgan to cruise, but then again I don't know how Morgan acts when his heart's been torn out of him. "Morgan?"

I wonder if someone's snatched the phone away from him. I can't even hear him breathing on the other end. Just those other male voices, deep authoritative voices, more of them than before. And they're not in a bar. I don't hear clinking glasses. *Something's terribly wrong.*

"Vittorio's dead," Morgan sounds like he's been anesthetized. "He's been murdered."

"What?"

"I'm calling from the First Precinct. The police brought

me here. They greeted me when I came home tonight and brought me here and now they're about to question me."

"Oh my God, what happened?" I lean against the edge of the reception desk. "Who did it? Do they know? How..."

"I *don't know* who would do this and *you* don't want to know what they did." It sounds like he's already been asked and told a few things. His voice is beginning to break. "It wasn't me. I couldn't..."

"I know you couldn't. I'm coming down there. Is there anyone else you want me to call?"

"I can't think."

"I'll be there as soon as I can," I reassure him. I look at my watch and calculate how soon I can get there. 12:10. If my timing is good and a train is rolling into the station when I get there, I can get downtown in ten minutes.

"Delilah," he warns, "be careful."

14

THE IRONY IS THAT MORGAN LIVES SO CLOSE TO THE PRECINCT HOUSE. *So safe.* Practically around the corner. He'd always tell me that he and Vittorio felt like they could practically leave the doors open. *Nothing* could happen, what with all those blue-and-whites cruising around at all hours.

He was talking about burglary. Not this.

Nothing was taken that I know of except a life.

I shift my weight on the hard wooden chair that I was gruffly told to sit in a half hour ago by a cop in uniform who ushered me upstairs and told me to wait. I wonder where they've got Morgan. The desk next to me is littered with pink forms. I stand up to stretch. The minute I do, I hear a voice out of nowhere saying, "Someone will be with you shortly." I wonder if the chair is rigged to some kind of silent alarm. The pressure of the hard wood made my butt fall asleep like it does during a tough pose, and I remain standing in defiance of the law.

I squint across the room at the map of the city on the wall and take a few steps closer to make out what the shaded divisions mean. As I do, a low voice stops me in my tracks. "Miss Price?"

"Yes?"

"Why don't you have a seat here..." He indicates the killer chair I just abandoned. "I'm Detective Quick. Mr. Merritt told us you're a friend of his."

"I want to see him," I insist. "Is he all right?"

"You'll be able to see him. We're just getting some background from him." He sits at the desk beside me and stares into me. This detective won't ever need bright lights to force a confession. His eyes will do fine.

"When can I see Morgan?"

"Soon. Right now I want to ask *you* a few questions." He rolls back the cuffs of his gray pinstriped shirt just past his wrists and takes a sip of black coffee from a Rangers mug, then sets it down between us. "Do you want something to drink? Coffee? Soda?"

I shake my head. "How is he?"

"Very shaken up. Mr. Merritt told us that you also knew the victim, Mr. Vittorio Scaccia."

"Yes. Not very well. I knew him through Morgan. He was Morgan's friend. I was just at their place last night. They seemed *so happy.*"

"Did you see either Mr. Merritt...Morgan or Mr. Scaccia since last night?"

"I saw Morgan this afternoon. Around three. He'd just gotten back from the Marathon."

"Mr. Scaccia wasn't with him?"

"Morgan's an artist. He came to his studio to work. Vittorio is...was a gourmet chef. His was a different sort of art. He never came to the school with Morgan. At least not that I know of, and we're both there a *lot.*"

"When you saw Morgan around three, he was alone?"

"He came in my studio to tell me he'd left some food for me in the fridge before he left to go to the Marathon. He was going to his studio..." I realize I don't remember him saying he was going to his studio. "And the next thing I know, he's calling me from *here.* What happened?"

"That's what we're trying to find out, Miss Price. It would really help us if you could tell me if you have any idea what time Morgan left the school tonight."

"He usually stays late, almost as late as I do, unless Vittorio has the night off; then he leaves earlier."

"How much earlier?"

I shrug. "It depends. Usually eight or nine."

"You didn't see him after three?"

I shake my head. A lot of the shaking is involuntary. "Maybe the guard did," I suggest.

"Is there any kind of register? Some place where you sign in and out?"

I shake my head. "People come and go at all hours. We get officially kicked out at midnight, but Morgan's usually never there that late."

"When you did see Morgan, how would you describe him?"

"What do you mean?"

"Did he still seem *happy*, Miss Price?"

Those eyes are unrelenting, boring into me from over the brim of his coffee mug as he raises it to his mouth again. I start to squirm in the chair. "I...I don't know. I guess I was too absorbed in my own work, my own troubles to notice. Would you *please* tell me what happened? Why are you asking me these questions about Morgan? He's the gentlest person I know. Particularly compared to some of the *others* I know." I grab the detective's coffee mug off the desk and sip nervously before either of us realizes what I've done. "Is he a suspect?"

"We're trying to get to the bottom of this, Miss Price, and right now we're just scraping the surface. Because of the nature of the crime, there are questions that have to be answered before we can rule out or zero in on anybody."

This man's use of the word *we* is driving me nuts. I have to keep looking around to verify that there are only two of us in this room. "Does he need a lawyer?"

Detective Quick leans back in his chair. "He hasn't asked for one."

"You're not going to arrest him or anything?"

"Morgan's been very cooperative so far. We're not giving him the third degree, Miss Price. It's just that certain questions need to be answered."

I lick my lips. "*I'd* like to ask a few questions."

He frowns. "Go ahead."

My eyes waver toward his shoulder holster and then I take a deep breath and meet his stare head-on. "*What happened?*"

All at once this man's fine features look pained, like *he's* the one sitting in the hot seat, or *hard* seat, as it were. He looks like he's been up all day and all night and he has seen way too much and wants to put an end to all the suffering in the city *now*. His dark brown hair looks uncombed, like it was blown around a bit when he arrived at the crime scene, or maybe it was mussed up earlier by some admiring woman's roving fingers. I look down at my own clay-stained fingers now. I'm bending and unbending them. I can't look at those eyes any more. It's been a long night and it's no longer beautiful.

"Mr. Scaccia's body was discovered shortly after ten on a loading dock in front of the building in which he occupied a loft with Morgan Merritt. He'd been stabbed numerous times and suffered other injuries."

"Oh my God, did Morgan...was he the one who found him like that?"

"The 911 operator received the call shortly after twenty-two hundred hours." Detective Quick glances down at a pad on the cluttered desk. "Twenty-two seventeen to be exact. It was phoned in anonymously. According to the scenario we've established so far, Morgan arrived after the Crime Scene Unit was already in place. The part that's a little fuzzy is why it took him as long as it did to get there when he supposedly left West Eighth Street before nine. How long did it take *you* to get here?"

"I didn't look at my watch."

I look at my watch now. It's 2:20.

"Maybe someone tried to rob him? He didn't understand much English. Maybe someone tried to rob him and he hesitated and whoever did it thought he was trying to resist..."

"We found his wallet on him, Miss Price. He had close to fifty dollars on him, two credit cards, a green card. He was wearing a gold ring on his right hand. We've pretty much ruled out robbery as the motive here."

"I can't imagine who would want to harm Vittorio. Not Morgan." I shake my head. "*Definitely* not Morgan."

"They were together for some time?"

"A year. Last night was their year anniversary. They had a party to celebrate." I'm having a hard time reading what Detective Quick is thinking about all this. He finishes the last of his coffee. "They were *happy*."

"It's possible that someone may not have been happy about them being so happy." His voice lowers. "An ex-lover. We're looking into that angle too."

"Yes, you never know what ex-lovers are capable of," I mumble.

"Did Mr. Merritt...Morgan ever mention anything to you about people in his or Mr. Scaccia's past resurfacing?" I ask.

"No," I say. *I'm the one having trouble in that department.* "There was some kind of problem Vittorio was having at the restaurant, with someone who worked with him. He was getting annoying phone calls." *Just like me.* "Didn't he—Morgan—tell you?"

"He mentioned it, yes."

"You're looking into that too, right?" Quick's jaw clenches in response. "Didn't anyone around there see anything?"

"Nobody we talked to so far. We're going to canvass the neighborhood thoroughly tomorrow." I envision all of the paintings in Morgan's loft being lined up along Franklin Street from West to Lafayette. Another guy in plain clothes that are bursting at the seams barrels out of a room down the hall and stops at the door. "I'm getting some water for Morgan *Le Fey* in there," he snarls. "Seems his mouth is dry."

Detective Quick shoots him a deprecating glance, then hunches toward me, trying to suck me up into his dark pupils and make like his fellow detective doesn't exist. *Quick thinking. Quick-tempered.* I wonder in what *other* ways his name suits him. "Here's my card." He pulls one out of his pocket and puts it on my outstretched palm. "In case you think of anything else that might be relevant to this case. If I'm not here, leave a message. I or someone else in this department will get back to you."

"Can I see Morgan now?"

The other detective pauses on his way back and raises his eyebrows at Detective Quick. "Hat trick, *you* want to talk with him some more?" Quick nods and turns back to me as he stands up. I didn't notice when he first came in how imposingly tall he is. As the night has ground on, I feel like I've shrunk in stature. Maybe *that's* it. Everything is too huge for me to handle. "I'm going to go in to see how Morgan's doing," he tells me. He doesn't sound like he's talking about his health. "I want you to wait out here. I'll let you know when you can see him. You sure you don't want some coffee?"

I'm reminded of a time a few years ago when I flew to Rome to study artifacts. The jumbo jet was grounded because of engine difficulty, and the stewardesses served up free champagne; when that happens, you *know* you're in for a long haul. I ended up being grounded for four hours. There's no telling how long I'll be stranded here.

"No," I shake my head. "No coffee. Thanks."

Detective Quick skims my shoulder with his hand as he

walks past me, a small gesture of comfort that at the same time is telling me, *Stay!*

That same hand displaying greater pressure wakes me up. "Miss Price!" I open my eyes and look up at him. My head is resting on a pillow of piled up pink forms on the desk. Some of them flutter to the floor when I move. He bends down to pick them up and puts them in a neat pile in the middle of the desk on top of a cream-colored file folder. "You can see Morgan now."

"You're through with him?"

"For now." His mouth is grim.

"Can he leave?" I stand up and start for the door. Detective Quick gently reels me in and steers me back toward the chair.

"Miss Price, Morgan is very disturbed by what's happened." He sits on the edge of the desk. "It's taken us hours to get anything coherent out of him. We're going to want to talk to him more, but he's not in any shape to help us right now."

"I *thought* you said he was cooperating..."

"I don't mean to imply that I believe he's purposefully holding anything back. There are a few gaps in his story. We're going to want to talk to him some more when he's calmed down. He's in a state of shock right now."

"I imagine *anyone* would be, under the circumstances," I insist.

"We still don't *know* all the circumstances, Miss Price."

"What are you telling me?"

"Do you know if Morgan has ever been under psychiatric care?"

"No," I shake my head. "I don't know. He's always seemed calmer than most of the other artists I hang with."

"Does he take any medication that you know of?"

"No."

"As long as you've known him, has he ever acted irrationally or exhibited violent or self-destructive tendencies?"

"No." I feel a sudden pang of guilt. What was it Morgan told me about how he felt looking through the windows of his studio when his work wasn't going well? *Makes you feel like jumping out.* But of course I didn't take that seriously. There were days when I joked about jumping into the kiln. I'd never do it. I'm feeling enough heat as it is. "Can I *see* him now?"

Detective Quick nods and ushers me down the hall. "Seeing as how you're a friend, maybe you could get him to compose himself long enough to be a little *more* cooperative with us. Okay, Miss Price?" he says softly before opening the door.

No ifs, ands, or maybes about it, Miss Price.

Morgan doesn't look up at first when I walk into the room. His head rests on the rectangular table in front of him; he looks like he's sleeping or pretending to be. I start to rush over to him, but Detective Quick pulls me back. "Morgan," he says, "you've got company."

The look on Morgan's face makes me start to rush over to him again. This time Detective Quick lets me go. "I'll give you a couple of minutes of privacy," he says, shutting the door behind him. I don't turn back to thank him. I cradle Morgan's head against me as he sobs convulsively into my stone-washed jeans. His arms encircle me clumsily and pull me closer to him like I'm the last life raft on a sinking ship. He's shedding so many tears the room may get flooded before the night is over. I'm fighting back tears myself and losing the battle. I bend over and whisper into his hair, "It's okay," a lame reassurance to be sure because things couldn't be less okay. My hands clutch him until finally his racking sobs stop and I only feel faint muscular tremors. "Morgan, I'm so sorry," I purr, "I'm so sorry about what happened..."

"They think I did it."

"You couldn't have done it. You would never do anything like that."

"Try telling *them.*"

"I did." I reach out and wipe some of his tears away with the back of my hand. "They seem more concerned with chronology than character right now. The detective I was just talking to said he couldn't understand why it took you so long to get home."

"The one who just left? The tall good-looking one?"

I nod. "Tell him. They'll let you go."

"Go where, Delilah?" he asks. "Home? Do you think I want to go back to that place?"

"You sure don't want to stay *here*." I look around, knowing we're being watched, even though the only faces I see are our own, reflected in the mirror on the wall in front of me. "It took me *ten minutes* to get here," I whisper self-consciously. "They *know* how long it takes to get from one place to the other. They probably have a *table* or something."

"I walked home. I took my time. I called Vittorio before I left and there was no answer. So I walked and I stopped on the way for a cup of coffee. I don't even remember *where* I stopped, Delilah, I was trying to figure out what possibly could have gone wrong since last night because last night we were so..."

"*Happy*," I mumble.

He begins to sob again. "And I didn't know what to expect, you know, when I got home. Whether Vittorio was going to be there or not or how things would be..."

I clutch him again.

"Who'd want to kill Vittorio?" Morgan wails.

"Someone from his past?" I suggest, considering what Detective Quick said to me about the ex-lovers angle. I don't mention the fleeting suspicion that Morgan brought up earlier of the existence of someone *not quite* ex. "Is there anyone he talked about who might have..."

"Not unless they came from Rome to do the hit. I was his first and only stateside love that I know of, and it's been a *year*, Delilah. The only mail or phone calls he got from

Rome were from his family in Malagrotta. *I* was the one who brought in the mail."

"Unless it went to the restaurant. What about whoever it was who was calling him from the restaurant? Do you think someone there could have..."

"That would *really* have made last night a feast to die for, wouldn't it?" Morgan sniffs. "I told them about it, but they don't buy it, even that porker who looks like he knows food, if nothing else. They said 'we'll look into it', but they're acting like they don't see anyone except me doing it. I could *never*... I don't think it was anyone else he knew either. No one who knew Vittorio would do what..."

"Maybe it was someone who *wanted* to know him. Someone he rejected." I lick my lips. "Someone who wouldn't take no for an answer. You just never know...what any one's going to do..."

"It was probably just someone who hates gays," Morgan says dully. "Nothing personal against Vittorio. It could have just as easily been me. It could have been him *and* me. If I'd gotten home sooner. I wish..."

"No!"

"...they'd find out who did this. Not waste precious time asking me, 'Now where was it you had this cup of coffee, *Mister* Merritt?' I think that's what *they* think, too. That it's *just* a *gay* thing. And I just happen to be gay and handy." He points to the door. "They hate gays too. That other detective, that Crisco in a can, said to me, 'What'd you say your name is? Morgan? As in Morgan le *Fey*? That was King Arthur's sister, you know, Morgan. Ever read about the Knights of the Round Table, Camelot, all that stuff?' and then he started rambling on how errant knights were killed in duels fought to preserve the honor of fair maidens. I couldn't follow *what* he was saying, but I knew he was trying to bait me, so I was careful about what I said." He puts his hands over his eyes.

"God, I wish I could help them, Delilah. If I hadn't dragged ass going home, maybe I would have seen something, been able to provide them with some sort of description, *something*, but by the time I got there, the area was already roped off with crime scene tape and they were pulling me aside and the next thing I knew, I was here. The whole thing is a blur. And you know what kills me? Once they get it through their thick heads that I didn't do it, I don't think they'll give a rat's ass who did. Just one less queer, as far as they're concerned."

I don't know what to say. I heard how the detective who interrogated Morgan referred to him outside. But I don't want to believe he represents the aggregate of the department. I wonder how many other victims that attitude could affect. I feel a chill go up my spine. "What are you going to do when they let you go?" I ask him. "Where are you going to stay?"

Morgan shakes his head. "I don't know. I'm not going back there except to pick up my things from the loft when they say it's okay. I think I'll go stay with a member of the family somewhere."

"Do you want me to call anyone for you?" I look around the room. "A lawyer?"

The door opens behind us at the mention of the word. Detective Quick storms in. He looks more ruffled than he was before, his sleeves pushed up more carelessly, and he immediately gestures to me to leave. "Wait for me outside," he says, "down the hall, where we were before."

"He didn't do it," I say.

"Down the hall, Miss Price." Detective Quick ushers me out of the room and shuts the door behind him.

The room isn't so quiet any more. Another detective is sitting at another desk scribbling notes as a woman with a black eye and a bloody lip mumbles incoherently. "When did you last see him?" he asks. The woman mumbles a brief answer. "You haven't heard from him since?" She shakes her head and dabs her lip with a soiled handkerchief. More writing. I turn away from them and close my eyes and keep them closed until I sense the immediate presence of someone hovering over me.

"Miss Price," Detective Quick clears his throat, "you can go home. We'll call you if we need further information from you. If you think of anything in the meantime, call the number on the card I gave you."

"What about Morgan?"

"Morgan's going to spend the night here."

"You're putting him in *jail*? No!" I try to rush back to the room where they're keeping him. Detective Quick deftly blocks my path, his arms outstretched in the stance of a basketball player thwarting an inbound pass.

"He's not going in lock-up. There's a cot in the CO's office. I'm going to let him get a few hours of sleep, then we'll talk to him some more and then, if we're reasonably satisfied with his account of what happened, he can leave. Does he have family here he can stay with?"

"No," I say, "they're all in Michigan. He's from Grand Rapids."

Detective Quick looks at me questioningly and I expect him to say something else, but he doesn't, not right away. "Come with me," he says finally, "I'll get you a ride home."

He leads the way down a flight of stairs and up to a group of three officers talking shop in front of a candy machine.

"So what'd you charge him with?" one of the officers asks, crumpling a Milky Way wrapper in his hand.

"Criminal trespass *and* disorderly conduct *and* resisting arrest *and* impersonating a human." The officer who's the center of all the attention nods to Detective Quick, then turns to me and keeps looking as he finishes his story. "And all the while he's telling me he's going to lawyer up, and I say fine, I'll bet I can get your lawyer on something too. Hey, Hat Trick, what's up?"

"This young lady needs a ride home," he says, then keeps walking, waving for me to follow him. "And I'm taking her. Come on, Miss Price, let's go."

15

THE UNMARKED CAR IS DEPARTMENT ISSUE AND MUST HAVE BEEN ISSUED A long time ago. The dark upholstery is stained and torn around the edges. I sink deeper into the cracked leather seat, wishing I could be swallowed into the foam filling, thinking how much better off I'd be, how much *safer* I'd feel, if *I* were the one sleeping on the cot in the precinct house or in the jail, for that matter. Detective Quick's eyes, darting in my direction every time he stops for a red light, look darker than anything inside the car or out. "You're holding back something," he says as we shoot past Broome Street. "What is it?"

"Hmm?"

"What is it you're not telling me?"

"It's not relevant."

He slams his foot on the brake pedal at the next intersection. The light is green. A horn blares nonstop behind us. He signals for cars to pass and pulls over. I hear tires crunch against the curb. "Why don't you let *me* decide what's relevant, Miss Price. This is a murder investigation. You never know *what* small piece of information could be relevant."

"What I'm thinking about has nothing to do with what you're investigating," I squirm in my seat. "My own personal problem. I feel guilty for dwelling on it, considering what happened tonight. It seems minor by comparison. Well, maybe *not* so minor. I don't know."

Bad choice of words. This confession of guilt sparks his interest for still more information. "Well then, why don't you take a load off your mind and tell me about it." This is not a suggestion. He lets the motor run, ostensibly for the heat, but the car isn't going anywhere. Not yet. He stretches his arm over the back of the seat like a guy on a date who's trying to get closer, only he stays at that arm's length. "Maybe it's something I can help you with."

"Maybe you can," I say. "I'm being stalked."

Whatever it was he expected me to say, this wasn't it. He checks out approaching vehicles, mostly taxis, in his rearview mirror and then aims his high beam stare at me. "Have you reported this to your local precinct?"

"They're aware of it."

"What's going on?"

"It started with someone calling and hanging up. Then he didn't hang up, he left voice mail messages instead. Then he progressed to wanting to talk to me in person and leaving *hand*written messages. Well, one anyway."

"You saved it, I hope? And the voice mails?"

I nod. "All that stuff. Yes, I've got it."

"Do you know who's been doing this, Miss Price? Is he an acquaintance of yours or..."

"I don't think I ever saw him before. Didn't recognize him if I had."

"You saw him, though? You spoke with him?"

"Someone came into the school yesterday...Saturday morning...and started talking to me, and a little while later I found a note tacked up on the bulletin board. I just figured he was the one who left the note. Not that many people go in and out that aren't students there. Not that many people who aren't associated with the place even know what it *is*."

I'm guessing Detective Quick never knew about it either,

before all this came up. Most of the abstract art I expect he sees is forensic in nature, blood spatters on a sidewalk probably the closest he's ever come to a Jackson Pollock. "What did he say?"

"He asked if there was an exhibit inside he could see, which there was, and if there was anything of mine on display, which there wasn't. He said his name was Curtis."

"First or last?"

"He said he was Curt and that it was short for Curtis. I assumed that was his first name." I shrug. "But I guess it could also be his last. Or his middle name, for that matter."

"What else?"

"He asked me about my work and when and where it was going to go up and I was caught off guard enough to tell him Soho, but not *exactly* where, not *exactly* when."

"He'll be able to find that out easily enough."

I nod wearily.

"Okay, Miss Price. Exactly where and when *is* this exhibit of yours going to go up?"

"Galleria Lafayette. That's just a fancy name for a loft space over on Lafayette Street. It opens on the first of December."

"Good. There's lots of time between now and then."

"I wish *I* felt that way."

"Has he threatened you?"

"He's insinuated that he's not going to give up," I tell him. "That's as good as a threat to me."

He puts the car in gear and pulls away from the curb. "What you should do," he continues, "is contact your local precinct—that would be the sixth—each and every time this person makes contact, save notes and messages, keep filing complaints so there's a paper trail to trace. You want to keep the heat on him. If he keeps it up, he can be picked up on a variety of charges. Aggravated harassment, menacing, disorderly conduct. And once he's picked up and IDed, you can go down to Centre Street and get an order of protection from Criminal Court."

I shudder, recalling Ivan's warning about that. I haven't even mentioned Ivan or how panicky I'm getting at the thought of another confrontation with *him*. He could be waiting for me right now. Now is not the time to bring him up. I remember another of his warnings. *You know how it's going to look, Delilah, asking for protection against two guys? Flaky. Very flaky.*

"How will a restraining order make any difference?" I mumble. "It's just a piece of paper."

"It's *something* to go on." I hear sudden anger in Detective Quick's voice, a pain response to my direct hit on a departmental nerve.

I'm in familiar territory now. The basketball courts are to my right. My keys slide out of my sweaty palms as Detective Quick veers the funereal car in front of my building. I pick them out of my lap and turn to him. "I don't want to end up like Vittorio."

"We don't know all the circumstances that led up to Vittorio's murder, Miss Price."

"But it could have been something like this."

"It could have been anything."

"Morgan couldn't have done it."

"We don't know who did it yet."

I look up at my windows. "It could happen to me."

"Come on," he says, turning off the motor, but not the lights. "I'll walk you up."

Detective Quick vaults out of the car. In what seems like less than a second, he's opening my door. *Quick moving.* I feel glued to the seat. "Come on," he says again, more impatiently this time. He looks to both sides as he escorts me up the stairs, past the wilting chrysanthemums in the concrete flower pot on the top stoop. My hands shake conspicuously as I fumble through my keys and drop them again.

Detective Quick picks them up. "Allow me. Which is the right key?"

I fumble through them and pick out the one that says Yale. "Here." I hand it to him.

He thrusts the key in the lock and gives it a quick turn. The beveled glass window rattles in its frame, and he doesn't even have to push the door in hard. He holds it open for me. I look up the stairs. "Will you walk me to my door?" I ask him. He follows me, holding on to my keys. I take them from him when I get to the top of the stairs and riffle through them and hold out the keys that say Independent and Best. Best to be independent. Better to not *be* in this situation. I hear a door open and it isn't mine. I see the fuzzy gray top of Mrs. David-off's head lean past her doorsill, then disappear just as fast as she clicks the door shut behind her. Detective Quick goes for the top lock first, then the bottom. "What about the one in the middle?"

"Kiwi." I take the keys from him. They feel warm from his hands. The letters on the key I'm looking for are worn and practically unreadable. He watches me as I wiggle it in the lock, gingerly push the door open, and flick on the light switch.

"Everything okay here?" he asks.

"Looks that way."

He walks in and looks around for corroboration, taking in the pieces of sculpture propped on every tabletop, segregated stacks of artist magazines and partially read newspapers in the corner, the unmade bed, and the mess in the kitchen area. The latter looks like a crime scene even to me, but no different than when I left it this morning.

"Why don't you check your voice mail too while I'm here? I'll wait."

I reach in my bag and retrieve it and remember why Morgan couldn't reach me earlier. "Seems I forgot to charge it," I tell him.

"Avoidance isn't necessarily the best policy, Miss Price. A dead phone isn't going to do you much good in an emergency situation. Or if someone wants to get in touch with you," he says.

"Depending on who's wanting to get in touch."

He clears his throat. "*I* may need to call you regarding the Scaccia case, Miss Price, and I wouldn't want to keep getting no answer and have to send an RMP here to investigate or to pick you up and bring you downtown."

"Who's an RMP?"

"A radio car. I wouldn't want you to have to sit in back, in the cage like a common criminal, *just* so that I can ask you some questions that could just as easily be handled over the phone."

"Okay, okay," I hold up my hands in surrender, "I'll leave my phone on and fully charged from now on."

"Good. Is Morgan planning to stay with you?"

"No, he said something about staying with some friends. Gay friends. He didn't say who."

"He's likely to contact you, though, concerning his whereabouts and to tell you where he can be reached, isn't he, Miss Price?"

I nod. "I should think so..."

He strides to the door and runs his hand along the array of locks suggestively before stepping out in the hall. "We'll be in touch, Miss Price."

16

SOMEBODY TOUCHES ME, JUST BRUSHES BY AND BUMPS MY ELBOW; THAT'S what wakes me up in the middle of a reclining pose. I don't know how long I've been asleep and the artists are smiling as they move their paint around with sable brushes. It's wonderful, this certainty that your subject isn't going to move very much. and after last night, I'm still life. Oranges and peaches would be more likely to roll around than I am right now. I was barely able to sign in at the desk. I didn't see a guard on duty on my way in; he or she was probably in the restroom, but I signed the book anyway. This is the only place I've ever had to do that, show an ID to the security guard *and* sign a ledger, and I didn't object; it made me feel safe. Now I'm too tired to feel *anything*. Except that touch.

I force myself to move around before lividity sets in. I go in the hall to use the phone and try reaching Sachi to tell her about what happened last night. Her outgoing voice mail greeting informs me, "*We* can't come to the phone right now..." I picture them fused together like Siamese twins, maybe sharing a common nose ring by now. This isn't the kind of news to break on an answering machine. I leave a message for her to call me later. I go back in the studio and walk from easel to easel, looking at all of the painting that was accomplished while I was in my comatose state. In some paintings I'm missing limbs; I'm faceless on others. The ones that are more complete startle me in their similarity. Very frequently, I look like a *zaftig* Rubens model on one canvas and one of Modigliani's waifs on another, as if the artists are painting their version of what they'd like me to be or what they'd like to be themselves. Big boobs and snake hips are the most common distortions. I have to look down at myself for confirmation that the body depicted isn't exactly the one I inhabit, but not today because in all these paintings, even the faceless, limbless ones, I look gaunt, like I haven't eaten in a month, and on those canvases where I *do* have a face, that face doesn't look very happy. My dirty blond hair *looks* unwashed, my eyes limned with dark shadows, my mouth tense and tight. I don't have to gaze in a mirror to know these neophyte artists are painting *exactly* how I'm looking and feeling.

The instructor walks around the room, raving about one canvas, criticizing another. "There's no sense of volume here." She traces the work in front of her with a blunt fingernail. "She looks flat, one-dimensional. Like road kill."

This work though illustrates more acumen than do most of the others. I *have* been run over. Repeatedly. The only thing I'm missing is tread marks.

17

WHEN I GET HOME, I'M DEAD TIRED BUT NOT TOO TIRED TO NOTICE THAT the concrete flower pot on the top stoop of the stairs is littered with cigarette butts and stems cut close to the soil are all that's left of Mrs. Davidoff's beloved chrysanthemums. I wonder if the same street person who smoked the Marlboros plucked the flowers. It's bad enough when they piss on them. I decide that after I get some sleep, say about three days' worth, I'll go out and buy some new blooms to beautify the decaying entrance. It might get her off my case for a day or two. Maybe even longer if I promise to do the watering.

I fumble with the keys and drop them. My whole body is stiff from the pose I held for so long. Maybe not long enough. At least I got a nap out of it. I insert the key on the second try and totter up the stairs almost noiselessly, tiptoeing like a prowler who doesn't belong here. I gasp when I reach the top of the stairs. Somebody dumped a heap of chrysanthemum blossoms at my doorstep in an arrangement that would make Martha Stewart lose her lunch. Yellow petals are scattered everywhere, and near them there's a note written on a sheet of paper torn from a yellow legal pad. I crouch to pick it up and read it:

I've picked you. You're mine. It's just a matter of weeding out the competition.

My hands shake as I quickly gather up the flowers—what
there is of them—by their short stems and squeeze them
in my fist. I thrust the note in my pocket and head down
the stairs and out of the building and keep walking. I turn
down West Tenth Street, clutching at the bundle of decapi-
tated chrysanthemums, and walk faster until I see a blue-and-
white, an *RMP*, pull out of a driveway and I know I'm close
to my destination. I run the rest of the way until I'm safely
inside and pull up breathlessly at the front desk, in front of a
big red STOP sign. I hold out the flowers to the first police
officer I see.

"For me?" he smiles quizzically.

"These were left for me," I babble, "like this, on the floor
in front of my doorstep, with this note..." I fish it out of my
pocket with trembling fingers and thrust it in the smirking
officer's face. I look around the room for either of the officers
who came to my place Friday night, a familiar face, someone
familiar with my situation. "Could I speak to Officer Veni-
son?"

This just prompts a bigger grin. I hear somebody somewhere behind the tall desk to my left say, "Didn't know he
was such a *dear*." I feel my face turn cadmium red medium.
"Vinson," I correct myself. "Officer *Vinson*." The officers con-
tinue to chuckle. Mixed in with their whispered giggles, I
hear the names Bambi and Thumper. "Somebody's stalking
me," I finally shout too loudly. "He left this pile of flowers at
my doorstep. He left this note. It's not the first note he's left
me. I want to file a complaint."

A man in plain clothes signals me to one side. He reminds
me of one of those hundreds-of-years-old men in the Cauca-
sus who stay young by eating yogurt and probably could use
some. He has a huge bushy gray mustache and a shaven head,

but is by no means even a half century old. The job must have
taken its toll. He looks very dour. I'm very grateful for dour.
Dour is exactly what I came here for. "Let's see the note," he
grumbles, and I hand it to him. He doesn't move a facial mus-
cle. "This isn't overtly threatening," he says solemnly, handing the note back to me. "Are you sure it isn't from some
boyfriend of yours just trying to be clever?"

Leaving flowers at my doorstep is very easily something
Ivan would do, but he would leave four dozen red sweetheart
roses mixed in with birds of paradise and white carnations,
all with stems attached, something I could stick in a vase and
add water to, thereby constantly reminding me of his existence. That's more his style. Not that that would be any less
threatening.

"These weren't left by any boyfriend," I insist. "These were
left by the guy who's been calling me and following me
around, I'm sure of it. He left me another note Saturday,
when I was working in the art studio over on West Eighth.
Now he's left this right at my front door. *Inside*. And defaced
private property besides!"

"You have the other note?"

"Not with me," I admit. "It's in my apartment. I didn't even
go inside. I just took off and rushed here as soon as I saw
this." I feel weak-kneed. "I don't even know if he got in my
apartment. He could have been waiting for me in my apartment."

"Was there any sign of forced entry?"

"I didn't look. I just ran."

"Well if, when you get around to looking, something looks
fishy, don't go inside, just go someplace else to call us. Okay
now, you say this person's been calling you *and* following
you. For how long?"

I shrug. "I wasn't aware of it until he started leaving messages. I was getting hang-up calls for...oh, I guess weeks, then

he began talking. And leaving messages when no one was home."

"What did he say?"

I babble what I can remember of the messages, watching the mustached cop's face, waiting for a reaction. His lips pucker like he's eaten something sour. "And yes," I assure him, "I saved the messages."

"Good thinking," he says. It's hard to tell what this cop is thinking.

Detective Quick was equally inscrutable last night. *Or was he?* I remember him losing it a couple of times, showing some emotion, and I wonder if I shouldn't have just called him instead of coming here. *Contact your local precinct* is what he advised me to do, so here I am doing what I was told and getting the distinct feeling that this centuries-old yogurt cop thinks I'm making an unnecessary stink over a well-intentioned if poorly packaged bouquet of dead flowers.

"What are you going to do about this?"

His mustache twitches like he's anticipating a sneeze. "Fill out a sixty-one," he says, signaling me to follow him. He leads the way up a flight of stairs, past stacks of filing cabinets, and stops in front of a door with a gold shield affixed to it, a magnification of the one dangling from a chain around his neck. He holds it open for me, slams it shut behind him, and ambles past me into a small office on the left. I follow him inside. He yanks a pink form out of a manila folder propped on top of the gun metal desk and barks questions at me, filling in the answers sloppily with a felt-tip pen. I cross and uncross my legs, fumbling through some of the answers, correcting myself a couple of times. The detective glares at me and reaches for a bottle of correction fluid. "I haven't had much sleep," I say. An apology.

"Things tend to get blown out of proportion when you're over-tired," he grumbles, block-printing the information I mixed up. A low blow.

I go through it all again, the account of every phone call that I can recall, the notes, the messages.

"This guy who's allegedly following you," he clears his throat. "Have you ever gotten a good look at him?"

I nod.

"Enough so you can describe him?"

"He's big."

"Well, *that's* a start."

I try to mimic cop talk. "Last seen wearing a dirty blue baseball cap, gray T-shirt…I think it was gray, and blue jeans. Indigo blue, you know, really dark. Blue eyes. Couldn't see the color of his hair, it was covered by the baseball cap."

"Eyebrows?"

"Excuse me?"

"Did you see the color of his eyebrows? That would give an approximation of hair color at least."

I shake my head. "He wore the cap low. I could barely see his eyes."

"How many times you seen him?"

"Only once that I know of," I say. Yogurt cop stops writing and raises his eyebrows. "But he was seen later that same day, tailing me back to West Eighth Street."

"By whom?"

I cough. "My ex-boyfriend."

"*Ex*-boyfriend. You're still on good terms?"

"Not exactly."

"Good enough though for him to be telling you this information." *Good enough for him to be leaving you flowers.*

"Bad enough that I had to call the cops on him three nights ago."

Yogurt cop's mustache is really twitching now. "What'd *he* do?"

I pull the hem of my dress down over my knees and run it back and forth through my fingers. "Threaten me, sort of.

He'd pushed me around before. I didn't know what he was going to do."

"Sounds like you got problems, sort of," he says impassively, making a new notation on the form he's working on. "You better give me the *ex*-boyfriend's name and number in case we got to get in touch with him."

"I'd really rather you didn't." I wet my lips. "He's not involved with *this*."

"He's a material witness. He saw the guy you say has been following you. We might need to talk to him."

Like when I'm dead? I grip the sides of the chair as I tell yogurt cop Ivan's name, rank, and cell phone number. "This note," he pokes at the note clenched in my hand with his pen. "It's not signed. Was the other?"

I shake my head. "No, it wasn't. But it's written the same way. On the same kind of paper too."

"Hold on to this stuff. We may need it later." He crosses his arms on the desk and looks at me with hungry hound-dog eyes. "This isn't a whole lot to go on, Miss Price. The most we could get this guy on now, even if we knew who he is—which we *don't*—is harassment in the second degree, which is a violation punishable by up to fifteen days in jail." I wince, and my reaction isn't lost on him. "Yeah, I know, but what you've got to have to get a tougher charge is proof of intent to harm, and you don't have it. What you do have here is a complaint form," he flutters it in my face, "and if this guy continues to harass you, you come in here and refer to the case number I'm going to give you and we fill out a follow-up and maybe we come up with more info and enough on him to get him out of your hair. You did the right thing coming here," he reassures me. "There just isn't a whole lot to go on."

"Can't I get a court order?"

"You don't know who to cite as the person the court is supposed to protect you from," he says. "You have to give them more to go on. Once the guy gets IDed, if it turns out

he's been in trouble before, we can get him on repeat offend-
er status. Meanwhile, keep the notes, keep the tapes, and if
you hear from him again," he hands me a piece of paper with
a row of digits written across it, "keep in touch. Ask to speak
to me and refer to this number."

"Just who do I ask for?"

He stands up to follow me out and pushes his chair back
with a screech that makes my teeth hurt. "Rubenstein."

Quick and Rubenstein. Makes me think of a Park Avenue law
firm.

I walk back up West 10th, turning around every time
I hear someone following me. Just past the laundromat, I
hear *psst! psst!* I clench my fists. *Psst!* Some guy who thinks
he's a real cobra. I turn around tentatively, afraid I'll see
Curtis behind me, wary that Ivan has tracked me down.
The only male I see is short and has a face riddled with
pock marks. *Like snakeskin.* "Hey, I seen you come out of the
police station," he says. "You seen a woman named Constan-
za in there? She's about my height, dark hair, built like *this.*"
He exaggerates her endowments wildly with his hands, like
some of the artists I've worked for do with their charcoal
pencils.

"I didn't see anyone in there," I mumble as I back away.
"Just police."

"I'll bet." I see the sparkle of a gold tooth. "So, baby, what'd
you get busted for?"

I walk faster. Busting loose is what I'm doing. Trying to
get away from everything. The sight of yet another blue-and-
white speeding southbound down Seventh Avenue, its siren
screaming, makes me cringe. *What is it this time?* At least it
quickly dispatches my pursuer in the other direction.

I look to my left down Waverly Place and instantly see
Mrs. Davidoff.

She's standing at the top of the stairs wearing a too-big-for-her blue floral house dress, her head bowed sadly over the empty flowerpot. She doesn't see me.

I turn right.

18

for her blue floral blouse that I just had blood stained over the empty flowerpot, the dozen bloom....

Here I am.

THERE'S A MESSAGE FOR ME FROM MORGAN WHEN I GET TO WEST EIGHTH Street.

He's at a friend's place, just got up, nothing added on the memo about how he can be reached, just that he'll call me later. Nothing from Sachi. A terse I CALLED—WILL CALL BACK from Ivan.

And somebody called and wanted to know HOW DID YOU LIKE THE FLOWERS?

Not Ivan, Louise the receptionist scrawled in addendum.

He won't leave his name.

"Is that all he said?" I ask. As if that's not enough. I wave the pink memo in Louise's face just as she hungrily tears off a piece of croissant and stuffs it in her mouth. "Someone...whoever left this message...just picked all the flowers from the pot on the stoop of my apartment house and left them at my door."

Her eyes widen and she holds up a finger as she quickly chews and swallows. "That is some weird shit, Delilah," she says, reaching for her coffee mug.

"When did he call?"

She looks at her watch and frowns. "About an hour ago?

I'm not sure. I've been swamped. Calls about the lecture Wednesday night."

"Did you notice anything unusual about the call?" All the time I've been spending in police stations is rubbing off on me.

Louise licks the confectionery sugar off her lips. "I'd say the call is pretty unusual in itself."

"I mean, background noise, static, stuff like that?"

"Can't say," Louise tears off another piece of croissant. "Want some?"

I shake my head. "Can I use the phone?"

She nods and chews luxuriantly, making disgusting yummy sounds. I dig in my fanny pack for Detective Quick's card and call the number he circled there, only to be told he's in court.

"When can I reach him?"

The woman on the other end sighs a non-committal, "Later." Like, *any time between five p.m. and midnight when I'm not here to deal with this.* She sounds like she could be eating a croissant too.

Calling the Sixth Precinct would be redundant. It's after four. Detective Rubenstein is probably still out on that case he was headed to when I left, or gone for the day, period. And I have nothing substantial to follow up on, no leads, nothing in handwriting, no voice to trace through the phone company, just a sinister message relayed through Louise, whose biggest concern is who the Bachelorette is going to pick for an all-too-short engagement tonight. And I'm not convinced that *any*one else is going to read this as being 'overtly threatening.'

"Any more messages?"

Louise looks up at me as she brushes her hands together, scattering buttery crumbs on a pile of unopened manila envelopes. "Gee, Delilah, I should think those were more than enough."

She's got a point.

I turn to go to the sculpture studio when the phone rings again. I hear Louise snap, "Hello?" Then she calls me back. "Morgan," she whispers, her hand over the mouthpiece.

I grab the receiver. "I tried calling before. Where've you been?" he asks, big brotherly as always, but today he sounds programmed. There is a deadness in his voice, and anyway, *he's* the one whose whereabouts are unknown; *he's* the one who's in trouble. He doesn't wait for me to answer. "I can't give you my number here," he says. "I don't even know how long I'll be here. But you'll be hearing from me; I'll stay in touch."

"But what if the police should ask me?"

"I should think they got what they wanted from me last night. Assurance that I wasn't their *man*," he says acidly. "But if something else occurs to them, you're not lying to them if you say you don't know where I am or how I can be reached." I hear clinking glasses in the background. I can guess where he is.

I hate to have to ask him the next question. "Are you hiding from the police, Morgan?" But better *that* than, *have you done something you can't tell anyone about?* Detective Quick or one of his partners against crime will be sure to get around to asking me more questions about why Morgan hasn't been in touch, why he can't be reached. I can't let him, *any* of them, think that I doubt Morgan's innocence. *I can't believe that I doubt Morgan's innocence.*

"I'm hiding from myself, Delilah," he says. "I can't think about what's happened. I want to be in *oblivion*, Delilah."

He's just understandably upset over what happened. He needs to feel cloistered, as in a cocoon; wherever it is that he is, he needs to feel nothing more can get to him, to hurt him. I feel embarrassed for having asked. As long as I've known Morgan, I've never known him to do anything impulsive or violent.

When I started going out with Ivan, he was a perfect gentleman. Then I let him move in with me. Then he changed. He raised his voice at me, began belittling me. He accused me of cheating on him with everyone. Then he shoved me into a wall.

How can I know what I don't see? Maybe anyone is capable of violence under certain circumstances.

Morgan hiccups. I wonder how many drinks he's had already, and it's just turning dark. I wonder if he's commiserating alone or if he's seeking solace with a stranger. I wonder if he routinely carries condoms on him, if he'll be sober enough to remember to use one if he needs it. *Big sisterly.* "Be careful," I implore him. *You know what I mean.* Then I shudder at the thought. He loved Vittorio. How could he just let some stranger ram it in him before Vittorio's body was cold? Unless there's something I don't know. *I don't want to know.*

Morgan chuckles dully. "Yeah," he says, like it's the last thing on his mind. "Gotta run, Delilah. Someone else wants to use the phone. I'll call you later. I'm not sure when." He clears his throat. "It'll have to be at random. Won't be any use putting a tracer on it," he hisses as a warning to whoever I might be forced to tell. Morgan's call is not exactly top priority for tracing in my book, but he's talking like he's still a suspect. *Is he?*

I don't get a chance to ask; we're disconnected.

Louise looks up at me questioningly. "What do the police want with Morgan? Some detective called and wanted to know whether I'd seen Morgan yesterday or today and who was on the desk last night. I gave him Ed's home number."

I don't know if she even knows what happened to Vittorio last night; when she handed me the message from Morgan's first call, she mentioned that she hadn't seen him all day and I didn't know what to say. There's even less I want to say now. "Morgan's lover was killed by someone last night. The police initially seemed to think he did it." *They might still think he did it. I'm not entirely sure any more that he didn't do it.*

"Oh, my God," Louise gasps, "Did they find out who *did?*"

"No."

"But what happened? Where? When? How?"

I shrug and turn to go in the sculpture studio. Let her read the who/what/where/when details in the paper. It's sure to be tabloid news, because the crime was committed in a gentrified part of town and remains unsolved. Nightmares sell papers in this city. God only knows why.

19

"WHY HAVEN'T I BEEN ABLE TO REACH YOU?" IVAN DEMANDS. "WHERE'VE you been?" He's keeping his voice on low simmer, but it could blow up the phone any second and I hold the phone a couple of inches away from my ear for my own protection. I can still hear him. "Your phone wasn't on. Again. I thought something happened to you, that that guy who's been following you..."

My hero. Oh, puke. I hold the phone a little farther away, bracing myself for the Grand Finale.

"...called the school and one of those other places where you work, on Twenty-Third Street, the emergency room at Downtown Hospital, Beth Israel." He pauses. "Bellevue."

"Did you call the city morgue too, while you were at it?"

"That's at Bellevue, Delilah,"

If someday someone has to run a tracer on Ivan, I'd suggest they start with Creedmoor Psychiatric Center. They won't have to go much further than that. Someday he's going to blow. *Blow my brains out.* Hearing his voice makes me feel like I'm on the Cyclone after one too many hot dogs at Nathan's. I tell him why I haven't been home and he sounds unconvinced, like I manufactured Vittorio's murder to cover up for other, more lurid activities. It's too pat, too *convenient* for him.

"In any case," I say, "I turned off my phone after the *last* time you called. Get the message?"

"Our messages seem to be crossing, Delilah. You didn't get mine. I *care* about you." His voice isn't oozing concern though, just anger that I would have the audacity to cut myself off from his grasp. "I worry, you know?" he continues. "I don't want anything to happen to you." *Unless I'm the one making it happen.*

Ivan worries a lot about what he can't control, whether it be the NYSE or me. I think that maybe when he gets over this rejection he should consider getting himself a pet to keep him company. Not a dog or cat; that would be too easy. A boa constrictor would be a good choice. He could probably even teach the snake a few things about how to squeeze the life out of people.

"I'll be okay," I tell him, wishing I wholeheartedly believed it. "I've *seen* Curtis, remember? I know who to be on the lookout for now."

Him and you.

"I filed a complaint. It's being looked into. All he has to do is show up on my doorstep again and he gets hauled off," I tell him. *And that goes for you too.*

"What do you mean, again?"

Shit. I suddenly rap on the wall loud enough for him to hear. "I've got to go," I tell him, "There's someone at the door."

"Who is it?"

"I don't know," I say, rapping harder. "Police. I think he said it's the police. Guy's holding up something so I can't see his face. Looks like a shield. Yeah, gold shield. It's a detective." I hold the phone away from my ear and kick the door a couple of times. "Just a minute," I call out, then lower my voice. "Look, I've got to go, Ivan. If I don't let him in, he'll kick the door down. I think he thinks Morgan's hiding out here."

"Is he?"

"I've got to go."

"I'll call back later."

"Don't bother."

"Oh, it's no bother," he says too sweetly.

I push the disconnect key in hard and notice the voice mail message bar on my phone flashing red as if auguring a national emergency. I push the playback button. Two messages to hire me to model, one of them from Heidi Obermeyer. A message from Pearl Paint to remind me to pick up a special order. A message from Detective Quick asking me to call him at the precinct at my earliest convenience. I feel exonerated. *See, Ivan, the police really do want to talk to me.*

I'm not so sure I want to talk to the police right now. Talking to Detective Quick on the phone will no doubt be easier than sitting across a desk from him, averting that stare that probably sears holes in the hearts of paper targets. I pull out his card, take a deep breath, and poke in his number. He picks up on the second ring. "Quick." I can't tell if he's merely identifying himself or issuing a command. Probably both.

"Delilah Price," I say.

"I need to get in touch with Morgan," he says succinctly. "He hasn't called us. Have you heard from him?"

"Yes."

"Good. Give me a number where he can be reached."

"I can't." I hear him take a deep breath. I have to be very careful with what I say and how I say it as I head him off at the pass. "I don't know where he can be reached. He didn't say where he was."

"Did you try asking?"

"It sounded like a bar," I tell him honestly. There are a *lot* of bars in this city. "What do you want him for now, anyway?" My question is spontaneous enough but the ensuing pause makes me wonder if Detective Quick assumes that Morgan put me up to asking that.

"I'd like him to come to the loft with us to see if he notices anything as missing. Also, we need a recent photo of the deceased to use in the canvass. The first twenty-four hours after a homicide are crucial for gathering evidence that may lead to nabbing our killer, Miss Price. You might impress Morgan with that when and if he gets in touch with you again. I *presume* he said he would?"

"Yes," I swallow hard. "I'm not holding back any information. I *just don't know.*"

"But you'll find out and then you'll tell us, won't you?"

"You don't want him to come in just so that you can arrest him?"

"As long as he didn't do anything wrong, he has nothing to worry about." I close my eyes and say a silent prayer. "We figure that he knows a lot more about what's supposed to be in the loft than we do; he lives there—at least he *did*—and we could use his help. He signed a statement last night giving us permission to go in the place. It's about the only thing he *did* do for us. Last night he wasn't much help at all."

"He doesn't sound much better now."

"In a bar, you said?" Detective Quick raises his voice over sudden commotion in the squad room.

"There are a *lot* of bars in this city," I remind him. If I mention the name of any one of the four or five places I surmise Morgan might have called me from, Quick would dispatch a blue-and-white there, *very quickly* too. But Morgan is probably long gone. "Look, Detective Quick, it might help if, when Morgan goes to the loft with you, he has a friend with him. He might go more willingly."

"You want to go?"

The thought of it nauseates me almost as much as Ivan's voice did. "Sure."

The truth is, I want this nightmare to be over for Morgan

and I want my nightmares to stop and if I do this, if I help the police nab Vittorio's killer, maybe then I'll feel like they'll be so grateful that they'll bend over backwards to arrest my stalker while they're at it. *Both stalkers.* As much as it undoes me, Quick's dark intensity is at the same time reassuring to me. He's not like any of the other cops I've met.

"I've been in the apartment a few times, so maybe I can be of some help even if Morgan doesn't..."

"Why wouldn't Morgan want to cooperate with us?"

My mouth goes dry. "I think he thinks he's being railroaded," I cough. "Because of the gay angle."

"We're not conducting a witch hunt; we're trying to find out who killed his companion. We're looking at the case from all angles." *Companion.* The word has a nice PC tone to it. I can imagine how Quick's partner last night referred to Morgan's *companion.*

"What about the staff in the restaurant? Haven't you checked *that* out?"

"Yes, we have checked that out and nobody we've talked to who works in that restaurant admits to having called Mr. Scaccia..."

"And you're taking their word for it."

"You're taking Morgan's word for it that someone *did* call."

"Someone called during the dinner party. I was there. Vittorio said it was a wrong number, but..."

"We're by no means finished with that aspect of the investigation, but there's nothing to implicate anyone who works there."

"Yet."

"That's right, not yet."

"Any other leads?" I ask hopefully.

"No. Though Mr. Scaccia was stabbed numerous times, I will tell you that the pattern isn't consistent with what is usual in crimes committed by gays. Of course there are variables. He could have been the target of a gay basher. We don't know the motive yet, but it wasn't robbery." He pauses. "I'm not saying Morgan is a strong suspect right now, but his not wanting to cooperate makes it look like he has something to hide."

"I'll urge him to come," I say. "I'll do what I can."

"You can do it," he says. The finality of his tone cautions me that I won't get clemency if I should fail. "Call me the minute you hear from him. Any time before ten a.m. tomorrow. We'll set something up."

"And if I *don't* hear from him by then?"

"Then you'll meet me in front of the First, anyway," he says, "At noon. We'll ride over to Franklin Street from here. In the meantime, think hard about where Morgan might be, Miss Price, and try to get in touch with him tonight and get him to come along voluntarily. For his own good. After all," his voice lowers, "if someone out there has a vendetta against gays and knew both of them, he might be a target too."

I didn't consider *this* angle. Maybe Morgan has all along and didn't want to tell me so I wouldn't have any more to worry about than I already do. But if that's the case, would he be staying with gay friends who would also be targets, who would make him more of a target? I make up my mind to contact everyone who was at the party Saturday night to see if anyone has seen him, if anyone knows where I can find him before the police beat me to it.

I start with Gary and Abel.

"Delilah, I still can't believe it. We're both in a state of shock here." Gary's voice is hushed. "What a freak thing. You're not safe anywhere. It said on the news that Vittorio was taking out the trash when it happened. The police didn't tell us anything. Poor Morgan, he's got to be devastated."

"You already talked to the police?"

"Oh, hours ago. Two plain clothes guys stopped by. They told us Morgan gave them the names of everyone who was at the loft Saturday night, flashed their fancy badges to make it official, and asked questions about who was at the party and how everyone was getting along. All very routine, they said, and then wanted to know where Morgan was, what *sex joint* they could find him in was what the fat one wanted to know."

"What did you tell them?"

"Darling, we haven't seen Morgan *or* Vittorio since yesterday morning at the Marathon and that's what we told them."

"Have you heard from him?"

"Yes," Gary says, "but he didn't say where he was. We both offered our condolences to him, naturally. We talked a little about why and who, but Morgan really wasn't up to it. He *did* tell us we'd probably get visited by the cops, but that they probably weren't going to bust their asses solving this by any means because he gets it up his."

"It sounds to *me* like they're trying to solve it," I say.

"It sounded to *us* like they wanted to bust *him*."

If they felt they had a case, they would have booked him last night: they had him and they let him go. I don't want to get into an argument. *You don't understand*, Gary will complain and maybe rightfully too, *you're straight*. I try to understand, but I'll never know firsthand what it's like to be looked down upon or ostracized or outright attacked because of who I choose to love.

I could be attacked at any minute by someone who unwisely chose to love *me* and isn't getting any back. I want to believe in the system right now.

"Have Morgan call me if you hear from him again," I say.

I don't make any more phone calls.

20

1010 WINS NEWS IS BRIMMING OVER WITH FRESHLY PERKED MURDERS ALL over the city. The badly decomposed body of a female found in the trunk of an abandoned car on West Street. A hit-and-run on East Houston. And across the river, a love triangle that led to a blood bath in Sunnyside. Vittorio's murder is already *old* news by this city's standards. I wonder what happens *after* that first twenty-four hours after a homicide which are supposedly *so crucial* for gathering evidence. I wonder if there is some kind of hourglass used to time just how long a detective can be expected to pursue a clunker of a case.

Vittorio's murder isn't even written up on page one, but on page five of the first tabloid I grab at the newsstand in front of the West Fourth Street subway station, even though the more recent murders were discovered too late to make the first edition, just as Vittorio's body was the night before last. I wonder about priorities. If Vittorio had been *straight,* someone *esteemed,* his demise would make page one in bold print; no stone would be left unturned looking for who did this. The last line of the story implores anyone having *any* information about this crime to call (800) 577-TIPS. All such stories end like this. I wonder if even one person will call in this case, if this really is the end of the line.

I fold the newspaper and tuck it under my arm as I start to go down the stairs to the subway. I don't look forward to telling Detective Quick that I haven't heard from Morgan since yesterday. *He's probably hung over. He's probably blocked a lot of it out. He'll come around. He's responsible.*

I can hear Quick now. Responsible for *what*, Miss Price?

I dig in my fanny pack for a MetroCard and swipe it at the turnstile only to find out I need to add more money to it. No back-up in my pockets either. I swing my nylon backpack off my shoulder and yank at the strings until it's open wide enough for me to get at my wallet without anyone else being able to grab it. I yank out a ten-dollar bill and hand that and the card to the attendant in the booth. Then I whirl around and walk into Curtis

"Hi," he says.

I don't want to say even *this* much to him. I start to walk around him. He does a little side step to his left, effectively blocking my path. I try the other way. He slides to his right and gives a little smile of pleasure, like he's doing the underground shuffle with me. I take a few steps backward and put a hand up like a cop stopping traffic, warning him not to advance.

"I just wanted to say I'm sorry about your friend," he says gesturing to the paper squeezed under my arm. "It's terrible to lose a friend. Especially like that. So unexpected. So undeserving. Obviously at the wrong place at the wrong time."

I nod, all the while making a quick study of him, the soiled sweatshirt, the dirty jeans, the same dirty baseball cap. I wonder what color hair he's hiding under there. I wonder *if* there's any hair under there. *How the hell does he know Vittorio was my friend?*

"If there's anything I can do..."

"I think you've done enough," I say.

"What do you mean?"

"The flowers were the absolute last straw!"

"Didn't you like them?"

I *don't believe* this guy. I take a deep breath and turn around and run up the stairs and around the corner. I drop the newspaper and don't reach down to get it. I don't turn around. I run all the way to the station between Broadway and Lafayette clenching my MetroCard in my fist and don't stop shaking until I come out of the subway station on Canal Street and see nothing but Asian women around me. No sign of Curtis here. As I walk westward, I approach the red metal stairs leading up to the familiar art emporium. I duck inside to look around and pick up my order while I'm at it. A diversionary tactic.

The line in Pearl Paint is longer than I anticipated, and when I finally get well past the corner of Varick Street, I see Detective Quick standing between the green lanterns at the entrance of the precinct, unhappily looking down at his watch, then up at me as I approach. "You're twenty minutes late."

I feel bad about the bundle of art supplies I'm carrying awkwardly under my arm and at a loss to explain myself. "It was in the neighborhood," I explain feebly.

"So you thought, why not try to kill two birds with one stone."

I leave that stone unturned. I fall in step behind him as he leads me to an unmarked car that is in markedly better condition than the first one I rode in with him. "I was followed," I tell him when he shuts his door, feeling like a fourth-grader fabricating a tale of why her homework wasn't done on time.

Quick looks in his rearview mirror, making sure that nobody is following him as he pulls into traffic.

"By whom?"

"The guy who's been stalking me. I would have been here sooner. I had to take a detour. You know, to get away from him." I lean into the cushy leather upholstery and take a deep breath. I tell him about the flowers left at my doorstep, the message left at the school, the complaint I filed, glancing over at him to see if he's buying it. I dig the piece of paper Rubenstein gave me out of my wallet and chant the case number twice like a mantra. "I talked to somebody called Rubenstein."

"Marty," he nods. "I know him."

"He said there's not much anyone can do right now unless Curtis makes some kind of move."

"That's true."

Quick hangs a sudden left turn and pulls up on the curb in front of a sign that says NO PARKING EVER in bold red.

That is, unless you're part of the blue.

"He's already entered my building and accosted me on the street, and I have a creepy feeling that he's done a lot more just to know all there is to know about me. I wouldn't call that being *stationary*."

I follow Quick and look up at the building where until Sunday night Morgan and Vittorio happily occupied a loft. Deflated black and orange balloons hang sadly from the rungs of the fire escape. Yellow plastic ribbon that looks like a party streamer sags to the ground. A garbage can heaving its contents on the loading dock blocks our path. Quick steps around the refuse. When I hesitate, he motions for me to follow him. "It's okay," he says, luring me away from the scene of the crime. "Come on."

He slides the cage door of the service elevator aside for me to enter, follows me in, and pushes the button for the top floor. "I take it you haven't heard from Morgan since we talked."

I shake my head.

He takes a deep breath. As the elevator ascends toward the roof, I see the very polished tips of black leather shoes tapping the floor impatiently, then an ill-fitting dark gray double-breasted suit, then the cadaverous face of a man who looks so bored that he's probably been tapping out the hours until he can start collecting his pension. The elevator creaks to a halt. Mr. Bored looks past me. "Already got the super to open up for us," he says, flapping a folded document that could be the signed statement from Morgan or a bench warrant. It looks like a take-home project for a beginner's origami class.

"Royko, you got anything?"

"Could be."

Quick turns to me. "Miss Price, we need a picture of Vittorio, a fairly recent one, to show around. Someone who might not have known him might recognize the person in the photo and be able to tell us something."

"Just look places where you think it's likely you might find what we want," Royko adds. "Chances are we already looked there. We looked everyplace else."

"What makes you think *I* can find a photo in here if *you* can't?"

"We weren't just looking for a *photo* the other night, Miss Price."

I lead the way into the loft where *just three nights ago* I was comfortably curled up on this white leather sofa. Now it might just as well be sheathed in plastic with a DO NOT REMOVE OR SIT ON UNDER PENALTY OF LAW warning tag attached. I cruise by the wall-to-wall paintings and stop at a familiar face. Vittorio. *Of course* Morgan would have painted him. Did he do it from a photo or did Vittorio pose for him? I reach for the painting. Quick clears his throat. "I don't think we can use anything quite as big as a canvas when we're conducting a canvass, Miss Price." He smiles at the idea of this though, a smile that makes me think of a dress accessory, not something he'd have occasion to wear often. It looks good on him.

There are paintings of me here too. I forgot about that. Royko gawks at them like a fourteen-year-old flipping through his first issue of *Penthouse*. Morgan's so good, so attentive to detail that my face is as identifiable as it would be in a photo. So are other parts of me that I suddenly wish were hidden with a layer of cobalt violet. I cross my arms in front of me. When at last Royko turns to me again, he brush strokes me with his eyes. Quick takes in the paintings too, but with the composure of a man who's seen other works of art in his lifetime.

"Morgan may have done that from a photo," I suggest, diverting attention away from the nudes of me to the portrait of a bare-to-the-chest Vittorio.

"Keep trying."

I wander into the kitchen area, scanning for graven images push-pinned to the cork board or lined up behind some yuppie appliance. My fingers tentatively skim through a mail basket. Royko looks around. He gestures to the wall behind me. "Nice exhibit of cutlery there."

I don't know anything about the knives, can't recall ever seeing the knives before. There they are stacked in a graduated rack above the butcher block counter, a family tree of cutting tools, and their flash under the fluorescent light seems leering.

Royko seems to be counting them off on his fingers *eeny-meeny-miny* style. "Nothing missing here."

"Doesn't seem that way."

"Maybe there's a photo in the bedroom," I say. The two men stay at the threshold. I hear snatches of their conversation as I rummage through a straw basket on top of the pine dresser, aware that they are aware of me being aware of them.

"What do you have for me?"

"This may be nothing, but the neighbor across the street says he heard someone saying 'Stay away! Stay away!' or something like that. After ten."

"Did he have an accent?"

"No, that's the thing, Hat trick, the guy doing the yelling *didn't have* no accent."

"Any luck, Miss Price?"

"No." I shrug haplessly, "Sorry." It's just that I'm afraid of what I might find or find out if I look too hard.

"Damn the fuck who tore out his damn passport photo," Royko grumbles. "Oops. Sorry."

Quick doesn't say anything, but his body language is telling me that I'm not off the hook. He tilts his head to the left. "Okay, let's go." He steps back to let me pass. The sudden brief closeness to him in the threshold makes my skin prickle. I don't dare look up at him, look at his eyes. I walk ahead of him and Royko, but I hear them tailing close behind. As I pass the wall of paintings again on the way out, I hear a speculative whisper: "You think there's more there than meets the eye?" No answer. Royko continues, "I've *never seen* nipples *that* big. Sure must've been cold." He chuckles. I'm sure not cold *now*. My cheeks burn like I've got a fever of 104.

21

"YOU COULD BE GETTING YOURSELF IN *BIG* TROUBLE IF YOU'RE WITHHOLDING information. Interfering with an investigation is obstruction of justice. If Morgan did something he shouldn't have in the heat of the moment and it turns out you've been protecting him, that's a felony." Detective Quick glowers at me as he starts the engine. "You'd have a criminal record. You could go to jail. Do you want that?"

"If you're so sure Morgan did something he shouldn't have, why didn't you arrest him Sunday? You had him there all night."

"Frankly I didn't feel we had anything solid against him, so we let him go. I told him before he left we'd want to talk to him some more. Now he pulls a vanishing act. It's not helping his credibility any. It's also possible Morgan was a witness to the crime, saw it happen and fended off an attack on himself. He might be hiding out because he's scared. If he'd let us know where he is, we could provide some protection and at the same time have a better shot at catching the killer. In *any* case, we want to talk to him further."

I turn away and wince as the car rolls off the curb with a thud. "I have no idea where Morgan is."

"This was a sham. Offering to come along to offer Morgan

moral support while he got us a photo. You probably knew all along that he wouldn't be coming along for the ride." He stops short for a light. "Don't *lie* to me, Miss Price."

"I'm telling the truth."

"But not the *whole* truth. You're leaving something out. You have to be a pretty good friend of Morgan's for him to have called you Sunday night. We gave him free access to the phone, but he didn't try anyone else. Just you."

"He trusts me."

"And yet you expect me to believe that he won't tell someone he *trusts* where he is and that you haven't heard from him since yesterday? Damn!" Quick blasts his horn at a cabby with a death wish who cuts in front of him. "*I'm* beginning to not trust you, Miss Price. *I'm* beginning to think that you come up with one story after the other to cover your ass." I bite my lip. "How can you expect us to take your complaints seriously when you ditz us around like this while there's a homicide investigation going on? Level with me, Miss Price. Fill in a missing piece of the jigsaw puzzle so maybe we can get a clearer picture."

I'm glad I don't know where Morgan is, what he's doing, *what he's done.* I could never hide the truth from this man. His eyes are focused on the street in front of him. I almost expect them to beam an express lane through the gridlock like lasers.

"The other night, when you asked me how I would describe Morgan Sunday afternoon, I told you I was too busy to notice. That wasn't exactly true. I *did* notice." I clear my throat. "When Morgan came by to see me after the Marathon, he seemed disturbed. He said Vittorio was being moody and left before the race was over. I said maybe he was just hung over. Everybody had been drinking a lot at the party the night before." *No one more than me.* "Maybe there was something he wasn't telling me or Vittorio wasn't telling *him,* but he *wasn't* exactly in a murderous rage. I didn't think anything of it."

"You thought enough of it to not tell us," he reminds me, and I sink deep into the looks-like-leather-but-sure-feels-like-Naugahyde seat, guilty as charged.

"I'm *sorry.*"

"Anything else?"

I shake my head vehemently, daring to meet his gaze head-on. His expression mellows. His grip on the steering wheel relaxes. I must have been validated by the lie detector he's got wired to his brain. He pulls into a space in front of the precinct and turns off the ignition. "I wish I could be of more help," I say. "Really."

Quick nods. "I wish *I* could be more helpful too, Miss Price, concerning *your* predicament, but you don't even know this person's full name yet, do you? If I had that, I could check him out for priors. Then too, Curtis could be using an alias. You *don't* remember ever seeing him before?"

"I'm not sure if I'd have known if I had." I shrug. "He's nondescript. There's no way I'd have noticed him before he began to pay me notice."

"He hasn't been enrolled in the school on West 8th Street or on their payroll in any capacity?"

"No way. I'd know. It's like a family there." Even if some of the members of the family are dysfunctional.

He lowers his voice like a priest in the confessional, but his tone is far from fatherly. "Is Morgan the only person you've posed for like that?"

Like without any clothes on.

"No," I say faintly. "I pose for different classes in different art schools all over the city, not just at West 8th Street. There are quite a few students in each class."

"How long have you been doing this?"

"Two and a half years."

"And he could have been one of them?"

"Yes, he could have," I admit, bracing myself for a you-should-know-better, what-do-you-expect lecture. "I honestly don't remember." *There have been so many of them.*

Quick opens his car door. He doesn't get out. "But you have no trouble recognizing him now, right?"

"None."

"You could pick him out of a line-up or ID him from a picture, if you had to?"

"Or draw him," I exclaim. "I could do that. I could draw Vittorio too. Sculpture is my forte, but I don't think life-size busts would be possible in short order. Or practical," I say, hoping to score another smile.

Quick keeps the smile in the closet, but looks at me with the reverence he probably reserves for rookies at the range who hit bull's eye on their first shot. "When can you have it ready for us?"

"Tonight," I say, though that's really pushing it. When I was taking advanced-level drawing classes in college, I had two days to produce a detailed portrait. I'm committing myself to finishing two in fewer than twelve hours. I should be committed for this. I get out of the car and grapple with my package of art supplies. Quick pauses at the corner before turning to go back through the doorway between the two green lanterns.

"I'll pick them up," he says, "Around ten. I have some other business to tend to in the neighborhood, if nothing else comes up."

I clear my throat. "I'm working until ten. In Brooklyn."

"Eleven, then," he says. "And let us know if you hear from Morgan in the meantime."

I nod.

"Where might a scared and lonely gay man go in this city to drown his sorrows, Miss Price?" I'm looking at him straight on. His eyes are like two welding torches, throwing sparks. If I don't talk, I'll be burned.

I give him several options, all conveniently located within a ten-block radius of my apartment. Morgan might drop in on any one or all of them if he's on a serious bender. Judging from the way he sounded on the phone yesterday though, I think he's probably bent too far out of shape to bar hop tonight. *Doing something far more dangerous, maybe.* If Quick comes up empty-handed, he won't like it. He'll show up at my apartment peeved and stare at me mercilessly, asking more questions, tolerating no lies.

I better make those drawings good.

22

THE JUMBO SKETCH PAD I'VE GOT PROPPED UP AGAINST MY KNEES KEEPS sliding off with every stop of the A train. "Sorry," I mumble at Canal Street as the corner of the pad hits the knee of the Chinese woman sitting next to me, who keeps looking down. "Sorry," I gasp at Park Place as the pad falls on someone's shoe. I start to look down too, even after picking the pad up. I squint at the drawing I'm working on. I already finished the one of Vittorio late this afternoon after stopping by my studio at West 8th Street to pick up the pad. I went to a back stairway and held the pad just like this and didn't drop it once. When I looked up, I saw only the reflection of my legs from the knees down in the dusty full-length mirror facing me. Here when I glance up, I see eyes. Closed eyes. Bloodshot eyes. *Beady criminal eyes* narrowing menacingly at me from over the rim of a furled paper bag.

Curtis' eyes are like this. Narrow. Hooded. I start sketching the lids with my charcoal pencil, trying not to smudge what I've done so far.

I hear a deep voice that sounds like it's spurting from the bottom of a bottle growl, "You drawing me?" insinuating he doesn't care to be an *objet d'art*.

He has nothing to worry about; he's far from it. I keep

my head down, keep drawing. The conductor garbles the name of the next stop over the intercom. The lights in the car flicker and flash on again. I look down at one brown and one black shoe with matching scuff marks. A gust of breath soured by cheap wine ripples the paper in front of me. "You better not be drawing *me*, bitch!"

I look up at him and grab the pad defensively. He reaches out for my hand and wrenches it back. I'm afraid next he's going to rip the drawing out and I'm going to have to start from scratch. I'm more afraid of *this* than of him hurting me somehow. A totally irrational fear. He's probably armed and dangerous; he's probably *wanted* for something; that's why the picture is freaking him out. He glances at the picture and backs away from it, letting go of my hand, but not before I drop my pencil. Just as the door slides open at Jay Street, the pencil drops to the floor and rolls out of the car and onto the tracks. Mr. Mismatched Shoes chuckles derisively, looking over his shoulder at me as he hurdles the gap onto the platform. "Don't be looking at *me*, *I* ain't getting it for you."

The door hisses shut. *Shit.* I hope there's a blue-and-white waiting for him when he gets up to street level. If I had time, I'd draw *him too.*

When I show up in class to model, I have to start off by panhandling for a #4 charcoal pencil that I can use to draw during my breaks and all someone has available is a #6, which I can't do fine lines with, it's like mush. I have to keep sharpening it to be able to do *any*thing with it until I start the shading. A few students in the class take a peek at what I'm working on. *Maybe they've seen him?*

No, he doesn't look familiar. Is he supposed to, they ask? Is he a model too? We sorely need male models, one woman says. There never seem to be enough to go around. It's a problem I can empathize with. No, I say, disappointing them, this guy is most definitely *not* model material.

"You're good," one of the artists says during one of my breaks. I'm not sure though whether he's complimenting my drawing or the subject of *his* drawing. His work is *definitely* good. A couple of people in the class seem surprised that I can draw a straight line at all, including the woman whose pencil I'm wearing down to a nub. Most of the artists in most of the classes I've worked for outside of West 8th Street have no idea I'm one of them. I've been asked more than once if I'm an actress trying to shed my inhibitions to do nude scenes. I *feel* like I'm acting tonight, putting on a show of bravado just to get through this until it's time to get home and hand over my drawings to Quick.

By ten o'clock every bone in my body is hurting, none more than the carpals and metacarpals in my left hand. I pull my turtleneck over my head and the label tickling my neck alerts me that I've got it on backwards. I pull my bibbed jeans on over it as is; it's all coming off again soon enough anyway. I notice on the subway coming home that I've slid the side buttons through the wrong holes. I try not to notice anything or anyone else. When I emerge from the subway and walk westward on 8th Street, passing shadows startle me. I start looking up and around and over my shoulder again. I press my drawing pad closer to my body and reach in my fanny pack with my free hand for my keys. I hold them in my palm as I approach the entrance to the school in case I need to duck inside in a hurry. I wheel around. *Nobody's there.* I keep walking toward home. When I finally turn the corner at Waverly Place, somebody *is* there, sitting on the front steps, waiting for me. The light is out in front of the building. I can't see him clearly. I immediately retreat around the corner and lean against a brownstone, waiting for a car to come by, hoping headlights will help me make out who it is. A banged-up Fiat flashes its beams on a figure with dark blond hair. Another form is coming up the street from the north. As he gets closer, I hold my breath. Even in the dark, I recognize Curtis' football player build and I can make out that he's wearing a different hat, a cap with some kind of insignia on it, but I can't see any more than that and I curse the darkness. "Hey, you," he bellows authoritatively to whoever is sitting on the stairs, "What are you doing here?"

"Waiting for somebody." The figure sitting on the steps stands up and I recognize Ivan's combative stance. It reopens old wounds. Just seeing it makes my hip ache. "What's it to you?"

The two of them, Ivan and Curtis, are standing in the middle of the sidewalk, in a showdown like in the climax of the movie High Noon, and I'm Grace Kelly, watching in the background, except it's closer to midnight and I don't have the prop that Grace had at *her* disposal. If I did, I think I'd blow *both* of them away.

A motorcycle picks this fine moment to roar by, flashing its Cyclops headlight on me. I have to back up fast so neither of them will see me. When it's good and dark again, I lean forward. I can't hear what either of them is saying now, but neither is backing down. Another car starts down Waverly Place. I can finally make out more. Dark jacket zipped up to the chin, dark blue pants, blue and gold insignia on the cap: stuff I've got to remember. Quick should be here soon. I wonder *how* soon. I look at my watch. It says ten twenty. The second hand isn't moving.

"No, no, get away."

"Shut up!"

"Stay away!"

I duck back into the shadows. What comes next is Saturday morning cartoon sound effects, somebody cracking their knuckles and scuffling and running and the screech of a car's brakes. I hear more scuffling and more angry voices and then sirens, short blasts of them that sound more like protests than wails. I inch my way forward and look around the corner to see. Two blue-and-whites are parked at ninety-degree angles from each other, cordoning off the street, a third, a dark unmarked vehicle with a single red rotating light resting precariously on the dashboard, parked on the curb between them. *A cop-car sandwich.* There are three uniforms shining their flashlights up and down the street, catching me in their beams. Detective Quick has Ivan's hands in his grasp. It almost looks like he's reading his palms. When I get closer, I see blood trickling down Ivan's wrists.

"This fellow says he's a *friend* of yours, Miss Price." Quick looks at me inquisitively.

"I know him, yes." This is about the only way I can confirm my familiarity with Ivan without choking on it.

Quick keeps looking at me. "I was about to turn into the street to wait for you when I saw someone sitting on the steps, so I went up the block and radioed for back-up."

"And missed the whole damn thing," Ivan hisses.

Two of the uniforms come to the foot of the stairs, and I recognize Vinson and Coolidge. Vinson looks at Ivan, then at me, then at Ivan again. "What were *you* doing here?" Vinson turns to me. "Did you *know* he was going to be here?"

I shake my head. Vinson doesn't look convinced, but turns back to Ivan. "What happened?"

"How come you guys always ask 'what happened?' after something happens? If you were in the goddamn neighborhood and thought something was wrong, why the fuck weren't you there *before* that asshole cut me?"

"Did you see what kind of weapon he used?"

"I asked *you* a question."

"You haven't answered my first one yet," Vinson says. "What were you doing here tonight?"

Coolidge clears his throat. "I thought we had an understanding that you were going to leave Miss Price alone after the other night."

Quick looks perplexed. He turns his attention to the doorway. "Why is this light out?" He goes up the stairs and looks up at the fixture, then down at the landing, and kicks something that tinkles against the railing.

"Nice and convenient for somebody sitting here who doesn't want to be seen," Vinson says, watching Ivan watch himself bleed, probably deciding whether he should administer first-aid or cuff him.

"Did you get a protective order against him?" Coolidge asks me. I shake my head. "Well, then, we can't press charges."

"*What* charges?" Ivan bellows. "If I *hadn't* been here, our pal who *you* let get away probably would have used his box-cutter on *her*."

"*Box*-cutter?"

"Something like that. Narrow with a retractable blade. He had it in his hand for only a minute. I didn't get a good look. Just enough to know it wasn't a knife."

"Did you defend yourself?"

"How the fuck do you think I got *this*?" Ivan holds his palms inches away from Vinson's face. Blood is every bit as dangerous as a gun or knife in this city. Vinson backs off and Coolidge steps in. His hands are sheathed in green plastic surgical gloves, just in case.

"Did you hurt your assailant in any way? Did you cut, scratch, punch him anywhere?"

"Who started it?"

"I *don't believe* this shit," Ivan sputters. "You guys were at her place Friday night, you heard the message that guy left for her on her voice mail. Well, now he's leaving more than just messages, he's staking her out, you see? I just happened to be in his way. Go ahead. Arrest me. Then who's going to be around to stop him *next* time he comes looking for her? *You guys?* Ha!" He wrings his hand in pain. "*You'll* probably be on Sixth Avenue choking down crullers."

Vinson and Coolidge both look like they've got a bad case of indigestion, but not from anything they've eaten. Ivan being here *may* have saved me from some harm and he *did* get wounded in the process, but I'm delighting in his discomfiture and not feeling guilty about it. I turn around and look at Quick. He's staying out of it for now but watching intently, like a line judge at the U.S. Open finals, ready to call the shots when he has to. My mouth goes dry when our eyes meet.

"*I* was here," Quick says.

"What business did *you* have with Delilah, anyhow?"

"An unrelated police matter," Quick says. "Routine."

Ivan looks at me and smirks. "Uh huh."

Vinson clears his throat. "You're telling us the guy who you confronted here is the same one who's been harassing Miss Price?"

"It's just a voice on the phone. How would you know, anyway?"

"I've seen him," I acknowledge, biting my lip. "It was him. I came around the corner and saw someone sitting on the stairs and backed up so I couldn't be seen. Then I heard two voices. When a car came by with its brights on, I saw enough to recognize *both* of them. I didn't see what happened after that. I stayed in hiding."

Vinson and Coolidge turn to me. "I thought you said you didn't know *who* the guy was."

"I didn't."

"And now you're saying you *do?*"

Vinson's skepticism grates on me. These guys don't believe anything *anyone* says. "Let's just say I've been *approached*," I say. I fumble through my sketch pad and flip to the last page I used, the drawing I just finished under such arduous conditions. "This is him."

Ivan whistles through his teeth. "Baby, I know you're fast, but this is ridiculous."

I wince. The cut in his hand may have torn tissue, but his digs at me never fail to sever a nerve.

"Let's see," Quick says, stepping between Vinson and

Coolidge, reaching for the pad. I did this drawing at *his* behest and feel relieved when he wrests control of it from them, takes the pad away from smudging, sweaty, bloody fingers. He studies it carefully. When at last he nods, I feel redeemed. "Seen him before?" he asks Ivan.

"Yeah, that's him."

"You're going to probably want this," Quick says to Vinson and Coolidge, tearing the sheet of paper out of the pad, looking up at me briefly as if to ask, *you don't mind?* Too bad if I *do.* "And I'll want a copy sent to me at the First."

"Oh no, you *can't Xerox* it," I protest, "I didn't spray fixative. It'll *smudge.*"

"It's *not* going to be on display in the *Met,* Miss Price," Quick reminds me, which is of little comfort to my artist's ego.

"Damn good drawing, though," Vinson says, "For someone who didn't know the guy from Adam a few days ago."

"Oh, it doesn't take Delilah long to do *any*one she has her mind set on."

Coolidge reaches for Ivan's arm. "Meanwhile you're coming with us."

"Where?"

"Beth Israel for starters. Have that hand looked at. May need some stitches."

"I don't think so," Ivan demurs. The blood on his hand is starting to cake. It looks like terra cotta.

Vinson scowls. "What, you're a *doctor* all of a sudden?"

"Well, you're coming anyway, those are the rules. We don't need you playing lawyer later on, trying to charge us with negligence."

"Unless you want to come to the station house with us. We can talk *there,* if you prefer. About pressing charges anyway," Vinson says.

"And a few *other* things," Coolidge adds.

"Thanks for the picture, Detective."

"Thank the *artist*," Quick says, nodding his head in my direction, paying me my due. As soon as the last of the blue-and-whites pulls away, he takes a few steps closer and gestures for me to follow him up the stairs. He pauses in the vestibule between the doors and looks down at me.

"Okay now, how about throwing some light on what happened here tonight, Miss Price?"

23

THE BRIGHT OVERHEAD CEILING LIGHT BURNS OUT THE MINUTE I OPEN THE door and flick it on.

"I'll change the bulb," Quick volunteers.

I open the utility cabinet under the sink and grope around inside. "I think I'm out of them."

I pull the chain on the antique lamp with the fringed shade suspended over the couch like a swooping bird. It can only accommodate a forty-watt bulb and isn't up to interrogation standards. Looking at him in this light with dark shadows filling the hollows in his face, Quick looks like he could forget about what he came here for, sit down, settle back, and fall asleep in an instant.

Appearances are deceiving.

"Let's have it," he says, reaching for my sketch pad. He flips through it looking for Vittorio, but not without looking at what else is inside: several other faces of models I've done for my sculpture, several nudes of both sexes and various proportions, some more detailed than others. When finally he comes to the drawing I did for him, he carefully tears it out of the book and crimps it in half, then in quarters. I wince. *More smudge.* He closes the sketch pad and hands it back to me. I drop it on the throw rug. Now that he's got what he came for, he wants more. He stares me down. *Let's have it.*

"I'm glad you came when you did," I say. "There's no telling what might have happened."

"How about telling me what *did* happen," Quick finally does sit on the couch, but not with the lassitude of someone about to fall asleep. *I know* that pose. He's comfortable with it; he could hold it all night. He pats the cushion next to him, compelling me to join him there and *too bad* if I still feel like standing. "And who it happened to."

I curl up against the arm of the couch for support while I brief him none too briefly on Ivan's part in this. Like an actor in repertory, I tell him, he played several parts. He was exceptionally good as The Charmer and The Button Down Wall Street Whiz. His portrayal of The Jealous Lover doesn't get such rave reviews from me. His latest role is The Bodyguard. I fill Quick in on the scenes we've played together: the shove into the wall, the frantic call to the police Friday night after I changed the locks on him, the incessant phone calls since. "And tonight he's sitting on the front stoop waiting for me to come home! I wouldn't ordinarily be happy to see Curtis come along, but tonight...yeah!"

"Is there a chance that Curtis and he know each other?"

"I don't think so." I shake my head vehemently, "Anyway, Curtis doesn't seem to be the kind of company Ivan likes to keep."

"They don't have to be squash partners to be in collusion on something like *this*. This could be a set-up between the two of them. Another *act*. Curtis playing The Bad Guy and Ivan The Concerned....*Ex?*"

I smile for the first time tonight. I like the way Quick has picked up on my metaphors. "*Definitely* ex," I confirm.

"He wasn't hurt *that* badly. As I said, he may have staged

this whole scene with Curtis to make himself look like The
Good Guy, to get you to let down your guard."

"I don't think..."

"So that you'd take him back."

"I'm never taking him back."

"He doesn't appear to be convinced."

"*Tell* me about it!"

"Miss Price..."

"De*lilah*," I insist wearily. Hearing Miss Price over and
over makes me think of a piece of merchandise with the
wrong tag attached. After what happened here tonight, I
wonder if he knows *what* tag to put on me.

"Pressing harassment charges against him might make
things a little clearer to him. Something you haven't done.
Why not?" I shrug and shift my weight, and my discomfiture
isn't lost on him. He bears down. "And why didn't you tell me
about this before?"

The light feels like a sun lamp scalding my face. "I was
worried about my credibility," I whimper. "Complaining
about *two* stalkers..."

"Yes, I can see why that would bother you, you've been *so*
credible up to now."

I bolt up and stand in front of him, folding my arms to
ward off any more barbs. "Ivan said nobody would take me
seriously if I complained about him *and* somebody else; that's
why I didn't tell you about him before now, and *how about*
that, for *once* he was *right*. I didn't even want to bring it
up with Rubenstein..." I wrap my arms around me tighter.
"When I did, he had this attitude...like he was thinking, 'How
bad can things be if the ex-boyfriend is still looking out for
her?' He didn't get it. He took down Ivan's name as a witness after I told him Ivan had seen Curtis and might be able
to identify him." I force a thin smile. "Which, what do you
know, he *did*. Well, he was good for something, at least."

"*I'll* talk to Rubenstein," Quick cuts in. "I'll fill him in on what happened here tonight. We're talking *assault* now. He'll take it seriously."

"What's he going to *do* about it?"

"The same thing *I'm* going to do. Have someone check the drawing you did of Curtis to see if it matches any photos of known perps with a similar MO. Post him on the wall along-side other wanteds we're on the lookout for. Fill out more paperwork." Quick grunts. "He'll like that."

"What about *Ivan?*"

"He walks. He didn't do anything wrong tonight. He simply defended himself, and in the *past,* when he *did,* you didn't press charges, Miss Price."

"De*l*ilah."

"You'll probably get a phone call from Marty. Probably not until later in the day. He's on the eight-to-four. What's that case number again?"

I take a deep breath and reach in my fanny pack where I stashed the piece of paper and give it to him. As he pulls a small ruled notepad from the inside pocket of his blue nylon windbreaker, I notice the gun in his shoulder holster. He jots down the case number on a page a third of the way in the pad. He's left-handed, I notice, and has long tapered fingers more befitting of a surgeon or an *artist* than a cop. He hands the paper back to me and gets up, but not to go, not yet. He looks over my shoulder at my cell phone. The red voice mail alert is flashing in tandem with an amber hazard light out-side. "Looks like you have some voice mail," he says. "Why don't you play it back?"

I push what I've come to call the panic button.

"Delilah, this is Morgan..."

Quick looks like, if he *could,* he'd reach in and pull Morgan out of the machine by his hair. I recall having heard a couple of cops call him Hat Trick and wonder if this has anything to do with the powers of magic. *Maybe he can.*

"I just wanted to let you know I'm okay..."

I close my eyes and whisper a prayer of thankfulness.

"...I'm in Park Slope..."

Quick reaches in his pocket for the pad again. He clicks his blue ball point with the same deliberation he probably uses to load his gun. He's waiting for an address with a *gotcha* gleam in his eyes.

"...I'll try calling again later..."

Click.

"You didn't mention any bars in *Brooklyn*, Miss Price."

"I don't know about any bars in Brooklyn." *Not true.* "Not the kind Morgan would go to." *Truer.* "Not the names of any anyway." The closest I can come to the truth. Quick should be able to forgive me this mental block since he seems to have his own where *my* name is concerned. "And anyway, he might not be calling from a bar..."

"*You* were in Brooklyn tonight, weren't you, Miss Price?"

Delilah, damn it!

"I wasn't *anywhere near* Park Slope. I was..." I cut myself off before I can say *baring my ass in front of a bunch of artists.* Quick would just remind me that Morgan is an artist. "Just over the river, in Clinton Hill."

"Ssshh..."

Click.

"That's him," I whisper, "that's Curtis."

Quick looks at me like he's appraising my own untapped powers of sorcery or thinks I'm crazy. *More* likely, he's thinking I'm trying to get him off *my* case and onto the case I *want* him to be working on. Which is *also* my case.

"He hasn't been leaving messages any more," I explain. "Last time he called, he said he was getting tired of one-way conversations."

"Maybe he's in a bind," Quick suggests. "Can't make calls as freely."

I shrug. "I've turned my phone off a few times."

"You told me he's still been leaving you notes though, right?"

I nod. "Right at my doorstep."

"I'd say that's pretty one-sided."

"*I'll* say."

"Let me see them."

"There are only two..." I say, realizing I sound apologetic as I place them in the outstretched palm of his hand.

He unfolds them, reads one, then the other, then holds them next to each other. "Looks like he used the same paper. The printing *could* have been copied out of a grade school primer. He didn't jot these in *a hurry*. They're too uniform, too neat for a spur-of-the-moment thing. He probably wrote these *way* before he left them for you, before he left *home*, in fact. Wherever home happens to be in *his* case. Nothing like this could be traced. *That* much he probably knows." He hands them back to me. "Did Rubenstein see these?"

"Just the second one. The one that came with the flowers, not exactly FTD. He told me to save everything."

"Okay now, what about the other messages?"

"Lots of hang-ups and one looong message." I say, sorry again for having so *little* in the way of evidence to offer him.

"Play it for me."

My fingers start trembling as I hit replay. I remember the contents of this message too well. I wonder how it's going to play with Quick, who looked at the paintings of me *so impassively* and then wanted to know, was Morgan the only person I had posed for *like that*. "You look good without your clothes on," Curtis begins, interrupted by a too-short screech of static. "You look good with them on too, but not half as good as you do naked. And I like the way you look at me when you're doing that slow strip of yours, like you're doing it just for me. One of these days, you *will* be, Delilah. Now that you've finally dumped that tightass, it'll be sooner than you think. I can't wait."

Click.

All this time I've looked every which way but up at Quick. I know he hasn't taken his eyes off me. I've never felt more undressed in my life. I cross my arms in front of me and look down at the parquet floor. My feet point forward and outward. *What a good pose this would be. I have to remember it.*

Quick moves toward the windows. He pulls up each shade and looks across the street, then left, then right, then up, as if Curtis, being the bird of prey that he is, might be peering down at me from an aerie. "No one can see in," I tell him. *At least not any more they can't.*

"When you're working," Quick says, "are the shades in the studio drawn?"

"Everything in the studio is drawn *but* the shades," I flinch when I look up at him and catch his reaction. "Or blinds or shutters. The students like natural light."

"What about *night* classes? Do they work by *moon*light?"

I shake my head.

"You worked tonight. Were the windows covered?"

It's a miracle that the windows were kept *closed*. "Maybe partially. I don't remember. I wasn't looking." I see the displeasure in his eyes. "I was concentrating on the drawing I was doing," I remind him.

"Next time you go to work in one of these places," he pauses, giving the slide projector in his mind time to change images, "take a look out the window at what buildings are nearby. Make a note of it if you notice anything unusual, like a vantage point someone may be using to get a better look. It wouldn't hurt to at least be observant," he cautions me, "because somebody *else* is certainly observing. How did Ivan feel about your work?" Again there is that pause before the word *work*, so palpable I could reach out and squeeze it. *Click.* *Another* image of me is projected in his mind, an even bluer nude than the one before.

"He hated it," I tell him.

"Did he ask you to stop?"

"*Several* times. And he didn't like it much better when the shoe was, or I should say *wasn't* on the *other* foot." Quick frowns and I elucidate. "Like when I had male models posing for *me* in *my* studio."

"Maybe he felt that *this* would make you stop."

"I stopped seeing him," I remind Quick. "So he really has no say in the matter."

"He still may not see things that way," Quick insists. "I may want to have a little talk with him after the boys in the Sixth are through taking his statement." A little man-to-man talk, I'm thinking, wonderful. I can hear Ivan now. *You're a man. How would you feel, Detective Quick, if it were your girl-friend, someone you hoped would be your wife someday, and she was posing naked in front of all those people all over the city? Have you seen any paintings of her in the course of your investigation? You must have. There are so damn many pictures of her floating around they might as well be plastered on the sides of buses and on the walls in subways. How would you feel, knowing she's alone in a studio with some naked guy who thinks he's a stud and never be sure she doesn't think he is too? How would you feel when you looked at her after that?*

I'm not sure how he'd feel or how he feels right now. I'm reluctant to give Quick Ivan's number, but I realize he can get it easily enough from the Sixth and it looks better if he gets it from me. The way things are right now, I couldn't be cast in a worse light, natural or otherwise. It just so happens that Wall Street is within First Precinct territory, Quick says when I give him Ivan's work address and phone number.

Very convenient. Right in the neighborhood. This is worse. I don't even want to think about what Ivan is going to have to say when he finds out that this isn't a business call, that the only investment Quick plans to make is in the interest of my safety. He reaches in his pocket and pulls out another of his cards and jots something on the back before handing it to me. "Here are a couple more numbers where I can be reached if I'm not at the precinct," he says. I glance at them. One of the numbers is prefixed by 718. I flip over the card. The name Patrick A. Quick is printed in the center of the card, in bas relief. *Patrick. A real cop name.* I look back up at him. *He doesn't look anything at all like a Patrick.* "One of these is my cell number. The other is another line." He doesn't indicate which is which. "In case you need to get in touch with me before four. If you think you're in immediate danger, call 911." I nod numbly. "Otherwise, call Rubenstein, then call me. You *have* the number at the Sixth?"

I point to the legend of numbers I pasted on the refrigerator door, a modern girl's urban-terrorism survival guide. I've added numbers to the list. I've Scotch-taped an auxiliary roster on the wall. Quick nods in approbation. "I'm glad you came when you did," I say again, edging near the door. "Thanks."

"I'll do what I can to help," Quick says as I undo the locks and turn the knob. "This isn't my jurisdiction. I'm here to follow up on a murder investigation and I'd welcome a little cooperation," he reminds me, as if I need reminding. My hands are so sweaty they slip all over the place. I know he's noticing this, knows how nervous I am, which makes me more nervous. Just as he steps over the threshold, he stops, turns back, leans against the door jamb and looks down at me. His proximity to me makes me feel like I'm about to break out in hives. If we'd been on a date, this would be his ploy to get a kiss, but there's something else he wants out of me. "Who does Morgan know in Park Slope?"

"Nobody that *I* know of." This is the truth. Nobody that Morgan knew of before tonight either, I'd be willing to wager. All Quick has to do is flip through the list of names of people who were at that party to know absolutely *none* of them live in Brooklyn. He's probably interviewed them all already. I can't be responsible for what they haven't told him or for any of the things Morgan never told me about his life. I went out with him and his friends to gay bars, we'd talk about art and diss old boyfriends, then we'd go home in different directions to different lifestyles. I didn't know *everything*. Morgan may be getting himself in as much peril as Vittorio was two nights ago, only his undoing probably won't be at the point of a sharp instrument, but in a drop of blood, a speck of semen, the kind of perp that Quick can't collar. Only protease inhibitors can.

Quick shifts his weight from one leg to the other. I flinch. Even the slightest sound out here is bound to rouse Mrs. Davidoff's curiosity. I'm surprised she hasn't made a grand entrance by now. This is her golden opportunity to complain to the police about me and she's blowing it big time. I wonder if she's been listening to all this through an eye cup suctioned to the wall. I wonder if she might be *dead*.

This interrogation, though, still has a beating pulse. "Listen, Miss Price, every time I talk to another of his friends, I get the same non-answers," Quick complains. "They don't know anything. It's like being pinned up against a brick wall of silence."

*Stone*wall, I think. This is where I've been told everything began.

I recall the detective who made reference to Morgan *Fair*child, Morgan Le *Fey*, who no doubt was the same one who asked Gary and Abel *what sex joint* Morgan could be found at. I wonder how Quick can be so surprised by the reticence he's encountered that seems to me to be, under the circumstances, entirely warranted. "Look, there's something you've got to understand," I say. "These friends of Morgan's *don't* exactly trust the police." *And I can't say I've blamed them most of the time.* "They've had a lot of bad experiences."

"One of theirs has been murdered. I'd say that's about as bad as an experience can get, wouldn't you?" Quick barks at me in the exasperated tone he'd use to reprimand a misbehaving child. *Yes, sir. No, sir. I won't say anything stupid like that again, sir.*

"What about the staff at the restaurant? You seem to be totally ignoring..."

"Clear the tables on that. Everyone we talked to has a rock solid alibi. Either they were working or have someone who can vouch for where they were on Sunday night. No one at that restaurant, no matter *how* upset they may have been over working an extra shift the night before, did Vittorio Scaccia."

He shoves his hands in his pockets and backs away from the doorway, toward the stairs, the jilted suitor retreating without the expected kiss. I don't want it to end like this. I want things to be straight between us. *You helped me, now I'll show you I'm willing to help you. So you'll help me again.* "I called a couple of Morgan's friends yesterday. I tried to get them to tell me where he was, but they couldn't."

"Or wouldn't."

"I'm an outsider too," I remind him. "Anyway, you've *got* the picture."

"Yes, Miss Price," he says solemnly, "I've got the picture." Just before he turns to go down the stairs, he gives me a look that lets me know it's not the eighteen by twenty-four inch sheet of drawing paper folded and tucked in his pocket that he's talking about.

24

THE RINGTONE OF THE CELL PHONE IS LIKE A LADDER LEADING ME OUT of a four-alarm nightmare to safety. I enjoy the ensuing feeling of relief for about ten seconds. I don't recognize the number, but lately I never do. I realize with a chill that the netherworld of my dream state was better cover.

"Why did you let that asshole back into your life?" Curtis barks. "I thought you were *through* with him."

"I am," I say.

"He was waiting for you tonight. *Expecting* you."

"Well, I wasn't expecting him. *Or* you. What were *you* doing there, Curtis?" I roll over on my side, curled up in a semi-fetal position to ward off imaginary blows.

"You're just lucky I *was* there," he insists. "There's no telling what he would have done to you if *I hadn't* come along."

"Why'd you hurt him?"

"Do you *care* that I hurt him. The guy beat the shit out of you!"

"He hasn't beaten me."

"How'd you get that *bruise* I saw then?" *How'd he see my*

damn bruise? "I knew I'd have to come to your rescue one of these nights if you stayed with him."

"I don't need you to rescue me. I can rescue myself, thank you."

"So why'd you call the cops on him last week?"

"It's *you* I called the cops on tonight, Curtis, not him."

"Do you still *care* about that prick, Delilah?"

"No. It's over between us, but that *doesn't* mean you can take the law in your own hands, hurt people without provocation..."

"That bastard still thinks he owns you." He emits a low chuckle. "I got *provoked.* I wasn't about to let him get anywhere *near* you. I wouldn't let *anyone* get near you."

"I don't want *you* near me, Curtis," I whimper, too tired to raise my voice. "For the last time, I'm telling you, stay away from me."

"Don't say that," he warns.

"It's going to get worse for you down the line if you won't leave me alone. I drew a picture of you. The police are on the lookout for you."

I hear a sharp burst of static. "You're even more talented than I thought," he says. "I'm impressed." The acid in his voice could burn through wires if I weren't wireless. "I wish you'd stop acting this way. You're spoiling *everything.* And I really want you to come to *my* sculpture exhibit."

"You didn't tell me *you* were a sculptor," I say. My mouth is so dry it's hard to get the words out. "What kind of work do you do?"

He pauses. "I guess you could say it's figurative."

"What medium do you use?"

An even longer pause. "Heavy metal."

"When does your exhibit open?"

He lowers his voice. "*That* depends on *you.* I want your input. A talented person like yourself."

"Well, you've *got* to have an opening date if you've got gallery space reserved, just like I have."

"First of December."

Same as *mine*. "And you've got to be advertising, right? You've got to have your *name* up there so people know whose work they're seeing. So I can do without the invite. Curtis, I can come see your work when your show opens and bring along anyone else I think might be interested." *Like a whole detachment from the NYPD. "*Curtis *what,* by the way. There may be more than one Curtis who's a sculptor."

"There won't be no ads with my name posted *any*where. My work is just available for private showing," he lowers his voice, "to those who *inspire* it."

"How many other private showings have you had?" How many other women have you harassed this way?

He clears his throat. "Two. The first one could have been better. I was *much* more pleased with the second. Artists get better as they go along. That's par for the course, *isn't* it, Delilah? You learn from your mistakes, you find what works and what doesn't. *This* one is going to be my best *yet.*"

I'm shaking like a Jello mold and not from the November chill blowing through the window frame. "In that case," I try to keep the trembling out of my voice, "I should think you'd *want* more people to see it. If you're a serious artist. How else do you expect to get recognition?"

"Just because I'm *inspired* by an exhibitionist doesn't mean I have to *become* one," he snaps. "Putting yourself on display *cheapens* you. *You* should know. You're paid, what, a measly fifteen, twenty dollars an hour to bare your body, the temple of your soul."

That's it, more or less. How the hell does he know how much I'm paid?

"You don't own your body any more, Delilah. You've given it to every one who's ever drawn or painted or sculpted you before me. That's a desecration. I'm not going to do that to my body of work. I'm not giving it up to anybody but *you*, the person who *inspired* it. You're all mine, baring yourself to me and me alone, and I'm showing it to you and only you. Once you see it, you'll never pose for another person," he says. "*Or* go to bed with anyone else."

I look at the mound of pillow and down comforter bunched up beside me. "You mind telling that to the person lying here next to me right now?"

"Lying bitch. There's no one there."

"How do *you* know?"

"I know. I'm keeping tabs. It won't do you any good to lie to me. I'm way ahead of you. I know everything about you, Delilah. Where you go. What you do. Who you see. How can I not? You're my *subject*. I've got to know as much about my subject as I possibly can if I want to do a good job. If I want to impress her with the final product." He clears his throat. "You won't be disappointed."

"You still haven't told me where or when it's going to be," I gasp. "This *exhibit* of yours that you're not exhibiting. There may be a conflict. If you tell me, I can at least arrange..."

"There won't be no conflict or arranging to be done," he vows. "I'll make sure you get there."

"You'll draw me a map, right?"

"Better than that," he says. I hear voices in the background and a muffled response to them by Curtis. "I have to go now," he announces, then lowers his voice again, "but I'll *be in touch*, Delilah."

Minutes pass and I still feel his voice all over me like sticky fingers.

If you think you're in immediate danger, Quick said, call 911. I lean on my elbows and peek through the gap between shade and window frame. No one's out there looking up. At least not that I can see. Just what would I tell the emergency operator anyway? *You've got to help me, I've just been invited to an art exhibit!* Uh-uh, can't do that. Otherwise I'm supposed to call Rubenstein, then call Quick. The big red LED display on my alarm clock says it's three twenty-eight. I can't call Rubenstein. He's not even on duty until eight, Quick told me. I don't particularly *want* to call Rubenstein, at least not until he's had a chance to talk with Quick.

The only person I *want* to talk to now is *Quick.*

But it's three twenty-eight, no, *three thirty-one* now, and he's probably fast asleep. I look at the mound of pillow and down comforter bunched up beside me. It was *Quick* I was thinking of when I told Curtis that lie about someone lying next to me. I wonder if someone is lying next to him. *I don't want to disturb him.* Thinking about him this way is disturbing in itself. *He's going to think I'm holding something back and I am.* The last thing I need, what with a crazy and an even crazier stalker, is another man in my life, even in fantasy, but for the minute or two I fantasized that it was him lying there next to me and not a lumpy lifeless mass of feathers, I felt incredibly protected. I wanted to put my hand on his bare shoulder and wake him, hand him the phone, and have him get rid of Curtis, then take care of my *other* needs. *It's been hard enough making direct eye contact up to now. How am I going to look at him after this, after imagining him naked in bed beside me, having sex with me?* He's already seen me nude in paintings, *several* of them, front and back views. I'm just trying to vicariously even the score. *Well, I can't help it, I'm scared. Just thinking about him makes me feel safer. And he's got a great physique and I'm an artist. And I'm horny.*

At least I can still prioritize.

But I still can't bring myself to call him at three forty-five a.m.

What I do is turn on the radio hoping that the announcers' voices will have a soothing effect on me, like hearing a bedtime story, but the lead story is *this:* "Police have identified the woman found in the trunk of an abandoned car on West Street late Monday night as twenty-nine year old Majesty Moore, who until her disappearance three weeks ago worked as a window display artist. Several display items were found in the car trunk with her. Police would not comment on the nature of the items found, but called it a *particularly heinous* crime and ask that anyone with any information contact detectives at the Sixth precinct or call (800) 577-TIPS."

Without missing a beat, the announcer starts to tell of a double-shooting in the Bronx. I turn off the radio and toss and turn in silence, very *unsoothed*. This woman, Majesty Moore, was a *window display* artist. *I'm* an artist on display. *Putting yourself on display cheapens you.* As I pull the covers around me tighter, the fantasy outline of Quick disappears. My hand reaches for my cell phone. *4:12. No, I can't do it.* I punch in the number of the Sixth precinct instead. A woman answers.

"I'm calling about the woman they found on West Street," I tell her. I hear a click as she transfers the call, upstairs no doubt, to whatever detective might be handy at this hour of the night. A voice strained by a virus or too many cigarettes croaks, "Sauer here," and he sounds it. "Can I help you?"

He might just as well be asking, *Can you help us?*

"About the woman they found on West Street..." I stammer. "Majesty Moore..."

"You know her?"

"No. I..."

"You *saw* something," he says.

"That's not why I'm calling," I say. "I heard about it on the news. I heard that she was a window display artist and that certain display items were found in the trunk with her..."

"And you're one of the people who hired her and think it's stuff that belongs to your store, right?" he growls. "Can't you vultures think of anything *else* to keep you up nights? Like maybe filing for Chapter 11?"

"Well, *is* it that kind of stuff?"

"Look, sweetheart, when you call this line, it's to *give* info, not *get* it. So either you know something about this case that you want to tell us or you know something about this case and you want to know what *we* know, in which case I ain't telling you nothing. Or you don't know nothing. Which is it?"

I roll on my back. "Look, I don't know anything about this case, but I've got this gut feeling," I tell him.

"You sure it's not something you ate? Oh, I got it, you one of those psychics? You want to come in and fondle these *display items* and tell us who did her based on that, huh?"

"Do you want to hear about it or do I have to wait until eight, until *Rubenstein* comes in?"

"What's Marty got to do with this? *I* caught Moore."

"Well, Rubenstein caught *me*."

"You mind telling me what the hell this is all about?"

Now we're getting somewhere. I feel like an old tape that's been rewound and replayed so much that the message is starting to warp. Sauer alternately uh-huhs and coughs as my story winds down to the phone call that still has me quivering. "When I heard about the display items in the trunk, it made me think of something Curtis said...that's the guy who's been calling *me*—" I gulp "—about artists displaying their work." I leave out specifics about the piece of work *I've* displayed. "I wondered if maybe there's a connection, if maybe he's the same one who..."

"This Curtis...is that his first name or last name?" The name in native New Yawkese sounds like 'Coitus.'

"I don't know. First name, I *imagine*. Using his last name would be too much of a giveaway if he's got a record..."

"Not necessarily. Curtis is a common enough last name.

Must be rows of them in the white pages, and I'd bet more than one or two have some kind of record for something, even if it's just scofflaws. Curtis isn't such a popular *first* name, you know. I can only think of *one*, off*hand*," he coughs, "and I don't think it's the guy who was with the Guardian Angels we're talking about. So what tipped you off? This guy mention Moore to you?"

"No, but I get a feeling he's done something like this before, that I'm not the first one he's come on to this way. At first I thought maybe it was just a fluke, that once he knew I wasn't interested, he'd go away, but it's gotten *worse*. *Now* he's telling me that he's had private showings of his work before and that they keep getting better and better..." I stammer.

Sauer interrupts. "Look, Miss, it sounds like you got something to worry about with this guy, but for all you know he could be a legit wacko artist who you've inspired. Just because the guy wants to show off his work to you don't mean he wants to off you. Probably just wants to impress you. I'll admit he has a funny way of going about it, but, let me tell you, there's all kinds. Maybe you better call later this morning and talk to Rubenstein about it, but as far as it having anything to do with Moore," he coughs, "that's not likely. I'll tell you this much, we got a strong suspicion it's someone she was seeing who did her. One of the guys she'd been seeing on and off liked to get rough, put her in the hospital a couple of times before. We're on the lookout for him now. Nine times out of ten, it's a boyfriend-girlfriend thing. Could be in your case too, did you consider that?" He doesn't let me answer. "But as long as you weren't dating Moore's old man," he clears his throat, "I don't think you got anything to worry about on that score. Of course only *you* know what the guys you date are capable of..."

"Yeah, yeah, I know."

All too well.

"Look, sweetheart, it's *very* late at night, you're upset, and your imagination's zooming all over the place. What you *don't* want to do is turn on the news. The *last* thing you want to listen to when you're upset like this is the *news*, for crissakes. Make yourself a cup of tea, turn on some *music*. My father was a cop too. After dealing with street crap all day, he'd come home, listen to *records*. Ferrante and Teicher, Mantovani, *that* kind of stuff; it would calm him right down. Of course they don't got records now, they got iPods. You probably never *heard* of Ferrante and Teicher, right? All I'm saying is calm down, try to get a few hours sleep, stop worrying about every bogey man who's out there. It ain't worth it, there are just too damn many of them and they're *not* all out to get *you*."

"Thanks," I say. "That's comforting."

"I'm a regular Ann Landers, huh? You going to listen to me and turn off that radio now?"

"Already did."

"Good girl. Don't want you getting spooked any more tonight." *Don't want you tying up the line any more tonight. Now* he's talking to me like I'm a house pet, a loyal lap dog who overenthusiastically chewed on the newspaper before bringing it to him, rendering it useless. After rolling it and hitting me over the head with it, he's acknowledged my good intentions, patted me on the head, and thrown me a Milk-Bone. *Good girl.* Click. He's left me to shiver in the cold of the basement. I wonder if Sauer is even going to *try* to put the bits and pieces of what I've told him together. *Probably not.* My hand still grips the receiver. When I think of who I *might* have called *instead*, I cradle the cell phone in my arms like a child would clutch a stuffed animal and ignore the operator's recorded plea to *please hang up now*.

25

"I'M SORRY, BUT DETECTIVE RUBENSTEIN ISN'T IN TODAY. HE'S GOT THE flu real bad." I immediately peg Sauer as the carrier, coughing in everyone's face. I wonder if I could get sick just from having talked on the phone with him. "Is this something someone *else* can help you with?"

Yes, it *is*, but he works in a different precinct and not until four this afternoon. It's only 9:10 a.m.

Quick *said* call Rubenstein, then call *him*. And I *did* call Rubenstein.

I take out the card with the phone numbers jotted on the back and punch in the one starting with 718. His message says that he is unable to come to the phone right now, but to *please* leave my name and number at the beep. I comply. *I've got something important to tell you*, I promise, and throw in the number at West Eighth Street for good measure. I'm going to have to spend some quality time there on my sculpture before I go off to model later today, and hope I have it in me to produce real quality work. My hands are shaking like the few dead leaves remaining on the trees in Washington Square, and I haven't even had a cup of coffee yet. *How am I even going to wield a fettling knife without cutting myself up in the process?* I take my time getting dressed, giving Quick a chance to call me back so we can talk in private before I leave. He doesn't. I don't call the other number.

There's more than just junk mail waiting for me when I run downstairs and open the door to the vestibule on my way out. "Surprise," Morgan says. That's an understatement. He's wearing the same lavender shirt and blue jeans he had on when I last saw him, but they look *cleaner* than they did then. His expression is clearer too. Now that the initial shock has worn off, maybe he's finally realized he has nothing to hide. *Or he's had enough time to launder all traces of complicity in the crime. Wherever* he was the last few days, he was well taken care of. He even seems to have gained weight. I'm beginning to wonder if Morgan has a penchant for chefs, even for one-night stands.

"Oh God, Morgan, I'm so happy to see you!" I throw my arms around Morgan's waist and hug him. The front door bangs into both of us as Mrs. Davidoff barges in carrying an overstuffed overnight bag in one hand and a Big Brown Bag from Bloomingdale's in the other. She's very much alive, that's for sure, and *not at all* happy to see *me*; she lets that be known with a loud heave as she pushes past us, exaggerating the beast of burden routine.

"Let me help you with those," Morgan says, reaching for her bags. She pulls back like she thinks Morgan's going to mug her; then, after a quick look up the stairs, she changes her mind and surrenders her cargo to his outstretched hands. He turns back and winks at me. *They're not all that heavy.* I move aside and let her go up the stairs ahead of me. Each step groans. When we get to the landing, she takes her packages from Morgan, turns around, and gives me a dirty look. "*Thank* you, young man," she says, looking at him, then warily at me, then at him again with real concern etched in her face, no doubt worried that his association with me might taint him.

"Would you like me to help you put these inside?"

"No, no, you don't need to," she says, really on the defensive now. *You've done enough, sonny.* After she closes the door behind her none too quietly, Morgan gives her a few minutes to get out of listening range.

"I'm not holding you up or anything, am I?"

"That doesn't matter. I was just heading over to the studio. It can wait. *Where've* you *been?*"

"It's a long story," he says. "Come on, let's walk over to West 8th together. I better claim my studio space before they give it up. We can talk on the way. You hungry?"

"Starved."

"We can make an Egg McMuffin pit stop on the way." He holds the front door open for me. I look left and right, up and down the street before ambling down the front stairs. The coast is clear and the flower pot is still barren. *I'm going to have to do something about that.* At the corner of Christopher Street, Morgan takes my arm. I jump at his touch. He gently wheels me around. "Delilah, you okay?"

"Uh uh," I shake my head.

"What's wrong?"

"It's a long story."

"I'll tell you *mine* if you tell me *yours.*"

"You first."

Morgan takes a deep breath. "Delilah, I...something inside me snapped the other night. I *really lost* it." I freeze in my tracks in the middle of Sixth Avenue. I can see the golden arches on the front of the restaurant, but wonder if I'm going to feel like eating *anything* after Morgan finishes what he's got to tell me. Taxis veer around us, their horns blaring. The breeze as they speed by blows my anorak open. I wonder if I'll live long enough to get all the way across the street. What we're headed for *doesn't* seem like it's going to be a Happy Meal.

"Lost it...*how?*"

"Coming home and seeing Vittorio like...like he was after..." he gulps. "It freaked me out." He drags me by my arm until we're standing on the curb in front of the basketball courts. "We were *so happy.* We were both tested for HIV before we started living together. AIDS was the *only* thing we were afraid of, Delilah, not some crazed character coming out of nowhere knifing one of us. Franklin Street seemed so safe, right near a *police* station. Actually, the police gave me a lot more to worry about, so Monday morning, after they got through with me, I took off." He holds the restaurant door open for me. "I got drunk. I get careless when I'm drunk, Delilah. Like you've never seen me before. I went from one bar to the next. I went to the john in almost every one and it *wasn't* to pee. I finally met this guy in the last place I went, on First Avenue. *Raoul.* He asked me, do I like Cajun? He took me to his place in Park Slope. Actually, I didn't even know where I was until I called you last night; *that's* how far gone I was. All this time he was alternately feeding me jambalaya and fucking me and maybe fucking the jambalaya too."

"What'd you like?"

I recoil, then realize the girl behind the counter simply wants to take our order. She looks so young she could probably get away with selling lemonade curbside without needing a vending license. She'd probably make more money that way. All I order is coffee, black. Morgan asks for the works and insists that I get a McMuffin too. He reaches in his back pocket and feels around with such force I see the fleshy tips of his fingers through the worn fabric. "I must have left my wallet in..." He closes his eyes. "Shit! He must've rolled me."

"Raoul?"

He nods in disgust.

"*I've* got money," I reassure him, pulling a ten out of my overstuffed fanny pack.

"I'll repay you."

"Don't worry about it."

After we get a seat in the corner facing the basketball courts, he takes up where he left off, all the while shoveling food in his mouth. "Late last night, I saw the light, literally. Raoul had this floodlight in the bathroom; even with the door partially closed, it was blinding me, so I got up to turn it off and walked in on Raoul shooting up. He has to use the floodlight, you see, to find a usable vein; he has more tracks on his arms than there are in Grand Central Station." He takes a sip of orange juice. "Guess where the money for *that* fix came from. Shit. Anyway, I got dressed and slipped out into the night. I ended up at Gary and Abel's doorstep with the morning paper. I tried calling *you*, but there was no answer..."

I look past Morgan's shoulder at a couple of teenagers shooting hoops across the street. I watch as the taller of the two makes what looks from this angle to be a sure shot. The ball arcs and seems almost to stop in space, then hits the rim and ricochets into the shorter boy's grasp. *Nothing can be taken for granted.* Meanwhile, Morgan is stuffing his mouth with food. I can't bear to watch. *How can he eat like that after putting his life on the line that way?* "Are you going to be okay?"

"I'm not going to do anything like *that* again," he says. "Not quite like that, anyway." That doesn't exactly answer my question and I realize he *can't* and won't be able to answer it for some time to come. AIDS was the *only* thing he was afraid of before Sunday night, and then it figured to be, at least at the time, the *least* of his worries. He's still acting a little too nonchalant, too glib, like a little boy who went wee-wee in public and got caught with his pants down, no big deal, nothing more serious than that. I have a feeling my telling him the police still want to talk to him will agitate him more. But if I don't tell him, there's no telling what damage Quick's impending appearance on the scene will do to our friendship. I look at my watch. If he got my message, he's probably already there, waiting for me. The last thing I want to do is walk in there with an unsuspecting Morgan in tow like a gift bounty I didn't have time to wrap.

"The police still haven't found out who killed Vittorio," I tell him. *He hasn't even asked.*

"Did you think they *would*, Delilah?" he shakes his head. "You watch too much TV."

"Only Channel 13," I assure him. "*Most* of the time."

"There, I told you *my* sordid story. *Your* turn."

"I was getting around to that." I gulp the last of my luke-warm coffee. "I'm being stalked."

"Oh my God, is Ivan the Terrible still up to his old tricks?"

"Yes, and he's not the *only* one. There's this other character following me, leaving me notes, calling me. He called me last night, in the middle of the night—it was closer to morn-ing actually—and I got the feeling from what he said...well it wasn't what he said, but how he said it, that he intends to snatch me off the street...make me part of his *exhibit*."

"He's an artist?"

"That's what *he* says. A con artist is what he is. Full of it. Crazy." I feel Morgan's hand tighten around mine as I start shaking. "I called the police about it, Morgan, I had to. After last night, I'm more terrified of this guy than ever." I gulp. "There might be a detective waiting to talk to me when we get over to West Eighth. I called the police before you came. I just wanted to forewarn you after that inquisition you said they put you through the other night."

"I trust the boys don't take the rubber hose with them when they make house calls," Morgan sneers. "Guess I should embrace the good old American justice system. In some countries, I'd have gotten the old shock rod up my ass. Except that fat pig cop who did most of the talking probably wouldn't take a chance with something like that even if he *could*: that is, if he knew *what one was*. He'd be too afraid it would turn me on."

"They still want to talk to you, though..."

"There's no APB out on me or anything, is there?" Morgan huffs dramatically.

"Well, no..."

"No problem then. This isn't the street where I live...er, *lived*. Different precinct, different dicks, if you'll excuse the expression. It's *not* like I'm going to see fat pig cop..."

"Nooo, not him."

I follow Morgan to the exit, dump our collective trash in the receptacle by the door, and follow him up Sixth Avenue past the basketball courts and curbside vendors hawking magazines stacked up on rickety card tables. Morgan stops to pick up a Village Voice from a dispenser on the corner. I wonder if it's the personals or the cover story on police brutality that he's interested in.

"Morgan, you're going to *have* to talk to them *sooner* or later," I remind him.

"Fine. I'll opt for later."

We walk the rest of the way to West Eighth Street. in silence broken only when we reach the vestibule. The density of cigarette smoke as usual makes me gag. I lead the way up the stairs past the shrunken head and take a deep breath and hold it. The only person in the foyer is Louise. She's skimming through a book on Donatello. "*Morgan!*" she squeals. She looks happy to see him, but nervous too. She cocks her head in Morgan's direction and raps a pen against the binding of her book like she's tapping out a code to someone just out of sight. I look around hastily, wondering if she's tipping someone off. Any minute I expect Quick to emerge from the doorway to my left leading to the gallery or maybe from the staircase across from the coffee station. A sudden clink of metal against metal behind me makes me jump. *Handcuffs.*

I whirl around and see a woman bustle by, lugging a portfolio and an array of keys dangling from a chain that looks like a baby's pacifier.

I ask the question that I dread asking: "Any messages for me?"

"Not since I've been here," Louise says. "Better check the board. *You*, on the other hand," she points her blue Bic at Morgan, "you've got a *ton* of messages."

"I'm sure." He takes the pile of pink slips from her, nodding, knowing without looking who the bulk of them are from. I put my hand on his arm above his wrist. He's so fully charged that vibrations radiate from him. I wish I could find his 'off' switch. I give his arm a squeeze. "I'm going to my studio," he says flatly, "if anyone should ask."

It's up to me to keep that someone from asking, if and when he shows up, and maybe I can still keep him from showing up, at least not right away. I gesture toward the phone. "May I?" Just as I reach across the desk for the keypad, the phone rings, and the suddenness of the ring makes me knock the receiver off the hook. Louise coos, "Hellooo?" and hands the receiver to me, whispering, "You must be psychic."

More than you know, I think. "This is Detective Patrick Quick, First Precinct Squad, I'd like to speak with Delilah Price..."

"It's me," I tell him.

"What's up?"

I glance up at Louise. She takes the hint and goes over to the coffee station. I tell him about the call I got from Curtis and the news report about Majesty Moore and the mysterious *display items* that I heard about *right after* the call from Curtis. "I called the Sixth and talked to some Sauerpuss who was just *tremen*dously unhelpful. I called back this morning, but Rubenstein was out sick. So I guess that means *you* won't be able to talk to him about what happened last night...right?"

"*I* can get through to him," he assures me. "I already spoke

to the desk sergeant. Your *ex*, it turns out, wasn't able to ID
any of the pictures they showed him there; nothing came
close to the drawing *you* did. I tried calling him too,"he says,
"It seems he didn't show up for work today and there was no
answer at his place. Have you heard from..."

"No, thank God, and I hope I don't!"

"Morgan?"

I look upward. "This hasn't got anything to do with Morgan. This has to do with *me*. I called everyone you told me
to call and nobody was able or willing to help me and now
you're asking me, have I heard from *Morgan*? Well, I'm
scared shitless, Detective Quick, and it's *not* Morgan I'm
scared of. I'm scared *for* him, but not of him. Your investigation must really be going nowhere if you're still after Morgan. He wouldn't hurt a fly. Meanwhile, whoever *did* kill
Vittorio is still out there and so is Ivan. So is Curtis, and I'm
scared."

"I ran a first-name last-name computer check on Curtis
and all I found out so far is that there are a *lot* of Curtises out
there. We'll see if we can narrow down the list of those with
priors who match up with his description and MO. Maybe
we can come up with an outstanding warrant on him too, but
I have to warn you, with what little we have to go on, all of
this is a long shot. We don't even know if his name, first *or*
last, actually *is* Curtis. He may be using an alias. I should have
the drawing you did dropped off to me by four. I ordered that
a copy of it and a description of him be sent to the CATCH
unit uptown. They may be able to match it up to a picture
there, ID him *that* way." He pauses. "I'm doing what I *can*,
but..."

"I'm *not* worried for nothing."

"No," he says, "I don't think you are. I'll get back to you as
soon as I have some information. Are you going to be there
all day?"

"Until later this afternoon."

"Then you'll be home?"

"No. Working uptown." For Heidi Obermeyer's class no less, an experience to be enjoyed under normal circumstances. Thinking of how Quick would react to my portraying a Biblical Delilah makes me blush. "Over on East Twenty-first..."

"You should be all right there," he reassures me in an In The Know tone. "Just remember what I told you about keeping the windows covered so nobody can see in. *Insist* on it."

"How long before this...catch unit gets back to you?" I'm picturing a line-up of cops wearing protective masks and oversized mitts crouching in wait for something big to come their way.

"It depends," he says. "I hope I'll be able to find out something before my tour ends tonight, but sometimes it can take days and we don't know yet if there's anything in their database on him *to* find out."

"Where are you?" I've been talking to him so much lately that I feel he's in the same room with me even when he isn't. *Like last night.* I blush again. "I mean, how do I get in touch with you if I *need* to?"

"I'm in Manhattan," he says, a signal for me to forget about 718 for now, but not much else; he could be *any*where. He could have been at the pay phone on the corner of Fifth Avenue *all this time,* waiting for me to hang up, giving me time to go to my studio before he storms in here to take Morgan in for more questioning. I can only hope *he's* the one who'll be asking the questions, if and when it comes to that.

"I'll be in the clay studio," I tell Louise, "but if anyone *else* should ask, you haven't seen me."

Louise nods. "Right."

I look over my shoulder, wondering who *has* seen me. Most of the time I was with Morgan I was off guard, looking at him, not for who else might be around, who might be lurking in doorways, following us here. The only person I anticipated seeing was Quick, and just the *thought* of him being here chased all the bad guys out of my subconscious.

Nobody is in the studio. Nobody is there to see me pick up a spare fettling knife, zig-zag saw and sabre saw and drop them in my roomy side pocket. They have light wooden handles, and under normal circumstances, when my hands aren't sweating and shaking, they're easy to hold. The test will be if I can keep my hand steady enough to use them if somebody should suddenly lunge at me. *Just tools of my trade*, I can say in my defense, *I'm a sculptor*. Before getting to work on my clay figures, I scoop up a cut-out tool sheathed in what looks like a test tube and drop *that* in my pocket too. *Just in case.*

26

I DON'T KNOW WHAT KIND OF PROGRESS QUICK IS MAKING WITH HIS investigations. It's after three p.m. and the only dents I've made in my sculpture are a few shallow impressions with a mold knife. I don't trust myself to be able to cut any deeper. I may need to deploy that energy later, out on the street. I reach into my pocket and reassure myself that the small bulge that the sculpting tools make next to my right thigh doesn't look suspicious. When I walk, they sound like lipstick cases lightly clicking against each other, not overly metallic.

Nobody is sitting behind the reception desk when I leave. As I walk down Eighth Street, I practice reaching for and letting go of those light wooden handles, stopping only when I pass two uniformed cops standing in front of the Astor Place subway entrance. I feel their eyes trailing me as I walk on toward Third Avenue. I feel like I might as well be carrying a loaded .38, like those things jiggling against my hip are bullets. *Potentially dangerous weapons is what they are.* I jam my hands deep into my pockets and pick up my pace. I look over my shoulder only after I get across the street and see them still at their post, blatantly checking out the shapely little ass of a girl with spiked green hair. I take a deep breath and strut the rest of the way to the bus stop. While I wait for the M102, I feel the point of a blade lightly prick my thigh through the layer of scrubbed denim. A blue-and-white whizzes by, its siren screaming, and I turn to the right to hide my cache as if *that's* what the fuss is all about. When I turn back to my left, a M102 heralds its arrival with a loud hiss. I step aside to wait for the door to open and glance to my left and gasp.

There's Curtis behind the tinted glass of the bookstore entrance watching me, waiting for me to get on this bus so he can get on too, so he can follow me to my destination, so he can– *God, what does he intend to do to me?* My hands grip the handles of the sculpting tools in my pocket. I feel like I'm traveling blind, not able to see which tool is which, not able to know which one will do the most harm. My first choice would be to go for his eyes with the zig zag saw, if I could keep *my* eyes open long enough to do the deed. *So he can't see what he's coming after.* But chances are I'd only have one shot at one eye, and unless he's already blind in the other, that's not going to be much help. The fettling knife or sabre saw could draw blood; *just how much* hinges on how much of a chance I have to strike before he springs on me. The cut-out tool, pointed at *just* the right place, could puncture an artery.

"You getting on this bus or ain't ya?" the driver snarls at me.

"No, no...sorry," I back away from the stairs and wave the bus away. I start walking north up Third Avenue, then spin around like I'm spotting a dancing step. As expected, Curtis barges out of the bookstore once I've gained about a half block on him. My hand grips the handle of one of the tools so hard that my knuckles throb. *I don't know what I'm dealing with here.* I don't see any uniforms on the street now. I wish to hell I did. It's the beginning of rush hour and I just passed up the last non-rush-hour bus and I'm sure going to be late getting to this class. *If I get there at all.*

I run up Third Avenue gasping for breath, looking over my shoulder to see how fast Curtis is catching up to me. I track his distorted reflection as it bobs from window to window, coming closer. Nobody pays any attention except when I bump into them. "Hey, look where you're..."

A gaggle of gum-chewing girls glare at me. I dart around them and trip on the curb and into the street. A taxi careens around the corner, brakes screeching. The driver screams something that sounds like "Bint!", whatever *that* means, and babbles on incomprehensibly when the cab stalls, blocking eastbound traffic. I don't dare look back until I get across the street. A clot of people at the curb momentarily blocks movement around the stalled taxi. I've lost sight of Curtis. Big blob that he is, I doubt that he can squeeze through, but I keep moving, just in case, my fingertips still brushing against the light wooden handles in my pocket. I take a time out before the next cross street to catch my breath and spot Curtis' stained Browns parka reflected in the window of a greengrocer halfway down the block. The light is with me this time, and I run the full length of the next block, bumping into more people, not looking back at all until I reach the curb and stop to catch my breath.

He's gaining on me.

Maybe he once played for a team called the Browns or he's a wannabe on that score too. I've underestimated his athletic prowess; this man can *move*. I sprint across East Thirteenth Street. in the path of another approaching taxi. Brakes shriek. I can't make out what *this* driver calls me. In an effort to avoid me, he erringly swerves toward me and his dented fender scrapes against my leg before I can make it all the way across. Another fever pitch of horns echoes behind me. I hear the crunch of metal hitting metal. More horns.

"*Stop* her!"

I don't know who's doing the shouting and I'm not turning back to look because I can tell by the diction it's not the cabby who's in close pursuit, who I need to trip up. My leg smarts where the cab hit me. I can imagine the bruise in the making. What I need is some ice. And there it is, right on cue, right in front of me, a greengrocer's fruit stand packed with ice, perfect little uniform cubes crammed around plastic cups filled with fruit cocktail. I scoop up a handful as if I'm going to press it against my throbbing calf and cup my hands in a funnel. The ice slithers through and out on the sidewalk in Curtis' anticipated path. I grab more ice and start throwing it, one handful after the other, creating a hailstorm underfoot. Passers-by rush around the squall. Some look at me warily; some don't dare. *It's not me that you need to worry about*, I want to scream, *it's him*. I see another M102 bus approaching the corner. *This is it, my only chance, I've got to get on that bus now*. I take a deep breath and the biggest armful of ice I can grab and heave it in front of me just before my retreat. Grapes and giant chunks of chilled pineapple fly through the air too. For added insurance, I grab a banana propped on the other side of the stand, quickly strip its peel, and toss it as Curtis comes closer. He starts to skid. I don't wait for him to fall. I scamper to the curb and jump on the first stair of the bus just as the door starts to hiss and closes behind me.

"You crazy, girl," the bus driver admonishes me. "You know that?" By talking to me like this, I know he knows that I'm not crazy enough to take a weapon out of my pocket and start slashing at him. *Not that I couldn't if I wanted to*. Maybe my behavior reminds him of something he's familiar with, a victim he knows. A sister. A wife.

The passengers avert their eyes, looking every which way but at me, like I'm not there. The driver looks at me nervously until I drop the exact change in the coin box, then figuring a fare is a fare, he directs his attention to the traffic ahead and ignores Curtis' dirty scraped knuckles banging on the door. The Korean grocer is there now too, waving his fists as the bus cuts away into the next lane.

"Thanks," I tell the driver. He ignores me. I edge away from the front of the bus and slide into an unoccupied handicapped seat, grimacing enough to make it seem legit. *My calf really could have used some of that ice.* Even if Curtis waits to board the next uptown bus, it's rush hour and the M102 makes limited stops during rush hours. My eyes skim street signs as they flash by so I can get off before the bus overshoots my stop. I don't want to have to do much backtracking. When the bus whizzes by East Twentieth Street, I get up and hover near the stairs just as it swerves to a stop at Twenty-Third. I wait until the door opens with a hydraulic wheeze and jump off, then turn to the bus driver to thank him one more time; he continues to stare straight ahead and the words get caught in my throat. I cough as the departing bus discharges exhaust in my face and back off, batting away the noxious fumes with both hands. I spin around and walk back toward the building on East Twenty-First where Heidi Obermeyer and her students are expecting me, where for two hours I can safely strip myself of my clothes and my defenses.

I'm already starting to unbutton my coverall as I walk into the studio, ready to mumble an apology for being late. My fingers yank off a button when I see Heidi Obermeyer in front of the window wearing a black vinyl peek-a-boo get-up that so cleaves to her that it makes her look like she's wrapped in cellophane. These students, given a choice, would probably *much* rather draw *her.*

"You're out of breath," she proclaims, oozing concern. I can tell by looking around the room that this condition isn't unique to me, just the mad chase down Third Avenue that it took for me to get here. The other spellbound students ogle her eagerly, waiting for her to bend over or stoop. She's used to the attention; she's knocked herself out to get it and now she's accepting it as her due and blissfully ignorant of it, or at least *pretending* to be. She puts her hand on my arm as I step out of the coverall . As expected, there's a huge all-the-colors-of-the-rainbow bruise on my calf. My shaking fingers go to work on the tiny mother-of-pearl buttons on my jersey. *Nobody in the room is even looking at me.*

What about somebody *out there?* There are no shades to draw, no partitions to pull in front of the picture window. *What a picture this makes.* The floodlights that Heidi has clamped onto several easels in the room are arranged like candles adorning a centerpiece, and *I'm it.* I fall to my knees ready to assume a reclining position, hoping that that will make me not visible to anyone in the building next door, that all any peeping Curtis can see is plastic-coated Heidi slinking from easel to easel. I settle into an *a la Ingres* pose, my right foot crossed over the massive bruise on my left calf, my head looking over my shoulder, more wary than come-hither. *Can anyone out there see me?*

Heidi sashays up to me during my first break. "You seem up-taght," she drawls, the gold stud at the tip of her tongue still making her sound like she's deep in the heart of Texas.

"I had a little problem getting here," I tell her. "Some guy who's been harassing me followed me." After I've pulled my jersey on, I look out the window again at a tier of fluorescent lights shining on bobbing heads. I can't make out any of their features; I wonder if any one of them can make out mine. "I wondered if he could be over there..."

"Not lahkly. Just a bunch of randy cops in training. That's the police academy for the city of New York over there. Don't pay them any heed. They lahk to *look*, that's all. Ah'd say you couldn't be *safer* raght about now."

It's later that I'm worried about, and even now I don't feel cavalier about the surveillance, even if it *is* by New York's soon-to-be-finest. Quick had to *know* about this; he *wasn't* just thinking about *Curtis* when he suggested I insist that the windows be kept covered. *I would, but there's nothing to cover them with.* It's one thing to be looked at by artists who paint a bowl of fruit with the same detachment and quite another to be slavered over like an overripe peach. I don't feel comfortable with this and it apparently shows. "You've moved," several of the artists in the class complain when I get back into the pose. "You weren't so hunched over before."

I gesture to my injured leg. "Sorry. I guess the pressure is getting to me."

"Oh my God, how'd you get that?" Heidi huddles over my leg, twisting her barely covered butt toward the exposed window. She cups the welt on my calf with the palm of her hand caressingly, mirroring the way I imagine those gawking in the building next door would spoon her buttocks after gleefully unwrapping her.

I wince. "While I was trying to get away from that guy I told you about, I got bumped into by a cab. I wasn't looking where I was going. I just had to keep moving."

Nobody in the room has stopped drawing. My guess is that Heidi has become a dominant part of the picture, a handmaid offering supplication. She rises slowly, then struts to a cabinet at the far side of the room and bends again as she reaches for something on a bottom shelf. She's wearing a black lace thong under this get-up and bends over just enough to let everyone in the room know it. She comes back with a grungy fuzzy pink blanket and wads it between my legs. "Does that feel bettah?"

I prop myself back into the original pose and concentrate on the adjacent white brick building as one light after the other flicks off. They remind me of winking eyes. I wonder how many recruits are still there in the dark staring into this studio with relish, maybe justifying their voyeurism by convincing themselves that it's part of the job, live theater training them how to recognize vice. I bet more than one trainee has had his hand in his pants by now. By the end of the class, all of the lights are out but I can't help but wonder if somebody's still home over there, waiting for a last flash of naked flesh. I crawl to a blind corner before climbing to my feet to dress myself. Heidi sidles over to me, a worried look on her face, a strand of her purple streaked hair standing up on end as if electrified. "Ah you going to be okay? Do you need some protection?" I hope she's not thinking about going out and calling over some of those recruits.

"I'll be okay," I say, not sure whether I'll be okay at all. I grab the handles of my sculpting tools in the palm of my hand and show them to her. "I brought these with me."

"By the time you get those out of your pocket, that guy's hands will be in your pocket and wherever *else* he wants them to be," she says. "Ah can get you something bettah. A gun. A nahce little LadySmith. It'll fit snugly raght in there." She points to my fanny pack. "Ah carry mine with me all the time."

I look her over from head to toe, wondering *where* can she possibly conceal *any* kind of weapon, no matter *how* small. She's got dipped-in-chocolate ammo dangling from her earlobes, and the laces on her Doc Martens are strung through what could be spent casings, but I can't even guess where she's packed this ladylike gun of hers and I don't intend to ask.

"In here," she says, reaching into the supply cabinet and dangling a purple satin pouch from its black cord strap. "That's how small it is." She unzips the pouch and pulls out a tube of hair pomade, a set of keys, a wad of silver foil packets branded TROJAN and RAMSES, and then her hand fits nicely around the rubber hand grip of a pistol that seems custom made for her, the perfect fashion accessory for a kinky Barbie doll.

"Where'd you *get* that?"

"Ah'm from Texas, remember? Here, see how easy it is to hold."

"I don't think..."

She pulls the cartridge out of the handle nonchalantly, like this is no bigger a deal than taking the refill out of a pen, and flicks a bullet out of a nook in front of the firing pin, then jams the empty gun into my hands. "See, it's not loaded and the chamber isn't rounded raght now. You're not going to *shoot* me, if *that's* what you're worried about."

The only gun I feel comfortable with is the green water pistol I use to shoot water at my sculptures to make the clay malleable, not this. Sweat from my palms makes the handle slippery, rubber grips or not. It may be small, as advertised, but even squeezing it with both hands, it feels as weighty as the charges against me would be if I were caught carrying this thing. I wonder if anyone from the academy is still looking over here now that the peep show is over. It would give them probable cause to stop and frisk both of us on our way out, something I'm not sure Heidi wouldn't immensely enjoy. I know *I* wouldn't.

Unless maybe it were Quick doing the frisking. Just thinking this makes me flush.

"You've got a real nahce hold on that. *Stop shaking* so much. You saw for yourself, it's *not loaded*. Here," she steps behind me and holds my wrists steady. "Take aim at that painting on the wall over there and just *laghtly* squeeze the trigger. Lahk *this*." She makes a popping sound with her pursed lips.

"No...I can't...I *can't* shoot a Renoir, I mean, I can't do this. I *can't* shoot a gun; it isn't in me." I drop my hands, pointing the gun to the floor.

"Well, at least you know what it's lahk." Heidi takes the gun from me and slides the cartridge back in with a thrust of a vampish nail until it makes a satisfying *click*. She drops the loaded gun in her satin bag the same way she'd probably toss a lipstick. "But if things should get worse and you change your mahnd, let me know and ah can take you somewhere to practice shooting *real* bullets. Ah promise you won't be defacing any great mastahs."

"Thanks," I say, "I will." I know I won't.

Heidi walks me through the corridor like a school monitor. When we get outside, she waves good-bye and heads east down Twenty-First Street, her purple satin pouch filled with condoms and hair goo and a gun swinging benignly around her neck like a sightseer's camera case.

I turn away and see a familiar dark car parked curbside, its driver beckoning me toward him with a hand gesture that isn't quite a wave, his gold shield beaming amber, reflecting the overhead mercury vapor light straight in my eyes. "Delilah!" he shouts at me as if I haven't noticed him. If he yelled "Freeze!" and pointed his gun at me, he couldn't have rendered me more immobile than he has by calling me Delilah. My heart starts beating the way it does when I gulp down a triple cappuccino. I wonder what he's doing here, what he's seen. He gestures toward the passenger door, reaches over, and pushes it until it's wide open, like a gaping mouth. He pats the torn upholstery of the seat next to him. "Want a ride?" I better make it *quick* is what he's implying. There is no question whatsoever that I'm going to take him up on the offer without even asking him where it is he's taking me.

27

THE FIRST RED LIGHT HE STOPS AT GIVES HIM THE GREEN LIGHT TO TURN TO me and start talking. "I'm taking you to the First," he says. "I want you to look at some pictures." Tucked in the console between the seats is a manila envelope marked CITY OF NEW YORK: OFFICIAL USE ONLY.

"Of Curtis?"

"That's what you're going to tell me."

I gesture toward the envelope. "Is this them?" I ask. He nods. I reach for it. "Not here. When we get to the First." He gently pushes my hand away. "I *can't* just show you *these* pictures. I'm going to show you *several* pictures of *several* perps and you're going to try to pick him out of the pile. Like you would in a line-up."

"Those *are* pictures of him. You're sure of it or I wouldn't *be* here," I say. "If those are pictures of him, it means they had to be taken for a *reason*. *What* reason? What did he *do?*"

Quick runs the next red light and glares at me like I'm to blame. "We'll discuss it when we get downtown," he says, and turns on the radio to some the-doctor-will-see-you-now music. The kind of music Sauer told me his father listened to after dealing with street crap all day. The kind of music I hang up on when I'm forced to listen to it when put on hold.

Quick scowls at it too. "Royko," he grumbles barely audibly and pops the buttons under the dial until he finds a station he can live with for the rest of the ride. Willie Nelson appropriately enough croaks 'On the Road Again.' I try to picture Quick relaxed and on the open road, his hair tousled from the breeze, his shirt unbuttoned, his tie tossed on the back seat. I know what it would take to get *me* to relax and that what Quick is bound to tell me when we get to the First is likely to have the opposite effect. *It's something he doesn't dare tell me in a moving vehicle.*

"Curtis followed me again this afternoon," I tell him. "He chased after me for blocks before I could get away." I struggle to keep my voice calm. I don't tell him *how* I got away, how I caused an accident, how I literally upset the apple cart just before boarding the bus at East Fourteenth, or any of my other misdemeanors. He swerves around the corner at Seventh Avenue and changes lanes abruptly, missing a cab by inches. "He's wanted for something more than just *following* me, isn't he?"

Quick runs another red light.

"I have a *right to know,*" I protest.

"I'll *tell* you," he promises, "when we get where we're going." He reaches in his pocket and takes out a package of peppermint-flavored Carefree, probably wishing the brand described *him.* "Want some gum?" He hands me the package and I take out two sticks, one for me and one for him, and put the package on the dashboard. He nods his thanks and pops the stick in his mouth and starts chewing energetically, signaling End Of Conversation. I fold the gum in half and then in quarters and suck on it almost as if I expect it to melt. The pungent burst of flavor makes me think of mouthwash. Quick shoots through a yellow light and just as abruptly slows up to stop at the next light at the intersection of Christopher Street even before it turns. He scopes Sheridan Square to his left and the cigar shop across the street to his right and then he steals a look at me, probably contemplating how what he's got to tell me is going to play with me. Once he's been caught at it, he doesn't turn away. I decide to try to force a confession of my own. "Is this standard procedure? Coming uptown, out of your jurisdiction, to pick me up?" I ask.

"My first order of business was picking these pictures up," he says, patting the envelope.

"At the Academy?"

"No, on Thirteenth. It's at two-thirty, three doors down from where you said you were going to be."

My sigh of relief is audible, like an emphysemic's wheeze. "So you thought, why not try to kill two birds with one stone." Quick begins to smile. "Has Curtis killed anyone?" I ask.

I've committed overkill. "We're almost there" is all Quick will say. His jaw tightens. He doesn't seem to be chewing the gum any more. I wonder if he's swallowed it. The car picks up speed past Houston Street as Seventh Avenue becomes Varick Street. Quick looks like just another dogged rush hour commuter, eager to get home. As we shoot past Canal Street, I recognize the giant ad for some Italian cheese painted on the wall above and behind the entrance to the precinct house. The car jerks to a stop at the curb. Quick pulls the envelope out of its niche next to his seat and tucks it under his arm as he gets out of the car. As I walk up to the sidewalk to follow him in, I suddenly remember what I've got in my pocket, I hear the *click click click* of the sculpting tools rattling against each other with every step I take. I jam my hands in both pockets to silence them, to not arouse his suspicion, to not invite a body search. *At least not while these tools are on my body.*

28

ONCE HE PASSES THROUGH THE GREEN-GLOBED DOORWAY, QUICK ACTS like the Wizard of Oz returning to Emerald City, in charge of *every*thing. He pauses at the foot of the stairs to his left. "Want a candy bar before we go up?" he asks me. I shake my head and start following him slowly, scanning the array of WANTED fliers posted on the wall, some with photos, some with drawings, a veritable gallery of rogues. Quick turns around at the top of the stairs and waits for me. "This way," he says, leading me down the narrow hallway. He pauses in front of the detective squad room. "Take a seat in here," he says, gesturing to a room to the right that would best be described as Spartan were it not for the large-screen TV propped on top of a no-doubt fully-stocked refrigerator, pulling out a chair, not letting go of that manila envelope.

"Hat trick, that you?"

Quick points his index finger at me. "I'll be right back," he promises. He might as well be saying, "Stay!" I recognize the overweight guy pausing for breath at the top of the stairs. It's the defective detective, the one Morgan referred to this morning as *fat pig cop*. He looks down the hall, but I can't tell if it's me or maybe the refrigerator behind me that he's ogling. I slump in the hard wooden seat Quick pulled out for me and try to distract myself from the reason I'm here by studying them. Quite a pair. Physically, they're the Laurel and Hardy of law enforcement. After an hour or two of heavy questioning from the likes of Ollie in solitary, the sudden appearance of someone like Stan probably elicits relief and quite a few confessions. Right now they're acting out what I suppose is their own routine, a variation of Who's On First at the First.

"The Flyers are facing off against your guys in the Garden tonight and you're not there."

"Neither is Callahan. He's benched. His shoulder's acting up again."

"They need you more than *ever*, Hat trick."

"My apologies to Bam-Bam. Can't do it. I've got pressing business *here* to take care of."

"All the better for Giroux."

Quick momentarily turns his back to me and turns down the volume. A burst of ribald laughter tips me off that they're speaking locker roomese. Suddenly both detectives turn and look down the hall at me looking at them. I shift my gaze to the rectangular wooden table in front of me and read the many sets of initials gouged deep into the waxy veneer. The voices in the hallway lower to murmurs as the two begin to walk back toward me. Quick pauses at the doorway and holds up the envelope. "It'll just be another few minutes. I'm going to get the rest of the photos. The coffee maker is broken, but there's soda and juice in the fridge if you want..."

"All I *want* is to know what you've got to tell me."

Quick nods. "You will," he assures me in a tone that makes me wish this seat came equipped with a safety belt, to secure me during the moment of impact. The other detective, who I realize must be his partner on this case, stands guard in the doorway. "I hear you're a regular Rembrandt," he says. I shrug. "Hat trick's got the picture you drew hanging on display right by his desk in the squad room. You got to get him to show you."

I hear metallic drawers screech open and clang shut and something rustling in the squad room next door and then more footsteps galloping up the stairs. Another detective struts down the hall toward the squad room, his eyes casing me before he veers to his left. "Who's the babe?"

I hear whispering in response, then more screeching, then silence. Quick comes around the corner carrying a loose-leaf binder in one hand and the manila envelope in the other. "Just another minute," he says, unwinding the string securing the top flap. He turns his back to me the way a doctor does when filling a syringe, sparing the patient the sight of the needle until it's time to stick it in. I hear Quick turn plastic pages and then pause to slide in the pictures. My mouth goes dry. "Can I have some of that soda now?" I croak.

Quick places the book open in front of me. "Let me know if anyone looks familiar," he says. He opens the door to the refrigerator and looks inside. "Diet ginger ale all right?" He doesn't wait for an answer, splashes some into a paper cone cup and hands it to me. "Take your time," he admonishes me as I flip from page to page and back again. "They weren't taken yesterday. They may not leap out at you."

"I'm worried about flesh-and-blood Curtis leaping out at me," I retort. "Not five-by-seven glossies." I'm aware of Quick and his partner studying my reactions to this and that picture as I use my fingers to crop a mustache here, the beginnings of a beard there, trying to imagine what twenty extra pounds will do to a formerly scrawny face. I flip to the next page and gasp. Half the ginger ale sloshes over the rim of the cup and onto the plastic envelope. A droplet falls on a corner of the actual photo and does a slow fizz, marking it for life.

"That's him," I say.

Quick nods and turns to his partner for confirmation that

he too witnessed what I've just done. "I been telling her she's a regular Rembrandt," the partner responds.

"Thanks, John."

"No prob," he says. "Thank *you*, Miss Rembrandt."

I nod, wondering if that's the only artist's name he knows. Quick goes out in the hall with him, says a few more things I can't hear, then comes back in the room and shuts the door behind him. "How'd you happen to come up with a picture of him so *quickly?*" I blush and stammer over my choice of adjective. "After all, you said, based on the flimsy information I had..."

"The computer uptown compared the drawing you did and the description we gave to several photos on file and came up with the match." He closes the book and pushes it to the side. "There's more."

"More pictures?"

"No. More I have to tell you." He pulls over another hardwood chair with masking tape wrapped around two spokes and sits to my left. I detect a trace of peppermint when he leans forward and wonder again if he swallowed the gum. "Some uniforms used your picture on a recanvass of Franklin Street late this morning and someone IDed it."

All of a sudden we're back on Franklin Street. I feel like I'm on a film reel set on rewind. "You mean someone recognized Vittorio and *saw* something?"

"Someone recognized the picture, Delilah, but it *wasn't* the one of Vittorio Scaccia. The drawing I gave to the uniforms from the Sixth last night was faxed here and the guys doing the canvass got the two drawings mixed up, picked up the wrong one on their way over there." He gulps. "Or I should say, as it turns out, the *right* one."

"What are you saying?"

"After looking at the drawing you did of Curtis, the house guest of a neighbor IDed him as being in the vicinity of the loading dock around the time Vittorio was murdered Sunday night."

"*Curtis*," I sputter.

"This witness thought he was on private security duty, he claimed, because he wasn't wearing street clothes. He was wearing a uniform and had on a cap with some kind of insignia..."

"The same one he had on last night..."

"And he was having a very loud altercation with somebody there who, based on the description this guy gave, we *believe* was Vittorio. Our witness thought at the time that the *security guard*—Curtis—had stopped Vittorio for a simple trespass and went on his merry way. He didn't associate that with what happened on the loading dock. Or so he said. We checked with a couple of companies that have provided security service in this area and neither of them had contracted *anyone* to work *any*where on Franklin Street Sunday night at the time in question. He showed up in a uniform and didn't think anyone would question his presence there, and if not for your picture being shown around, no one might have even remembered him. A uniform blends right into the urban scene, particularly at *night*. People *trust* uniforms." Quick pauses and gives me a chance to swallow this and the rest of my ginger ale before continuing. "You said before that you couldn't be sure if you'd ever seen him before he made his presence known to you, that he was nondescript. Don't you think it's possible you might have bypassed him, coming in or going out of West Eighth Street or any one of the other places where you work and not noticed because he blended in with the scenery," Quick's eyes hold me captive. "Because at the time he was wearing a *uniform?*"

I shrug. "Someone wearing a uniform can walk into an office and gain access to information he shouldn't have any business knowing, right?" I feel like I've been punched in the stomach. "Like my home address, my cell number, not to mention the names and addresses and numbers of everyone else...including Morgan and Vittorio. *Why* would Curtis kill *Vittorio?*" My hand crumples the paper cone cup into a sticky ball.

"In one of those notes he left you, he said something about getting rid of the competition..."

"*Weeding out* the competition. *That* came with the *flowers.*"

"Did he have any reason to believe that you had become involved with Vittorio?"

"Vittorio was *gay.*"

"He might not have known that."

"Why wouldn't he? He seems to know everything *else* about me and everyone I'm close to. He *told* me so." I suddenly remember bumping into Curtis in the subway station yesterday and what he said to me. *I'm sorry about your friend. It's terrible to lose a friend, especially like that. So unexpected. So undeserving. Obviously at the wrong place at the wrong time.* I choke up. "Could I have some more soda?"

Quick goes over to the refrigerator and reaches in for the two-liter bottle on the top shelf. I hold out the crumpled wad of paper in my fist. "I think I'm going to need another cup too...while you're there."

He stands over me while handing me the cup. I feel like I'm in the shadow of a giant, strong-rooted Sequoia. "Did he mention Vittorio to you at all when you spoke to him those few times?"

"He said he was *sorry about my friend,*" I concede. "Yesterday, in the subway station, when I was on my way to meet you here. And I wondered how he even knew I *knew* Vittorio, but that was before he told me that he knows where I go, what I do, who I see. The only person in my life he seemed obsessed with was Ivan. He apparently called my home number quite a lot when I wasn't home when this...*infatuation* of his began, to get Ivan riled up, to rouse his suspicions.

Enough so that he resorted to physical force..." I remind him. "Every time Curtis called me, even in the message he left on my voice mail, the one you heard, he dwelled on my involvement with *Ivan*, always referring to him as that *tight-ass stockbroker*. Even after I told him I was involved with someone else."

"*Are* you?"

"No," I say. "I just told him that, hoping that would get rid of him."

"*When* did you tell him that?"

I bite my lip. "Saturday night was the first time...when I got home from the dinner party at Morgan and Vittorio's loft. I was *very* drunk when he called, I'm not sure if I can remember exactly..."

"Try."

"I think I said something like I'd had a special date and he was wasting his time. He said it couldn't have been *that* special because I wasn't dressed for anything like that."

"He knew what you were wearing, so he obviously saw you coming or going."

I suddenly remember what else I said. It didn't really matter what I wore since I wasn't going to stay dressed once I got there. Or something like that.

"Do you remember seeing Curtis, seeing *anyone in a uniform*, on your way home from that party Saturday night?"

"I took a cab...I went to a bar across from Sheridan Square to use the phone because I forgot to charge mine, then I went home and one of my neighbors told me that *I*van had been there looking for me, but no Curtis...there may have been *some*one in a uniform around, but I don't remember."

"Near your place or near Franklin Street?"

"I don't remember."

"Did you leave the party by yourself Saturday night?"

"Morgan called me a cab and Vittorio waited outside with

me and..." I cover my face with my hands. The ginger ale mixed with a sudden wash of tears leaves a burning streak of fizz down my throat. "Oh God."

"What?"

"I kissed him good night before I got in the cab." I whimper. "It wasn't a tongue-to-tonsils kiss or anything like that, it was just a—" I bring the tip of my index finger to the hollow of my cheek and give it a light swipe "—*brush* of my lips kind of thing, but it *was* a kiss." I gulp. "Are you trying to tell me that Curtis may have seen it and thought...my God, in *that* case, I'm just as guilty as *he* is, I gave Vittorio the kiss of death!"

"All I'm saying is that there's good reason to believe Curtis is guilty of a *lot* more than disorderly conduct, and we're going to have a nice long talk with him," he promises, "once we find him."

"That shouldn't be too hard. I keep bumping into him. Him and Ivan." Follow me and he's yours is what I 'm telling him. Follow me. Don't let me out of your sight for a minute. I don't know what will happen to me if you do.

"We haven't found Ivan yet either," he adds. "Have you heard from him since last night?"

I shake my head numbly. I know I didn't give Ivan the kiss of death, except metaphorically, something he refused to accept. *So what* if something has happened to him too. *So what!* I'm too anesthetized to react to any more.

"What we did find out when we got this," he slaps the book filled with pictures, "is that Curtis moved from his last known address and left no forwarding address, so his landlady was stuck with a lot of dead mail that she put aside for him and started to read one day when her afternoon soaps got preempted. She complained to the Thirteenth because some of it was *dirty*. Some of the mail she found lying around *also* turned out to be addressed to other people who were on record as having been victims of various crimes. He was booked for one of them in '05. That's how we got the mug shots. He didn't do time, though. The complainant dropped the charges."

"What *was* he charged with?"

"Aggravated sexual assault."

"Oh..."

"It was a gray case to begin with. One of the guys who worked it was there when I picked up the pictures, and he gave me some background. The girl met him in a bar. He was drunk and she was even drunker. He was in a *uniform*. She *trusted* him."

"He was posing as a security guard even back then?"

"He was a cadet in the academy back then."

"The *police* academy?" I recall that assembly line of bobbing heads bouncing under the fluorescent lights late this afternoon.

"He didn't last too long. The assault charges may have been dropped, but it got him noticed downtown, and *not* for commendation. Too many questions were raised about his conduct. There were apparently some psych problems."

"Apparently," I whisper.

"The return address on some of the mail sent to him at his old address was One Police Plaza. So based on this bundle of mail the landlady brought in, the Thirteenth got interested in him as a suspect in some of these other crimes and issued a want card on him."

"Is that the police equivalent of issuing a *contract* on somebody?"

"It means if he gets picked up for anything anywhere else in the city, we get notified. And it turns out his name *really is* Curtis, A variation of it, anyway."

"Curtis *what?*"

He shakes his head. "I want you to just keep calling him

Curtis. I don't want him to know that you know any more than you did before I picked you up tonight."

"So I get to die in ignorance..."

"You're *not* going to die and you're by no means ignorant." The sudden declaration of admiration in his eyes and his voice enthralls me. "If it weren't for you and your drawing, we wouldn't have a make on this guy," he reminds me, as if I need reminding. "We'd still be dragging ass talking about disorderly conduct charges and not doing anything about it."

"You'd *still* be looking to pin Vittorio's murder on *Morgan.*"

"I still need to talk with Morgan, Delilah. In case he saw something."

"*He* doesn't know where Curtis is."

"Do you happen to know where *Mor*gan is?"

I nod. "He showed up at my doorstep this morning and walked over to West Eighth Street with me. He's probably still in his studio."

Quick pulls his notepad out of his pocket and clicks his pen into ready position. "Do you happen to know where he's staying?"

"With his friends Gary and Abel over on Wooster Street. They have a landline. It's an unlisted number. I believe you *have* it."

"Give it to me, just in case I *don't.*"

I grope around in my bag for my address book and hesitate before handing it over to him. "Under 'W,' I tell him. "It's the only one there. Aside from the dry cleaner." Quick takes his time flipping through the pages to get to the end of the alphabet like he has *every right* to. My life has become an open book to him. He finally jots down the needed phone number and hands the book back to me without bothering with X-Y-Z. I drop it back in my bag.

"Do you have someone *you* can stay with?" Quick asks me. "A friend or relative, preferably in another part of town?"

I shake my head. My 'closest' female friend Sachi has been inaccessible for so many days now that I'm beginning to wonder if this latest guy of hers who moved in with her turned out to be a space alien who not only swept her off her feet but also off to some distant planet. My gay male friends may not be friends of mine any more after they figure out that I share at least some of the blame for what happened to Vittorio and aided and abetted the police to boot. A trip to see the old folks at home outside Frankfort and hear about how it *serves me right, I should have stayed home and made someone a good Kentucky farm wife* is out of the question. I imagine I *could* call Heidi. She'd be more than willing to provide bed and breakfast and bullets. I shake my head again. Staying with her, even just for an overnighter, would make me look like I'd just leapt out of a Munch painting. "No, I tell Quick, "there's no one."

Except for you. You live in another part of town.

The scream of a siren outside makes me flinch. Living in this constant state of anxiety may do me in before Curtis even has a chance to lay his hands on me. Quick stands up and signals me to follow him into the squad room.

"I knew her when I worked the seven-five," one detective says, flipping through a newspaper. "I mean, knew *of* her. When you heard the boys were going down the block for some hot Toddie, you *knew* it wasn't for a drink."

"Like mother, like daughter."

"Don't know. Seems to me she was *trying* to keep the girl *straight.* Sent her off to live with an aunt when she was open for business, then picked her up when she was *through* for the day. Kid turned out all right."

"Yeah, right. Kid turned out *dead.*"

The first thing I see when I walk in behind Quick is the

front page of the *Post* masking a detective's face with the picture of a beautiful young black woman wearing a tiara and an equally dazzling smile. She looks like a queen. Alongside the photo, the headline announces DEATH OF HER MAJESTY in big bold print. I get it. It's the window display artist who was murdered, who I heard was IDed late last night, and I lean over the desk to try to read more. Quick notices and guides me away. The pressure of his fingertips on my arm lingers even after he successfully maneuvers me where he wants me, boxed in, unable to read any more distressing headlines. I notice that the drawing I did of Curtis is indeed tacked on the wall above Quick's desk. So are a lot of pictures of other perps. So is a Sierra Club calendar with dates circled, with indecipherable jottings flowing out of several boxes.

Quick picks up the phone on his desk. "I'm going to notify the Sixth to keep an eye on your place," he tells me. "Actually, as many eyes as they can spare. They've got a make on Curtis. That's all that I can... yes, hi, this is Patrick Quick, First squad, who's on for Rubenstein? Yeah, I'll hold." He drums his long, elegant fingers against the side of his desk. I watch as the detective across the aisle folds the *Post* and discards it in the waste paper basket with the ease he probably wishes it took to clean out his docket of cases. When Quick begins mumbling in earnest and I'm sure that somebody on the other end has garnered his full attention, I reach in the waste basket and pull the paper out, flipping to the full story spread on page five. A reporter got the mother's side of the story. Majesty was her only child, a go-getter who grew up and out of East New York and moved on to Cooper Union and the showrooms of Fifth Avenue stores before someone went and got her. As far as *who* got her, the official police wonk they've quoted would only say *several leads are being investigated.* No specifics about a belligerent boyfriend, though Margaret Toddie, the mother, "expressed remorse over some of her daughter's social blunders." A wrong turn down a one-way street is a *blunder;* I'd use a bit stronger terminology to describe sticking with a man who put her in the hospital twice, as Sauer told me Majesty's boyfriend had done. There is *no mention whatsoever* made of display items.

"Has anyone found out who did this?" I ask.

Both of the other detectives in the room look right over my head at Quick. He reaches over my shoulder and takes the paper out of my hands. "Not yet," he says. "Come on, I'm getting you a ride home."

I follow him into the narrow corridor. "Was any of that mail you said the landlady found addressed to Majesty Moore?"

He turns around at the top of the stairs. "*Most* of the mail apparently was pulled from addresses in his immediate neighborhood, near Gramercy Park. That's how the Thirteenth caught *that* end of it. They're still going through it. Months of *his* accumulated mail and then these *souvenirs* of his." He pauses. "Have you been aware of any mail *you* should have been receiving but haven't?"

I shake my head and follow him down the stairs. I almost trip trying to keep up with him. "You said you were *getting* me a ride home. Does that mean *you're* not...?"

"Can't tonight. I'm going to be tied up here for a while. You'll be all right." He stops short in front of a bank of black and tan filing cabinets, across from a desk that reminds me of a judge's bench. A banner hanging above it announces THE FIRST PRECINCT IS PROUD TO BE AT YOUR SERVICE. I imagine that most civilians who have had occasion to stand before this desk have little reason to be proud and have not done their community a service. "Wait here a sec." Quick gestures to a row of blue plastic chairs lined up against the wall. I remain standing. Two uniformed officers swagger past the front desk on their way to the candy machine. Quick stands in front of it. "Got a big favor to ask of you," he says, motioning them to one side. The two uniforms turn toward me and grin, nodding like bobblehead dolls. "Sure, sure," I hear them reply.

Quick comes back over to me. "These two officers are going to drop you off at your place and make sure you get in all right."

"What about once I'm in? Will I be all right *then?*"

"If you have any problems, call the Sixth first. They're going to have a car cruising around Waverly; they'll be able to respond right away. Let me know too, if anything happens. If I'm not here, use my cell number. Is there anyone in your building who you think might keep an eye on things?"

I nod, picturing Mrs. Davidoff leaning against her door, squinting through the peephole. "Yes, I have a neighbor like that."

"Good," he says. "In *any* case, I'll be in touch," he promises, and does touch me, lightly, on my shoulder. I walk away from him wanting him to be more in touch. "Oh, and Rodriguez,"

The two uniforms escorting me turn around. I wonder if *both* of them are named Rodriguez.

"Be sure to radio in the *minute* you complete your assignment," he barks at them.

"*Ten-four*, Detective," they shout back.

29

WHEN I GET OUT OF THE RADIO CAR IN FRONT OF MY BUILDING, A. Rodriguez smiles tersely, his hand already grabbing his radio transmitter to notify Quick that he's done his duty. Z. Rodriguez, no relation to A., walks me up the stairs while I fumble in the dark for the right key and try to keep from dropping it. The Z stands for Zixto, he told me on the way home; he was so named because he was the sixth of seven sons. "In that case you should have been called *Sex*to," A. Rodriguez quipped. "Guess your parents figured that would make you too sexy for your own good."

"The seventh was supposed to be lucky," he said, pretending to ignore his partner. I wondered about the others' names, not his use of the past tense. "Some lucky. He got blown away by a drug dealer when he was thirteen. *Just thirteen!* That's how come I became a cop." He brushes his knuckles against his silver shield. "*I* gotta be the lucky one *now*."

I decide to let Zixto try his luck with my key because my hands are shaking so bad I can't fit it in the lock. He gives the door a shove and steps aside for me to enter, handing me my keys. He climbs up the stairs behind me and waits while I fumble with the array of locks. I hear a door open and it isn't mine. And then *my* door springs open *too easily.* I realize it was unlocked to begin with. "Somebody's *been* here!" I gasp.

"You *sure?* You didn't just forget to lock up on your way out or...?" Zixto Rodriguez looks at me for confirmation, all the while blocking my way, making sure I can't dart past him and go in.

"There's *no way!*" I cry. "There's *no way* I'd do that with what's been going on. *No way!*"

Zixto runs his hand along the side of the door and frowns. "Little bit of chipping here."

The door next door slams shut. "Mrs. Davidoff...."

"That your neighbor?"

I nod and try to squeeze past him to take a better look at my apartment. He pushes me to one side. "Stay here," he says and taps his transmitter. "Alonzo, we got a possible ten-thirty-one here." He reaches for his gun and I slink further back and get pushed to the other side by A. Rodriguez as he gallops to the top of the stairs. Both officers advance into my apartment with their guns drawn. I lose sight of them as they split off into different rooms. When they come back to the door, it's in alphabetical order, A. followed by Z., and their guns are tucked back in their holsters. It's okay to start breathing normally again. "Okay, you can come in now; whoever was here is gone now. Fire escape window's locked, so that's out as point of entry, unless he's Houdini. Must've pried the door or had some help. Alonzo, check out the neighbor." Zixto points his thumb toward the wall Mrs. Davidoff is probably leaning her ear against. "You," he signals me to come in, "take a look around. The place doesn't *seem* to have been tossed much. Notice if anything's missing?"

"Not offhand." I start a slow tour, aware of Zixto watching. I wonder if he still suspects that I carelessly forgot to lock the door. I can hear Mrs. Davidoff in the hallway being interviewed by A. Rodriguez. "Not hard to believe it would come to this, what with all the men parading in and out of here at all hours," she says too loudly, for my benefit. Zixto looks at me like he's wondering if he indeed could get lucky, even if he *isn't* the seventh son.

"Have you seen anyone other than the other tenants in or near the building *today?*" A. Rodriguez asks her. "Delivery man, mailman, FTD florist?"

I cringe, thinking about the mums I have yet to replace. *"Police officer?"* I suggest, picturing the former cadet who was kicked out of the Police Academy wearing a fake badge on his cap, probably carrying a fake search warrant. If no one was around to present it to, he probably jimmied my door open with the box cutter he keeps in his pocket, the best place to keep the tools of one's trade. A. and Z. Rodriguez glower at me.

"I was out all day. I came home after seven," Mrs. Davidoff says. "I didn't hear or see anyone or anything then. I turned on the TV in time for the rest of Jeopardy and then I watched Wheel of Fortune. There was no banging on the door. *That* I'd *hear*. That and what goes on when she's *with* them."

"So it could have been *before* she came home," I say softly to Zixto to try to take his mind off banging noises. A. Rodriguez is advising Mrs. Davidoff to be sure to keep her door locked at all times. "This is a safe neighborhood, but you can *still* get something like *this*. You never know."

"I know I don't keep *her* kind of *company*," Mrs. Davidoff sniffs, looking over her shoulder at the TV during a break in commercials. "There was never any kind of trouble in this building *before*. You never know *what* you're going to get with sublets."

"You're subletting this apartment, Mrs. Davidoff?"

"No, *she's* the temp."

"This is pretty nice. How long you been living here?" Zixto asks me, stepping inside again, looking around.

"A little over a year. I'm living out the rest of the tenants' two-year lease. They're in Japan. I'm in hock." I laugh nervously. "Actually I'm doing better than I was when I *first* moved in. I inherited their rent control. I've been doing *okay*. That is, okay until now."

"Anything missing that belongs to them?"

I suddenly notice a dustless space on the floor that was formerly occupied by a plaster bust I had done of Ivan. He didn't sit for it. I did it from a series of pictures we posed for in a photo booth at Coney Island in the early days when we had fun together. The sculpture turned out to be a bust; the head was disproportionately huge and hardened too fast, and I kept it as a reminder of failure on all fronts. "Ivan," I say. "Ivan's missing." *Indeed he is.*

"A dog? A cat?" Zixto looks down at his feet. "You're not gonna tell me it's a *snake*, are you?"

"It's inanimate. A sculpture I did. A plaster bust." Zixto's eyes suddenly fixate on the straps of my coverall. "Probably the *worst* piece of work I ever created," I admit. I start to feel queasy wondering about the fate of some of the best work I've ever created, Glad-bagged and locked up in the clay studio at West Eighth Street. I count to ten. The building is secured, there's a guard on duty. *Who's on duty tonight? A guard who maybe likes to play with knives?* I have visions of heads rolling, not all of them plaster. When my cell phone suddenly rings, I jump and go to pieces like overbaked terra cotta.

"Go ahead and answer. We'll wait," Zixto Rodriguez says, still looking around the room nervously, anticipating the appearance of an imaginary snake.

"Are you home?" Quick asks. "Are the officers still there?"

I hand my phone to Zixto. "We had some trouble here," I hear Zixto explain as he retreats to the bedroom so I can't hear everything he says. He returns after only a couple of minutes. "He wants to talk to you." Zixto holds the receiver out to me.

"You're going to be okay," he says without asking if I am. "He must have gotten in *long* before I called the Sixth. They know who they're looking for now and they'll be patrolling on and around Waverly all night. He won't be able to get close. Did he *take* anything?"

"Just a piece of sculpture," I mumble. "A head I did of Ivan a long time ago." I pause to wipe away a tear. *I never shed a tear over Ivan. Except when he hurt me.* "I'm worried about my *other* sculptures. The ones over at West Eighth Street. If he can get in *here*, he can get in *there* too. He can get in *anywhere he wants* when he's wearing a *uniform.*" I take a deep breath and announce, "I've got a show to think about. I've already put a lot of work into this. I want to go see if my sculptures are all right."

"No," Quick snaps, "Not tonight you're not. Wait until morning. I'll pick you up at your place and take you there. Ten o'clock all right?" He doesn't expect me to say no. "Put Rodriguez back on."

I hand the phone to Zixto and wonder if Quick knows which one he's talking to. Zixto does a lot of nodding and uh-huhing, looking up at me from time to time. Alonzo comes back in the apartment. "No one saw nada," he re- ports dismally. Zixto mumbles this information into the mouthpiece and nods again. "Okay, okay, we're on our way." He hangs up. "Guys from the Sixth are gonna be taking over for us. Quick said to tell you, just stay put, you'll be okay."

I lock the door after them and turn on the radio. "All news, all the time," I'm promised. *None of it good*, they might as well add as a disclaimer. I start to undress. *Double shooting in the Bronx.* Off comes the coverall. I take the sculpting tools out of my pocket and lay them out on my bedside table. *Twenty-nine year old man stabbed in front of ATM on Madison Avenue, robbery believed to be the motive.* Off comes the jersey. *SWAT team called to hostage situation on Linden Boulevard.* I unhook my bra. *Baby thrown out of a fifth story window into a dump-ster, fifteen-year-old mother being sought for questioning.* I reach behind the bathroom door for the oversized T-shirt I've been wearing to bed the last couple of nights. It isn't there. *I'll be okay, I'll be okay, I'll be okay.* At least there are no messages on my answering machine for a change. I turn the radio dial to a Spanish station where the *only* word I under-stand at the top of the hour is *noticias,* then pick up my cell phone to call Morgan. I'm a friend of his, *I* want to be the one to tell him the latest before the police get in touch with him, but *how* am I going to tell him *this? I have good news and bad news. The good news is the police know who killed Vittorio and know it wasn't you. The bad news is he's after me and anyone who comes near me and that's why Vittorio got whacked.* Gary answers the phone on the fourth ring. "Morgan just stepped out," he says when I ask for him. There's a serrated edge to his voice that could cut through metal. I guess Quick beat me to the punch. I feel guilty for having given him Gary's unlisted number. *I had to. He's the police.* Gary must *feel* like he was punched. Morgan too. I begin to worry about what sort of dessert is on his menu tonight.

"Would you have him call me when he gets back? Please?"

"He may not be back until late," Gary says. "I don't know where he went. He may not be back tonight at all."

"When he *does* come back..."

"I'll tell him," Gary says, and hangs up.

I turn up the volume and peek under the shade at the street below. I see a blue-and-white down there, cruis-ing around to make sure I'm safe. I don't see anyone *else.* I pull the covers over my head, muting the sounds of a soothing salsa beat and the sirens in the distance that always seem to be there, barely audible but *there,* like white noise. I consider calling Quick with an updated inventory of what's been stolen as a pretext to hear some comforting words, but the only ones that I know would make me feel better are *I'll be right over.*

30

I start firing questions at him. I didn't hear from *either one of them* last night, I tell him, Curtis *or* Ivan. Did you catch Curtis? Did you get in touch with Ivan? It's nine thirty a.m. and I haven't slept. I switch the phone from one sweaty hand to the other. I'm wearing a dress for a change, a blue jean dress with a white Peter Pan collar and pockets that are almost deeper than the dress is long, all the better to conceal my sculpting tools. I'm worried that he might withdraw his offer to take me to check the condition of the sculptures I'm working on for my show. Quick goes so silent on me that I can't even hear him breathing any more. I wonder if we've been cut off, and then he says it, *I'll be right over*, and hangs up.

Right over can mean anything from fifteen minutes to an hour depending on the volume of traffic he's got to deal with on the way, so I kill time by calling Rubenstein at the Sixth to see if I can get anything out of *him* before Quick gets to him. "*I'm* sorry, he's out."

"He's still sick?" I wonder if maybe the yogurt I pictured him eating non-stop got to him.

"No, he's *in*, but he's out in the field." I picture him in the middle of Sheep Meadow playing catch. "Is there someone else who can help you?"

That someone else knocks on the door a half hour of pacing later. The only thing that's changed about him is his clothes; he looks as stoical as he did last night, if not more, and I feel self-conscious about having fantasized about him again. He gives the apartment a cursory wide-angle once-over and then focuses on me. "Are you ready?" I expect him to add *for what I have to tell you?* I nod. He follows me to the door and waits while I lock up. I hear a soft click next door. "That's Mrs. Davidoff, my neighbor," I say to Quick too loudly, for her benefit. "*She's* the one who keeps an eye on things."

"But she didn't see anything yesterday."

"Right."

I lead the way downstairs, conscious of him looming a couple of steps behind me, wondering if my dress is riding up my ass in back, if I should reach behind me and tug at it or if that would seem like a *too*-obvious ploy for attention. I'm not used to wearing dresses and being chauffeured about in police cars. *There's a whole lot going on in my life now that I'm not used to.* Before he starts the motor, Quick reaches his long arm around the head rest and retrieves a brown paper bag from the back seat. "Bagel?" He unfurls it. "There's cinnamon raisin, pumpernickel, and whole wheat."

I reach in the grab bag and pull out a still-warm cinnamon raisin. He takes the whole wheat. "Did you want *this* one?"

He shakes his head and tears off a piece of his bagel before shifting into drive. "Sorry there's nothing to put on it."

"The bagel's fine as is," I mumble through chews. "Thanks."

"There's more I have to tell you," he says. I drop the bagel in my lap. He turns onto West Eighth Street, almost hitting the curb in front of the bookstore, and keeps to the right, slowing to a standstill behind a blue-and-white. "Looks like we've got company," he says, not seeming at all surprised when Rubenstein comes out the double doors and strolls over to the car. Quick hands him the brown bag. "They didn't have onion. Hope you like pumpernickel," he says.

Rubenstein fishes the bagel out of the bag and gives it a dead herring stare. "I can live with it," he finally decides, taking a tentative bite. He notices me. "You were over at West Tenth a couple of days ago," he says. "Boyfriend pushed you around or something like that, wasn't it?"

"*Some*thing like that." I rub my hand up and down my arm. Every mention of Ivan makes something hurt, even now.

"She wants to see if her work is okay." Quick gestures us toward the building. My hands are shaking so much I can't even *find* my keys. I have to buzz us in. Louise looks past me at Quick lagging behind and doesn't stop looking. She licks her lips. Rubenstein turns to Quick. "What d'*you* have?" I hear him ask and I know he's not talking about bagels. They remind me of two four-star generals contesting each other's war strategy as they huddle closer and closer to the statuary at the top of the stairs and further away from me so that all I can make out is "task force." Quick all at once turns and shoots a look at me that pierces like a bullet.

"Who's Mr. G.Q. over there?" Louise purrs.

"That's Detective *P.Q.*," I say. "Patrick Quick, First Precinct."

"Appropriately named. Wouldn't mind a quickie with him." Louise's pupils are so dilated that I wonder if the two detectives will suspect her of being under the influence of something other than caffeine and hormones. "Or something more enduring. So is *he* here about the note *too*?"

"*What* note?"

"The note for you that was left behind where the armatures were, the ones that got stolen..."

"*What* armatures got stolen? Louise, what are you talking about?"

"A couple of armatures disappeared during the night. You

know Hannah, that bleached blond who can't go anywhere without her iPod? Well, she took her ear buds out long enough to complain to me about it when I got here this morning and I called in a complaint, but I didn't expect anyone to take it seriously. I mean, *armatures?* Besides," Louise lowers her voice so the two cops can't hear her, "she was convinced it was an inside job. She *specifically* mentioned *you* as her chief suspect."

I roll my eyes and Louise nods knowingly. "So what's with the note? Where is it?"

"*He's* got it," she points to Rubenstein. "When I found it, I called back, and about ten minutes later he's here asking for it. So I gave it to him."

"What'd it say?"

"It was in an envelope. Heavy vellum, like the kind you'd put an invitation in. It looked like whoever left it had had an open cut; there was dried blood all over it and it had your name on the front of it, and considering what's been happening..."

Something is *definitely* happening. Two detectives from two different precincts are here, evidence enough that they've got a *lot* more on their agendas than stolen art supplies unless the items in question are directly connected to what they happen to be investigating. "Yeah, I agree. Who'd want to take armatures," I shout. "They're nothing of value. Just *display* items." Both Quick and Rubenstein turn and glower at me. "I'm going to check and see if my sculptures are all right," I announce for everybody's benefit, and walk straight to the back door and open it. The modeling stands are still lined up against the wall, sheathed in black plastic; they *seem* untouched. I walk up to one and pull a corner of the bag up gingerly, the way a coroner would to get an ID on a corpse. The featureless face of a Vestal Virgin greets me. I drop the plastic and move on to the next and then the next.

I wheel around and see Quick in the doorway. "Everything seems okay here," I say woodenly. *Except for me. I am anything but okay.* He gestures for me to come back in the lobby, and I back away from my bodybagged figures and walk right up to Quick, so close that I can see a nick just under his chin, I can practically sniff the antiseptic that he dabbed on it. "But everything's *not* okay, is it? Or else *both* of you wouldn't be here. Or even *you*. I mean, you've got more important things to do than *this*, right?" I turn to Rubenstein. "This *note*. It's an invitation," I mumble, "to a *private* art opening." I don't have to be Karnac the Magnificent to divine *that*. "Can't I at least *see* it?"

The look that Rubenstein gives Quick fills me with the same prescience of doom as the chime and flashing light alerting me that I have new voicemail messages has lately. There's something I don't want to hear here and I've just pushed the PLAY button. Quick takes my arm and leads me to the right, stopping in front of a reproduction of a Van Gogh. "Can't let you do that, Delilah," he says somberly. "It's evidence. We're sending it out to the lab to be analyzed. See if it *is* in fact blood, and if so, whose it is."

"In the meantime," Rubenstein says, "while we're looking for the person who we think might be behind this, maybe it would be a good idea if you could get out of town for a few days..."

"I can't do that."

"Why not?"

"I've got a *show* opening. There's a lot of work I've got to do."

"That's not for *weeks*," Quick argues. "This wouldn't be for long."

"Long enough for me to fall behind. Do you think my work's going to get done by itself? I can't skip town and then just slap this stuff together. Rome wasn't built in one day regardless of how this exhibit is billed. I *can't.*"

Besides, there is absolutely nowhere I can go.

There's a limit to how much protection we can provide if you stay at Waverly Place," Quick says. "I might be able to arrange something temporary for you," he adds *sotto voce.* "I should know by the end of the day. Have to make a few phone calls. I don't like the idea of you staying at your place alone."

"I don't like the fact that you're not telling me everything."

"What I will tell you is it seems last night wasn't the first time Curtis paid you a courtesy call when you weren't home. He said so in the note. Among other things. We *don't know* everything, Delilah. If we did, we'd crack this case in an hour and every other case we've caught and this city would have a near-zero crime rate, but that's not the case. There's a *possibility* that this person who you know as Curtis may be implicated in another..."

"The Majesty Moore investigation?"

"That's being looked into," Quick concedes. "We're reviewing a *few* unsolved cases, not just Moore, to see if we like Curtis for any one of them. We *already* want him for questioning in regard to Vittorio's death. I can't tell you what I don't know for sure. What I *do* know is I want you out of the neighborhood, at least for a couple of days."

"I *still* have to go out to *work,*" I remind him.

Quick's eyes cloud over like he's been hit in the head by a brick. "I don't think that's such a good idea," he says and I know right away that the image he's projected *isn't* one of me modeling *clay.* He looks askance at Rubenstein. "I'm breaking protocol by doing this, Delilah," he whispers. "This is the best I can do. I can't promise twenty-four hour protection, but I think you'll be reasonably safe. If you go traipsing from one part of town to the other, you *may not* be."

"I've got to work on my sculptures. In *there*." I jab my thumb in the direction of the clay studio. "And work for a drawing class tomorrow. *Also* here. I can't afford to *not work*. But it'll be here, in this building. That's all the job assignments I have for the rest of the week. So far. But what if I get more in the future?" This is one f word I like the sound of. I want to feel like I *have* a future to think about here.

"If you have to go out, use your cell phone. I want you to keep it with you whenever you *do* have to go out, and don't forget to have it charged. If you see Curtis, you hit 911 *immediately* and give your location. *Don't forget* to give your location, you got that, Delilah?" He's talking to me like he would to a child again. "What are your plans for the rest of the day?"

"I was planning to stay here for a few hours. In *there*." I point toward the clay studio again.

Quick nods and walks over to the reception desk. Louise parts her M.A.C.ed-up Russian Red lips, but it's the phone that he's interested in. He helps himself to it and stretches the cord to the limit so no one can overhear a word, his brow furrowing like the fate of the free world is resting on this call. *Or at least mine.* Rubenstein pokes my shoulder and signals me back to the ersatz Van Gogh. "You want to lay low for a couple of days," he says. I nod. *No shit, Sherlock!* Quick rejoins us. "Okay, it's all set. I'll come by here later to take you where you're going to be staying. In the meantime you stay *here*. I don't want you going *any*place, got that?"

"Not even to eat?"

Quick turns toward Louise, whose lips pucker in readiness to say "Yes" to anything he might suggest. "Does someone relieve you here when you get a lunch break?" he asks her. She nods, but before she has a chance to salivate, he adds, "Good. When you go out, can you pick up a sandwich for Miss Price so she can eat it in her studio?"

"*No* problem," Louise acquiesces.

"And make sure whoever relieves you is informed about the situation. Nobody who doesn't belong here gets in without credentials, and that includes security personnel. If anyone *tries*, call the Sixth." Quick turns to me. "I don't want you going *any*place until I get back." He follows Rubenstein down the stairs.

"*I* sure wouldn't," Louise sighs, not too subtly rising out of her seat to get a last look, "if he were coming back for *me*."

I cross my arms in front of me. "I don't even know where he's *taking* me."

"With a guy who looks like *that,* I wouldn't think it would make much difference if it were Heaven or Hoboken."

I'm tempted to ask *how about if he said he was taking you to Riker's Island?* but the look on her face tells me she'd still be willing to pack for the one-way trip. "So what *do* you want for lunch, Delilah?" Louise asks me, putting on a Mona Lisa smile, and I realize I must have that prisoner-of-lust look on my face too.

"I'm not hungry," I say as I saunter off to the clay studio. I pause in front of the door, then spin around and add huskily, "At *least* not *yet*." I don't stick around to see Louise's reaction.

My reaction to Louise's predatory moves on Quick surprises me. This is a potential threat to my *life* that he was here about, and here I am carrying on like a woman warding off a rival from *my man*. My hand clutches a fettling knife. I rip away at black plastic until the Vestal Virgin is once again exposed, the one that I asked Louise to pose for, and I start to whittle away clay and give her a face, one that I notice after an hour of nonstop carving looks *nothing at all* like Louise and *very* much like *me*. As is always the case, when I get into my work, really get into it, I lose track of time and space. The only thing palpable to me is the cool clay that I'm modeling with mold knives and spatulas and fingertips. When the door suddenly slams behind me, I nick my thumb with the serrated edge of a sabre saw. Before I have a chance to squeal in pain, I look up and see Quick. How many hours have passed since he left, anyway? At least four, according to my watch, and maybe more since the hands aren't moving. I need a new battery if I'm going to get anywhere on time. I turn back to Quick. The expression on his face is enough to make time stop. I can feel my heartbeat vibrate like a souped-up V-8 engine and put down my tools before I can do further damage to myself. "Are you ready?" he asks me, not moving from the door.

For what? is what I'm wondering. I don't know what the right answer is, *yes* or *no.* "I need to wrap my sculpture first."

"It looks like it's coming along good."

"Thanks." A compliment from him under any other circumstances would be enough to give me wet dreams. Right now all I feel is wet, but in a mucky clothes-stuck-to-me way. "I won't be long."

He stands erect against the threshold, unmoving, like the statue of a sentry gracing some public park, minus the requisite bayonet. What he's got instead is his semi-automatic tucked in his shoulder holster. I feel self-conscious picking up my neon-green water pistol to wet down the clay and look over my shoulder at him, expecting the sight of the plastic gun to draw a laugh, but his expression remains sober. The muscles in his jaw twitch, but not in good humor. *What am I getting ready for here?* My finger nervously pumps the white plastic trigger, shooting more water before I've fully turned back to my sculpture, spraying the work table, barely missing the front of Quick's blue pinstriped oxford shirt. He doesn't flinch. *I* do. "Did I get you? I'm sorry."

He shakes his head. "Done?"

"*Almost.*" I put the water pistol down on the work table, gather the torn black plastic sheathing, wrap it around the sculpture from top to bottom and knot it. "*Now* I'm done."

"Okay," he holds the door open for me. "Let's go."

As we walk past the reception desk, Louise's eyes follow Quick as he leads the way. He turns back to make sure *I'm* the one who's trailing behind him. Louise clears her throat. "If anyone wants to know how to reach you, what do I tell them?"

"The same thing you would have told them yesterday," Quick snaps.

"I'll call in for my messages," I promise. "Tell Morgan..."

Quick spins me around and propels me to the stairwell before I can say another word. "She'll be in touch," Quick says succinctly, this time following me to make sure I don't turn around again. I stop at the door and tilt my head up until I see him looming over me as he opens it, signaling that it's time we ride off together into the sunset.

31

It's Brooklyn we're riding off to, Quick tells me as the sun begins to set behind us. He opens the passenger door of a blue Volvo that almost but not quite matches the denim of my dress. "This is *my* car," he says. I clamber in, expecting to fight for seat space with a lot of personal belongings since it's not police issue, but aside from a neat bundle of brochures of some sort bound with a rubber band that he quickly tosses on the back seat, and a Daily News opened to the Sports section, the interior is so uncluttered that it could pass as a rental car from Avis. There are no other clues about what makes Quick tick, except maybe that he likes the color blue.

"You're going to be staying at my sister's place on Henry Street," he tells me as he starts the motor. "It's nice and quiet there. You'll like it."

"How about your sister? Is *she* going to like it? My being there, getting in her way?"

"You won't be in anyone's way." The muscles in his jaw tighten conspicuously as he checks out the view of oncoming traffic in the rearview mirror. "She's not there right now."

"Then my guess would be that she'd like it even *less*."

He gestures to the safety belt dangling to my right. "Buckle up," he orders, hinting that I better prepare myself for bumps and jolts along the way, and not necessarily just those caused by road surface and vehicular traffic conditions. "She knows you're going to be there," he says as he jerks the steering wheel to the right. "I spoke to her. She's okay with it, Delilah." The car continues to lurch forward. "There's a few things I have to tell you about before we get there."

I tighten the shoulder strap preparing myself for a crash.

"While you're in Brooklyn, we want to plant a decoy in your place, set a trap. We've got a female officer, about your coloring and build, who's going to mimic your movements. If Curtis makes an appearance, we nail him, and she's going to make damn sure he can't resist making an appearance." He doesn't say *how*. "I'm going to need your house keys. You're not going back there until we take care of it on our end. If you do, you'll be jeopardizing your own safety and *hers* as *well*." He turns to me. "The life of a *cop*."

I half expect him to start reciting my rights, feeling like I'm guilty before the fact. There is no worse crime than *this*. I fish out my keys and clench them in my palm before handing them over. "Why couldn't I just stay there then? I'd obviously have police protection. Why try to con me that I wouldn't be safe and then tell me 'oh, by the way, we've got a female cop we want to put up in your place while you're *else*where.' Don't I get to have any say in this?"

"You get to say 'yes.' It has to be this way, Delilah. Trust me." He takes the keys before I have a chance to drop them and puts them in his pocket. "You should be safe at my sister's place as long as you stay put. Even if you don't, you'll be *some*what safer than you would be at Waverly Place right now. I know some people in the Eight-Four; they keep an eye on the place. If you need help, you'll get it. I don't live too far away, but I may not be home much." He veers off gridlocked Houston Street and onto the FDR Drive entrance ramp and guns the gas pedal as he cuts into the left lane. "I'll keep you informed."

"Just like you've *been* doing?"

"I can't tell you what I don't know for sure," he reminds me. He turns onto the Brooklyn Bridge entrance ramp.

"What you're *not* telling me is telling *enough*." I say. "I overheard you saying something about a task force this morning. How big *is* this?"

"It's getting bigger. Majesty Moore got an invitation a lot like the one you got today the day before she disappeared, Delilah. It was one of the things that were found in the trunk of the car along with her remains."

"What were some of the other things?"

"Mannequin parts. Heads, torsos, limbs." He frowns. "A model stand that was probably used to prop one up in a store window. And of course what was left of Miss Moore."

"How did she die?"

He turns to me and I notice his hand momentarily slip off the steering wheel. "She was impaled with part of the model stand."

The horizon starts to look wavy to me and I'm not even looking down at the East River below. I close my eyes. *A couple of armatures disappeared during the night. Armatures made of twisted wire. All the better to* pierce *you with, my dear.* I feel Quick turn a sharp right and open my eyes. The buildings to the left and right of me are shorter and browner than the ones directly across the river that now have a tantalizing glow; from this distance, they look like long strands of tinsel lit by tiny bulbs. Quick turns up one street and down another, forced to find a legal alternate-side-of-the-street parking space for the Volvo like the rest of the mere mortals in this city. I feel like I'm going around in circles, and *not* just because of being driven around the block a few times. *She was impaled with the model stand.* Quick suddenly pulls up to a vacated space in front of a pastoral courtyard and adroitly backs into it, making the tight squeeze in one try. He turns off the motor and turns to me. "Are you okay?"

I shrug.

He gets out of the car and comes around to open the passenger door for me. "It's only a couple of blocks," he says, slamming the car door behind me, setting off a sharp trill that blends in with the bird sounds emanating from the trees behind the wrought-iron fence. He stops for a minute in front of the fence, looking in almost as if expecting to see someone he knows there, then steers me ahead of him and to the left, past brick and brownstone buildings barricaded by more wrought-iron gates. He turns again, this time to the right. The neighborhood looks pricey. I start to wonder about his sister. She must have a damn good job to be able to afford to live here. I wonder again where *he* lives. *Not too far away.* He stops in front of a brick building that looks a lot like the one I just left this morning on Waverly Place. "This is nice." I hesitate in front of the concrete stairs. "You're sure it's no trouble?"

"We don't want *you* to get in trouble," he says, gesturing with a jerk of his head to follow him. The hallway smells of cabbage. He sidesteps a ten-speed bike affixed to the banister with a U-bar and leads the way up the stairs. Two flights of stairs. *Three* flights of stairs. All the way to the top and I can still smell cabbage when I catch my breath. He opens the door with no hesitation and walks in like *he* owns the place. "*That's* funny," he says, his hand brushing the collar of a down coat slung over a metal café chair. Not *ha-ha* funny, I take it; he's not exactly smiling. I tiptoe in behind him. He goes from room to room. "Alison?" he calls softly. "Allie?" He turns back to me. "My sister's coat," he says, gesturing to it. "She's not supposed to be here."

"Maybe *I* shouldn't be..."

He puts his hand up like he might if he were assigned to

traffic duty, totally in control, but *is* he *really?* He backs up and walks into another room. "Allie!" I hear a brief scuffle, a soft female voice uttering something incomprehensible, a toilet being flushed. Quick emerges from the bathroom with his sleeves rolled up to his elbows and picks up his cell phone. "Medical emergency, send an ambulance." He barks out the number of the building before putting the phone down and going back where he came from. He reappears again. "I'll go down to let them in."

"I can do that. Stay with her."

"Just open the door and come right back up here," he commands. I nod. *Four flights.* I hear the toilet flush again. I shut the door behind me and descend into the cabbage patch. *I've just left the stew up there.* The EMS wagon jerks to a screeching stop just as I open the front door, and a couple of paramedics scramble out. "All the way up?" one asks with surprising familiarity as the other hauls a stretcher out of the back of the wagon. He takes a sip of coffee from a plastic mug that says PATIENCE IS A VIRTUE BUT NOT WHEN I HAVE PATIENTS, then puts it down on the curb, freeing his hands to take more apparatus out of the wagon. I half expect him to tell me to watch it for him while he's gone, and I do. I pick up the mug and bring it into the foyer with me while I wait at the foot of the stairs.

Quick bounds down two flights ahead of the paramedics and gestures for me to stand back. I hear a soft moan and turn away until I hear the front door being opened. A couple of uniformed cops stand like stone lions on both sides of the entryway. When I look back, I see Quick talking softly to them, then to the paramedics. All I can make out is "Atlantic Avenue" before he turns back to me. "Here's the key." He holds it out in his palm. "Don't drop it and don't go anywhere except upstairs. Lock yourself in and wait until you hear from me. I'll try to stop back here after I check on her." He looks over his shoulder. "Or I'll call from the hospital. Don't set foot out of this place."

"Is she going to be all right?"

"She *should* be," he says softly. His wearied tone suggests that a *lot* of things should be other than the way they are. "It's a long story. She somehow managed to walk out of rehab. I've got to get her set up someplace else once she gets clean. In the meantime, I don't want you leaving this place until things are secured, Delilah, not for anything, and don't tell anyone where you are. *Anyone*, got that? If you get a message from Curtis *or* Ivan, you call my cell number immediately. We don't know where Curtis is, or Ivan either for that matter, not since Tuesday night after he left the Sixth. Nobody's seen *or* heard from him and I'd still like to know why. The two may be connected." He rattles the door. "I've got to go. I'll be in touch."

A *hug* is what I need, not a mere touch. Quick looks like he needs it too, maybe more than me. *But not now.* I have to cross my arms to keep myself from crossing that boundary, and wonder if I ever will.

The pictures his sister has on display on her faux-rococo mantel represent another threshold I'm not sure I'm entitled to invade, but I do, without even pausing to take off my coat. There are several snapshots of a young woman who I presume is Alison, in a prom dress, in a cap and gown, in advanced state of pregnancy. I *don't* see any pictures of her with a child. To my right is a studio shot of her standing next to her brother when he was still in uniform, his hand gripping her arm authoritatively, their expressions equally austere. There are some pictures of him by himself too, also in uniform, probably taken when he was fresh out of the Academy; he looks green in them, and not just because of shifting dyes. I'm getting a picture of the family dynamic here. *Someone to watch over me.* Except that in some way he has failed and

I've witnessed the failure, and he's in no small way berating himself now. Another item framed in black on a table beside the fireplace catches my eye, an issue of Playbill turned to the credits page, where the name Alison Quick is circled in red under the listing for set design.

I look out the window and see a blue-and-white cruise by. Someone is indeed watching over *me*. Quick didn't waste any time getting things in place. Even during a personal crisis, he's being Robocop.

And *I'm* being *nosy*. Total security can have its boring moments. I need to do *something* to pass the time until Quick comes back. As if looking at the pictures on and near the mantel wasn't enough, I start to explore the rest of the apartment, looking for the fire escape exit in case I need to use it. *It must be in the bedroom, the most dangerous place for the metal stairwell to be. Someone's more likely to get in than need to get out.* I glance in and what I see makes me think of a fifth floor display in Bloomingdale's: an all-too-perfectly made bed, a polished chest of drawers, a clothes tree in the corner. I wonder when was the last time Alison set foot in this room. The bathroom across the hall looks like a set not of *anyone's* design: black and gold paisley towels scattered on the floor; bottles with unscrewed caps; a burned-out light bulb. *That's not the* only *thing in this apartment that's burned out.*

That reminds me to keep looking for the fire escape exit. Make sure it's locked. I'm beginning to think like Quick now. I walk to the end of the hall, to the kitchen, which is more compact than the galley on a plane. The exit I'm looking for is right in front of me: a grated door leading out to a small balcony overhanging an alley. All I can see is coils of green hose down there; it makes me think of a viper pit. And thinking of snakes reminds me to check my voice mail, as if one thing has to do with the other. *Maybe it does. It all depends on what messages I have.* Just one message this time, from Heidi

Obermeyer, asking me if I can work for her Friday afternoon class. This is one assignment I'm going to have to turn down; I'm already hired for that time slot, at West 8th Street, and I don't even know if can make *that* one.

The minute I hang up, the phone rings. I let it ring three times before I realize it's got to be Quick and pick up. "It's me," Quick says. "Why'd it take so long to answer the phone? What's going on? Where *were* you?"

"The bathroom," I say before realizing this wasn't the greatest thing to say and a lie to boot. The truth is I'm not sure what I was expected to say or do if it *wasn't* him, but it's too late for *that* now.

"Looks like I'm not going to be able to stop by until later. A *lot* later, I'm afraid, not till the end of my tour. I'm still at the hospital." On cue, I hear a muffled voice paging Doctor Somebody-or-other over the intercom in the background. "I've got to go straight from here to work, and things have a way of cropping up late at night."

"How's your sister doing?"

He clears his throat. "She's stabilized. I can't talk now. I've got to get some things taken care of on this end. I'll call back later. In the meantime, stay inside, don't go *any*where."

Not even in the bathroom. Which is the *first* place I go. Which makes it *not* such a lie that I said I was in there in the first place. *There are no windows in here. At least no one can get at me.* As I step over the towels, my heel skids on something. I pick up a wax paper envelope scaled down to Barbie Doll Dream Kitchen size. Except the powdery residue in that wrapper has probably been at least partially responsible for turning Alison Quick's life into a nightmare. I wonder what I should do with this piece of evidence that Quick in his angst somehow managed to overlook. I kick it under the heap of towels. *I didn't see it. It's up to him to tell me. And he's going to have to eventually tell me a lot more to account for what I did see.*

32

"I HAVE TO TELL YOU SOMETHING," QUICK SAYS, SHUTTING THE DOOR behind him. I rub my eyes groggily. I fell asleep on the couch hours ago; *how many* hours ago I don't know, it's dark out now, and it seems as though it was still light when I curled up on the couch, but it gets dark by five. Quick said he wouldn't be back until the end of his tour, which I translated to mean some time after midnight. A glance at my watch now tells me it's still early afternoon, then I remember it needs a new battery. "No, don't get up. Stay there," he says. When he comes closer, I can see *his* watch, the hour hand pointing to nine. What he has to tell me, I suddenly realize, has nothing to do with his sister.

"I got a phone call a little while ago from someone I know up in the Seventeenth," he says. "Unrelated to all of this, but he mentioned something about a stabbing late last night in front of an ATM on Madison Avenue. The vic was DOA at New York Hospital. The motive *believed* to be robbery. Cash was gone, but the wallet was left behind, credit cards, a BlackBerry. Gave a home address outside of Greenwich and work address on Wall Street, which it turns out is the same one you gave me Tuesday night," Quick sits down. "It was Ivan, Delilah."

The only response I can express is a nod. "You're sure." I *know* he's sure, or he wouldn't be telling me this.

"His family drove in from Connecticut early this afternoon to make a positive ID," he reports, watching me, waiting for my emotional seams to split.

"Well, I guess that's why I haven't heard from him." I take a deep breath. "Any clue who did it?"

"You don't seem upset." I wonder if he's rehearsing what he's going to write in that little notebook in his pocket. *Ex-girlfriend who was abused by victim in the recent past did not seem upset.*

"Are you thinking maybe *I* did it?"

"I *know* where you were last night at the estimated time of death, Delilah. You were at the precinct house with me, looking at mug shots. I *know* you didn't do it." He's still looking at me the way I imagine he's looked at hundreds of people under interrogation, waiting for them to deliver the goods. What I have to say isn't so good. "So maybe *now* I can safely confess there's this small part of me that's not sorry someone else *did*. Are you happy now?"

"No," he says, "I'm not."

"I'm not happy either. *Or* particularly *sad*. I guess that's normal." I shrug. "I'm supposed to be in shock, right?" I suddenly think of the plaster head taken from the apartment last night. "Do they know who did it?"

"No witnesses as of yet. The guys at the Seventeenth are canvassing the area. There'll be pictures in the papers, appeals for anyone who saw anything to call the TIPS hot line. What I was told was that things got a little savage, like maybe the vic fought like hell to hold onto his money." *Yes, yes, I can see Ivan doing that.* "Or the perp had a mean streak. Ivan was missing a few fingers." He clears his throat. "*Vittorio* was missing a few fingers."

"You didn't tell me..." I gulp. "What you *are* telling me is that the guy they want is the same guy *you* want, the guy I *didn't* want. Curtis."

"What I'm telling you is you've got to do exactly as I tell you," Quick says. "And the first thing is to put 911 on speed dial. Add my numbers, the number for the Sixth for when you're going to be at West Eighth. Fourth is the Eight-Four. When you're ready to leave tomorrow, you call me and you *keep* calling every step of the way so we know your location. I don't think you should have any trouble *here*, but I'm not ruling out anything."

"While you're at it, don't rule out that anyone who's gone near me has been a target," I say. "That makes Morgan a target too. And *you.*" *So be careful.*

"I haven't had any success getting through to Morgan. One way or the other, he isn't getting the message. As for *me*, it's nothing I'm not used to. People are always gunning for cops." He unzips his jacket to remind me that he's armed and wearing body armor.

"What's going on with that decoy you've got staying in *my* place?" Aside from the fact she's wearing *my* clothes, using *my* moisturizer, sleeping in *my* bed, intercepting *my* mail.

"Nothing I can tell you yet. The minute Curtis shows up on her doorstep—and he *will*—we nail him." Oh, and so it's *her doorstep* now *too.* "Meanwhile, *both* of you get police protection until this thing blows. She's part of the Task Force we've set up and the Eight-Four is watching this place *and* you until you cross over into Manhattan tomorrow, then *we* take over. I'll get you over there myself if I can. I've got to get back to the First now," he says. "Lock up after me." He hovers by the door, so close that I can tell by his breath that he's been chewing gum again. My mouth waters. "If you need anything," he gestures toward my cell phone, "call."

*Any*thing? I impulsively reach for his hand and give it a

light squeeze. He surprises me by returning the squeeze, not pulling away. "I will," I promise, "if I need anything. I'll call."

There's need in his eyes *too* all right, but duty comes first.

The first thing I do when he leaves is call Morgan. I *have* to give the phone a trial run. Gary cuts me short. "He's not here."

"Is he still in his studio?"

"Don't know."

"Or *with* somebody. Gareeee..."

"*You* still with the *cop*, Delilah?"

"Morgan's off the hook as far as the cops are concerned. They don't want to talk to him, Gary, *I* do."

"Why are they still calling here then? You think maybe one of them wants a *date?*"

"They're calling because he might be in danger. Gary, just tell me where he is. He's got to be warned."

"I *still* don't know where he *is*, Delilah. Maybe your *friend* can investigate the matter more fully."

"My *friend* has enough to investigate. Somebody who thinks he can't have me any *other* way is killing everyone who comes near me, may be trying to kill *me too...* "

"It must be hell to be straight and beautiful. Glad I'm neither. Glad I don't know anyone else who *is. Ciao, bella.*"

My fingers tremble with rage as I punch in the number of the reception desk at West Eighth Street. It's *Gary* who's blowing me off, *not* Morgan, I remind myself. *Unless I hear differently from him.* "Who d'you want to talk to?" the night desk guard asks. I don't recognize who it is by his voice. I don't want to ask for Morgan by name. I'll see him tomorrow, anyway, in the drawing studio while I'm posing. I'll talk to him then. *If* he's *there.*

I imagine Lady Detective, *whoever* that person is who's raiding *my* refrigerator, reading *my* piled-up back issues of *Vogue* and *Time Out New York,* would alert the task force if

Curtis left any notes for me, that they'd work on it on the other side of the river and leave me out of it unless they had no choice but to warn me of impending danger. And I must be safe because my cell phone isn't ringing. I *don't want* to be in the know right now. I *want* to feel I can trust Quick and the force to take the matter to task. *I want a good night's sleep. I might need it.*

33

"I'm sorry, but Detective Quick's not here right now. He's out in the field." The receptionist at the First Precinct sounds very much like the one at the Sixth, same monotone, same New Yawk accent so thick you could spread it on a bagel and choke on it. "Is this something someone *else* can help you with?" *Same lines even.*

I haven't got time to wait for her to put someone else on the line. One thing I forgot to ask Quick for last night was his sister's alarm clock and a *map,* and now I have less than an hour to get to West Eighth Street in time to pose for that drawing class. Lucky for me I didn't sleep all that great anyway. I kept waking up and thinking of Ivan, picturing Ivan missing a few fingers, fingers that once penetrated me, grabbed me, left bruises on me, shuddering because he's dead and because I *don't feel bad,* even though it's because of me that he's dead. *He could just as easily have killed me one day if I'd stayed with him.*

I can't stay in the apartment another minute or I'm going to be late for this class. I stash my cell phone in my nylon pocketbook and lock the door behind me. The hallway still smells of cabbage. When I get to the front door, I don't see any blue-and-whites around and I remember Quick's admonition to me: *Keep calling every step of the way.* I need protection. I need *directions.* I fish the phone out of my bag and punch in the abbreviated code connecting me to the local precinct. Great thing about this phone, I can make tracks while I'm using it, save time. "I'm at the intersection of Henry and Clark Street," I report. "Henry and Pineapple. Henry and Orange...

"Whoa, I can't keep up with you, where you going?"

"West Eighth Street. Which subway do I..."

"You *just passed* a subway stop at Clark Street. You want to go *where?*"

"West Eighth Street. I *think* I'm supposed to have a police escort. I haven't seen anyone..."

"Go to the High Street station. Got that? You want the *High Street* station, near Cadman Plaza. Keep walking the direction you're going, go right."

I expect to see a blue-and-white when I get there, but I don't. *They must be in an unmarked car.* I look over my shoulder before descending the stairs to the platforms below, wrestle my MetroCard out of my change purse. I miss my fanny pack. *Why'd I have to wear a damn dress.*

"Service on the A and C *mumble mumble* between *mumble mumble* Street and Lefferts Boulevard *mumble mumble mumble* smoky conditions," a raspy voice squawks over the loudspeaker. "Damn trains ain't runnin'," a homeless man leaning against the pay phone swears. He looks like he could be anywhere from thirty-five to seventy years old, could have been waiting here to take the train for half a lifetime. "Ain't seen no trains for *two hours* now." His voice suddenly blares into song, makes me jump. "You *can't* take the A Train. You *can't* take the A Train," he wails off-key. I leap out of the way as he staggers up and down the platform, picking up speed, waving his arms up and down like he's desperately trying to take off through the tunnel on his own steam. "You *CAN'T* take the A Train," he screeches in my ear.

I don't even *want* to take the A Train any more. I turn around and go back through the exit and up the stairs, looking over my shoulder for the promised police protection. I don't see anything that even *remotely* resembles an unmarked car. I'm getting to be an expert at detecting those; I've been in enough of them in the last week. I whip out the phone again, call the Eight-Four again. The same voice answers. I hang up on him. I call back the First, hope Quick is back by now. This time a male voice answers, but it's not his. "Royko."

I remember him, the toe-tapper who waited for Quick outside of Morgan's loft a couple of days ago and the way he looked at those paintings of me. I have the sudden urge to cross my arms over my chest. "Quick's not here," he grumbles. I don't identify myself. I reach in my bag and fish out the *other* numbers Quick gave me, his cell number, his home number. I take a deep breath and call the home number. *Give your location.* "I've left the High Street subway station," I report after a long *beeeep*. "The train isn't running, so I'm going to have to walk across the bridge, I guess, and then take a train from City Hall up to Astor Place. I don't know if anyone's watching me. I haven't seen anyone." I look from left to right at the line-up of cars parked around me as I walk by; there's nobody *in* them. "Are *you* watching me?"

Is *Curtis* watching me?

No, I remind myself, he's watching someone who he *thinks* is me. Maybe he's been *caught* already, handcuffed, put in the back of a radio car. Maybe that's where Quick is now, making imprints of Curtis' inky fingers. As I start up the walkway spanning the Brooklyn Bridge, I check my voice mail messages. Maybe someone will actually tell me, "you *can* go home again."

I look behind me. The Brooklyn landscape shrinks in contrast to the gilded Manhattan skyline framed by myriad cables. *Blip-blip-blip.* A guy in flashy red shorts and Rollerblades to match whizzes by to my left and turns back to give me a preemptory smile. I wonder if *he's* an undercover cop assigned to watch me. How better to *not* be obvious than to appear *too* obvious. My cell phone rings before I have a chance to speculate where he'd keep *his* gun.

"*Surprise,* Delilah. Did you think I'd *forgotten* you? No chance of that. That slut that's parading around your apartment half-naked *pretending* to be you isn't even a close second. I've seen *you* go *all the way,* remember. I see you *now.*" Curtis pauses. "Isn't that blue jean dress you're wearing a little too *short,* Delilah? You can see up it from the back, you know. It doesn't cover much. Not that you ever cared about covering anything anyway. You're a piece of meat that people just drool over. Like *prime rib.*" I look over my shoulder frantically. No uniforms of any kind around, not even *bogus* uniforms. "You can't see me. Don't strain your neck. You've got to *pose* soon, *don't* you? *After* which you'll be posing strictly for *me.* My art exhibit is ready. I *sent* you an invitation. I'm looking forward to showing it to you," his voice becomes a menacing whisper, "real soon."

Traffic whizzes below to the left and right of me and I look up at the gray arch over my head and behind me. I start to call 911. The phone slips out of my sweaty hands and crashes face down onto the bike lane of the wooden walkway. A black ten-speed sideswipes it. I run after it. "*Watch* it!" another biker yells out. I jump out of his way. Before I can retrieve my phone, it skittles under the metal barrier rimming the walkway and crashes to the roadway below.

The Manhattan skyline looms closer through the web of cables, but so far I don't see a sign of *any* of the police protection I've been promised. I do see a yellow call box ahead and I run over to it. It surprises me that it's not *look-at-me* red.

What *doesn't* surprise me is that it's out of order when I need it the most. *Where is Curtis watching me from? Is he behind me?* I keep walking, looking over my shoulder at shadows, dreading the appearance of a *very* big one, and a squeal bursts out of me as I feel the impact of a head-on collision. Whoever it is *is* big, *very* big. I freeze. I can't even spin around to confront my attacker face to face. I'm too paralyzed by panic to make a sound, to get past that first squeal of surprise and have it escalate to a *bona fide* scream.

"You mind? I'm trying to take a picture here," my would-be perp intones in a high-pitched nasal female voice. I spin around. She's easily as big as Curtis and giving me a *look* that could kill, waving a disposable camera in my face. "You *could* watch where you're going, you know. You just made my arms move and this was the last shot on the roll."

"I'm sorry."

"Hal, never mind, you can relax now, the film's all used up, she made my arms move," she shouts at the scowling man standing at the base of the gray stone arch, waiting for her to click the shutter. His expression doesn't change, but his eyes tell me he's relieved that I've inadvertently released him from the torture of holding the pose. I could tell him a *lot* about torture, but I haven't the time. I keep walking by them and pick up my pace. Cars zip along the FDR Drive. The green exit sign to my right points to Park Row. I start to run, not entirely sure whether I'm running away from danger or right smack into it. *I'm almost there.* I turn around one last time. Fingers suddenly grab my forearm, propel me forward. A scream catches in my throat. "*No!*" is all I can sputter. When I dare to look, a gold shield is thrust practically up to my nose and Rubenstein is holding it, looking more dour than I've ever seen him. I know all too well his acerbic expression has nothing to do with yogurt or anything *else* he's eaten. "It's okay, Miss Price," he grumbles, "we're the good guys."

I look around and don't see anyone else I recognize. "Where's Quick?"

"He's been tied up all morning. Some kind of unexpected personal business, but he's back now. He radioed me to meet you here, take you where you're going." He jerks his head in the direction of the dark blue junker blocking the exit ramp. "I'm afraid I got some bad news," he says as I get in the car. He waves off a driver giving him the finger. "The operation over on Waverly was *completely* blown; our boy knows she isn't you."

"*Duh!*" I mumble as he struts around to the driver's side.

"So it looks like we're going to get him while he's in the process of thinking he's going to get at *you*. Did you see him while you were crossing the bridge?"

"He saw *me*. He said…"

"Annie told us what he said. We got people in cars *all around* here."

"I didn't see *anyone*."

Rubenstein jerks the car into reverse. "We got West Eighth blocked in. We know who we want, shouldn't be hard *now*." *Shouldn't* be, but what happens to me if it *is*? "Bastard's killed five that we know of now. Time to shut that mother-fucker down." He glances in my direction. "Sorry."

I'm not. I start to count off all the dead bodies that have been accounted for on the fingers of my left hand like I'm playing *this little piggy went to market*. Majesty Moore, Vitto-rio, Ivan. I squeeze them together. "*Five*? How'd you come up with *five*?"

He's not about to tell me. "I'm going to drop you a couple of blocks *from* West Eighth. We got cars in place *all over the place* and someone's going to tail you. When he moves, we move." Rubenstein's moving at top speed *now*, along the FDR, almost bypassing the Houston Street exit. The sound of screeching brakes as he cuts lanes makes me gnash my teeth.

"Meanwhile, you just go about your business, do just like you always do. We got you covered."

Rubenstein, true to his word, drops me off on University Place across from the park. "Walk straight up and to the left on Eighth, keep going till you get there," he instructs me. I wonder how much manpower is backing him up and how much it's going to cost the city of New York to carry out the whole operation. *Better that than to wonder where Curtis is.* A guy in flashy red shorts and Rollerblades to match whizzes by to my right and I do a double-take as I recognize him from our earlier encounter on the Brooklyn Bridge. Maybe he *is* an undercover cop assigned to watch me. Maybe that cabby parked by the curb isn't a cabby after all. Maybe the guy at the pay phone on the corner of Fifth Avenue is giving my position to someone on a cell phone half a block away. I start to relax as I turn into the familiar doorway framed by rococo stone columns.

Louise is nowhere to be seen. In her place is a guard in uniform. All I see is the uniform at first, and I feel a sudden wave of nausea grip me before I've had the chance to take a good look and realize that this guard doesn't look anything like Curtis; he's about fifty pounds lighter than Curtis. Probably a uniform posing as a *different kind of* uniform. I clutch my hand over my stomach and take deep breaths. "I'm late for an art class," I explain as I head past him, so he'll know who I am as if he doesn't already. I glimpse Louise in the vestibule to my left making fresh coffee as I start for the stairs. She scowls and dumps the filtered grounds in the trash. I hurry up the stairs and into the second-floor drawing studio. "Well, look who's finally here," Morgan announces, "everybody's favorite target of obsession." I stop dead in my tracks, but not because of Morgan's greeting. Standing there among the crowd of disgruntled artists impatiently honing their #4 charcoal pencils is Quick, a huge Morilla newsprint pad propped up on an easel in front of him. He greets me with a perfunctory nod.

Rubenstein definitely wasn't kidding when he said *we got you covered*. Except that I'm going to be *uncovered*. *Literally*.

"What are you *doing* here?" I whisper at him. He holds a pencil aloft. The hand grip of his semi-automatic protrudes from under his windbreaker. "Aren't there any *female* cops who could be doing this?" I hiss under my breath as I start to unbutton my dress.

"None who can *draw*." He seems genuinely surprised that I would object to him being here while I'm working. If it were a crime in a strip club he was investigating, *no one* would question his presence there. *Bare flesh is bare flesh, right?*

I gape in his direction, my mouth forming a perfect O as in *oh, shit!*

"That going to be your pose, Delilah?" one of the artists asks me.

This all reminds me of days, before all this began, when I was nude and feeling *very naked* standing before an uptown studio class, because people who had no business being there criss-crossed in and out with their tool kits, copping a peek at me until the security guard on duty shooed them out. *Who was the security guard on duty uptown anyway? This* is *worse*, of course, a *lot* worse, punishment from the gods for having fantasized about Quick that way in the *first* place. Except in my fantasies *he* was the one getting undressed and I was helping him. There's nothing remotely egalitarian about *this* set-up and it sucks. I can't even object. He's not some electrician making like he's checking for faulty wiring. He's here to *protect* me. Either *he* stays or Curtis gets me.

My dress flutters to the floor.

I feel self-conscious about feeling self-conscious. *It's not supposed to be this way*. Most artists see their models' body parts as geometric shapes, measured for proportion from eraser tip to pencil point of their charcoal pencils—at least they're *supposed* to, *at least I* do. I'm there to be drawn or painted or sculpted, not judged. While I'm modeling, I feel like I'm closed off from my audience by that fourth wall of theater lore.

But not today. I feel like Quick is looking me over through a huge picture window. He's going through all the motions like everyone else in the room, squinting, sketching, erasing, and I have to give him credit for *that.* What's more, he seems *not at all* self-conscious about me stealing looks at *him.* It seems to goad him into making heavier pencil strokes. My skin prickles at the soft swoosh sound of charcoal making contact with paper. Each geometric circle of breast, triangle of pubic area tingles as he captures it. I have no need for a space heater today. Fifteen minutes into the pose, I feel like I've spent an hour in a sauna. Twenty-five minutes and I'm in Dante's Inferno. At the half-hour, a cell phone rings. Quick drops his pencil and whips out his Droid and walks into the hall. When he returns, he says, "Remember what I said about your phone."

"I don't have it any more. I uh...dropped it off the bridge."

His glare tells me that *this* is what I should feel shame about. "Don't go anywhere." *Like where would I go?* Footsteps echo in the hall, sounding like thundering hooves as they come closer. The guard from downstairs stops at the threshold and chokes out, "Ten-Thirteen down the street! Officer down!"

Quick reaches for his semi-automatic and holds it facing down at his side as he darts out of the studio past the gawking uniform, who takes a few seconds to recover before following him.

"I'll say *this* much for him," Morgan says as he smudges and erases, "he *sure can draw.*"

Quick's easel is set up so that no one else in the room can

see it, so it's not artistic aptitude that Morgan's talking about. I'm curious enough to steal a glimpse at Quick's newsprint pad, and what I see surprises me. My arms and legs are in true proportion to the rest of my body. Nothing in his sketch of me is exaggerated or diminished. *He really does know how to draw.* I pick up his pencil before anyone else can get their hands on it. He may want it back later. I don't know where he's gone or what's going on, but the wails of one siren after the other pierce the silence of artists at work. After a few minutes of trying to ignore it, everyone around me packs up their wares and herds into the hallways and down the stairs to take in the street scene.

I'm the last one to leave. I've got to get dressed.

I hear murmuring in the hallway about "some cop bleeding all over the place, right up on the corner of Fifth," and for the first time this morning chills teem up and down my spine. My fingers tremble as they force each button through its matching denim hole. I'm breathing the way I would after running a marathon. I hear stirring behind me and look up expecting to see artists coming back in the room to claim their supplies, bring them back to their studios with them.

I only see one person in the doorway. I catch a glimpse of dark-spattered blue uniform, the glitter of gold badge that was probably bought in a police supply store or maybe ripped right off the heaving chest of some cop bleeding all over the place, right up on the corner of Fifth.

He's no artist.

34

I OPEN MY MOUTH TO SCREAM AS CURTIS GRABS ME, AND HE THRUSTS something between my teeth before I can get out a sound. My jaw clamps down on a ball of something cold. As I try to wriggle out of his grasp, something pokes the small of my back. It doesn't feel like a finger. "Move and I'll scoop out a chunk of you like clay." He jiggles the gag he's got wedged between my teeth with his thumb and index finger. I wonder what piece of work it was gouged from. "You're familiar with what carving instruments can do, aren't you, Delilah?" I feel a sharper poke. "I'm going to show you a first-rate exhibit of what carving instruments can do. You're going to be real impressed, I promise. First you're going to get us out of here. I'm going to take this out of your mouth so we don't attract undue attention. People around here oughta be *used* to seeing you with cops by now." He pauses as his fingers caress my lips. "Just remember," he whispers, "you make a sound and," *sharp* jab now, "you're shish-kebab."

"There are cops all over the place. You'll never get away with this."

"*Look* at me." He pounds his chest with both fists, a regular Tarzan, pats the badge, gestures to the triple triangle patch on his sleeve. "Who's gonna question a sergeant? Besides, they're all *way* too busy out there. Tending to one of their own who, last I looked, was bleeding like a *stuck pig*. Who d'you think's gonna come *first*, Delilah, you or him? Come on, lead the way."

Prodded by heavy metal and an iron fist, I steer Curtis toward the main stairwell. Staccato squawks of a police radio bleat somewhere down below.

Curtis reels me back in like a fish. "Isn't there *another* way out of here?" I feel the cold metal against my back now, a stinging sensation, and realize he's cut through fabric and nicked skin to boot. I have no choice but to lead him to the back of the drawing studio, where double doors lead out to a stairway that leads down to MacDougal Alley. I weave my way around the easels like a mouse careening through a maze, giving those footsteps I hear downstairs a chance to catch up. Curtis catches on, digs the tip of the blade a little further into my flesh. I see light from the top of the stairs. *Maybe I can trip him.* His arm goes around my waist as we descend the stairs, and he releases me only for as long as it takes to open the exit door.

"After *you*, m'lady." The tall black gate leading to the alley is closed, but not locked; all it takes is a shove and it swings open into the private cul-de-sac lined with row townhouses. I look up at each window of each house as Curtis propels me toward the black gate leading to the main street that I *know* is locked. Is anyone watching *this*? Even if they are, what are they going to make of this scene? The guy's in a uniform, in a *sergeant's* uniform, authoritatively leading me *out* of the alley, *away* from their pristine homes, into custody. *This could be the end of the road.* I hear so many sirens, so much shouting, all of it up on West Eighth Street, too far away to do me any good. *Help,* I need help *here!* I look over my shoulder.

Curtis slams me into the fence. "Climb!" he commands.

I wedge my foot in the space between the fence spokes

and hoist myself. He lifts from under my arms and throws me over on the other side. I scramble to my feet. "Oh no, you don't!" He hurdles the fence and tackles me before I can make it to the Capezio store across the street. He steers me to the left, down MacDougal, then jerks me to the right at the next block. People walking by look at me, then at him. "*Careful*, folks," he says genteely as he shoves me along, radiating protect-and-serve seriousness. Passers-by obligingly step off the curb, keeping their distance, careful not to interfere with justice. Doesn't it occur to *any* of them that it's pretty odd that there's only *one* officer making this supposed bust, odder still that this officer is leading me *away* from where the action is, *away* from where all the radio cars are parked? "What d'you know, we're on the street where you *live*, Delilah!" he exclaims, circling back to a gray Chevrolet Caprice when all the pedestrian traffic has cleared. He wrenches my arm as he fiddles with the trunk lock. "*When'd* you say this was broken into, Miss?" he bellows as another cluster of pedestrians sidle by us. I watch their backs, waiting for someone, *any one* of them to turn around, but *why should* they? The situation is *obviously* under control. Curtis swoops me up like a piece of luggage and hurtles me with full force into the steel jaws of the trunk before I can call out or even *try* to physically resist. The lid snaps down, forcing me into a fetal position with a thud.

This is it, I'm going to die.

When I was very little and there was a thunderstorm, I'd scream and hide in the closet. That way I wouldn't see the bright flashes of lightning, wouldn't hear the loud rumbles. It turned out to be the darkness that scared me more, particularly after being locked in there once as part of a perverse application of tough love. *Let's see if she minds thunderstorms as much once she gets out of there.* Nothing like getting over one fear by replacing it with another. This trunk space would make that broom closet seem almost the size of the Metropolitan Museum, even if I were in it now, fully-grown.

But I'm safer in this trunk than I'm going to be with Curtis once he lets me out. *If* he lets me out. Majesty Moore's body was found in a car trunk.

This is it, I'm going to die.

I grope around me, feeling around for wires I could disconnect to incapacitate the car, draw attention to it before it's too late for me, but as my hands pat the rough surface, all I feel is dampness against my skin. A sudden stop makes me cry out. *Can anyone hear me?* I pine over the cell phone I dropped over the edge of the Brooklyn Bridge. My only means of communication now is banging my fists on the metal roof over my head, hoping out there it sounds like something more than the ping-ping-ping of a faulty muffler. The rank smell under me makes me think of something that must have died a long time ago.

A siren seems to be coming closer and closer.

Please pull this car over, whoever you are.

I realize that it's *this* car that's equipped with the siren, making everyone move out of its way as it speeds me to my demise. *How the hell did Curtis get his hands on a car with a siren?*

I scrunch myself up even more, wincing as the car skims rough surface. I'm bearing the full brunt of bump-bump-bump vibrations that make me think we're crossing through a construction site or over cobblestones or bricks. I pound the roof even harder. If there are construction workers out there, maybe they'll hear. *Over the shriek of the siren? Forget it, I'm dead meat.*

My stomach churns as I recognize the smell permeating the trunk. Meat smells like this when it's been left out in the air to defrost too long and gone bad. A sharp turn pitches me against something sharp. I cry out and fold my arms under me protectively. The skin on my hands stings from friction burns. I couldn't hold a sculpting tool or a pencil or a cell phone if my life depended on it. My life *does* depend on it.

He's stopped. This is it.

I hear a car door slam. I could kick him when he swings open the trunk, just straighten out my legs like I'm stretching and catch him hard right in the nuts. My legs are tucked up under me now; all I have to do is swing on my back and jack-knife them out at him and he'll be Blue Boy while I make it to safety. I hold my breath at the sound of approaching foot-steps. *This is it.* A metallic click welcomes the key into the lock over my head and I see daylight and the flash of a white smock smeared with something that reminds me of clay. He must have pulled it over the uniform before he got out of the car. Curtis leans over me appraising the damage done to me *so* far, holding the tip of his knife up to the cleft in my chin. "Don't make a sound or you're going back in and *staying* there," he warns as he reaches in for me. I count one-two-three-*kick*. My legs stay locked in semi-fetal position and tin-gle painfully. Curtis grabs my left arm and thrusts his beefy other arm under my legs. I feel fingers reach up and give me a hurried grope in a part of me that isn't insensate. *Why'd I have to wear a damn dress.* I squirm and he swings me down to my feet. I stagger and fall.

"Get up!" he orders, looking around to see who might be watching. I follow his gaze and spot the big brown eyes of a black and white Holstein painted on the side of a white-washed building down the block, but no human eyes staring in this direction. *No witnesses.*

I make like I'm even more dazed than I am, looking up and down the street at boarded-up buildings, most of them scarred brick representing every shade of red. Even the *street surface* is overlaid unevenly in red brick, glistening with spillage from cars and trucks parked front to back against loading docks. Graffitied door grates are all that break the block pattern. A sign down the corner advertises Fresh Cuts.

"Get up before somebody comes!" Curtis hauls me to my feet and digs the point of the blade against my back to prompt me to *move* it, inflicting another fresh cut. I yelp. "And *shut up*, for Christ's sake."

"Where are you taking me?"

"*Apparently* you didn't read my invitation. Where's your *artistic curiosity*, Delilah? I'm disappointed in you. Well, once you see *this*, *you* aren't going to be disappointed." He pushes me in front of him toward a sealed door, pinning me against the building with the point of the blade. He reaches in his pocket with his free hand and retrieves a key ring that jingles like a tambourine as he riffles through the assortment of keys looking for the one he wants. "A private showing, just for *you, how about* that?" He inserts the key and pulls up the grate. I see a trio of men in white smocks just like *his* walking over to a truck parked in front of a dumpster at the corner and wonder what it would take to divert their attention from what they're doing. A show of legs, maybe. *Thank God I'm wearing a dress.* I wiggle my butt against the back of the building while Curtis shoves the metal door up and feel my dress ride up by inches. Not that there were that many inches of it there to begin with. I notice one giving another a hey-will-ya-look-at-*that* elbow poke while the third reaches into the cab to retrieve something. The wagon tilts back and relieves itself of its load of scraps into the dumpster. Curtis unlocks a glass-paned door and gives it a shove. "After you." He propels me inside with his bent knee and pulls a chain, lighting a bare bulb suspended from a ceiling beam.

I look around. No masterpieces here, not that I expected any; just piles of stripped lumber that once must have been walls. The damp floorboards creak under Curtis' heavy step as he retreats to pull a dark shade over the glass. I look down and see marbleized scraps of something that doesn't look like wood. I step around the pile and stoop down. Curtis gives me a yank, hurling me to the ground. The stench makes me glad I didn't have time to eat this morning. Nothing to throw up. Curtis takes my right arm and drags me along the blood-stained floorboards. He stops just short of a stairwell going down. "You want to see my work or don't you?"

I don't think the latter is an option here. I nod wearily and crawl over to the railing to get my balance before I can stand. Once I go downstairs, there's *no way* I'm going to get back up to safety. There's *no way* I'm going to get out of here alive.

This is it, I'm going to die.

Curtis thought ahead. He probably even stole the *flashlight* in his pocket from the cop he assaulted on Fifth Avenue. After making sure that I tramp in front of him, he lets the beam glance off every couple of steps so I won't fall and break my neck before I see his exhibit. A Soho gallery this *isn't*. It doesn't even come close to being an out-of-the-way Chelsea garage. Either Curtis thinks he can corner a new art market in this district as others have started to do or he's crazy. *Either way, he's crazy.* He pulls another ceiling chain. "Almost there, Delilah." He prods me in front of a door that makes me think of a safe. *I'm not going to be safe in there.* The rusty handle moans as he pushes down on it. I moan too. Curtis glares at me, then his look softens as he shoves the door open, as if he expects me to soften too, once I'm pleased by what I see inside. I don't see anything yet. The smell is enough to kill me. I hear thumping against the wall as Curtis fumbles around for the light switch and I take a step backward, then another. Fat fingers burrow deep into my arm. "Where d'you think you're going, huh?"

"Want to be in a position to get a better look," I croak.

"You'll see fine." He doesn't let go, just drags me along with him as he gropes along the wall. I close my eyes and then I hear a *click*, like the snap of a camera. *Someday somebody's going to snap this crime scene. I wish it would have been before I was part of it.* My teeth dig into my lower lip to keep from screaming. There's no telling *what* Curtis will do to me if I scream. The reek of meat long removed from hooks still haunts the room. Tacked on sheet rock is a mini-gallery of drawings of someone who might be me. They don't look much like me, but few drawings *ever have* looked much like me. Most of *these* look less like me than usual. I can picture some being torn out of sketch pads in unlocked studios. Where did he get them? How long has he had them? Did he do any of them himself? Mounted next to them are putrefied human fingers, five of them, spread in a way to suggest they were about to touch their subject but lopped off before they could defile her. I back away, but even before Curtis can stop me, my heel jams against something hard. I look down at the plaster head I did of Ivan, leaning on its side on a pillow of sawdust on the floor, its eyes gouged out. Next to them are two armatures, their wire heads unraveled, sticking upward and out, like the hair on Einstein's head, ready to receive clay. *Or a live body.* It doesn't take a genius to guess where they came from.

And this is his best show yet. That's how he advertised it to me on the phone three nights ago. *This* one is going to be my best *yet,* he promised, and I'm showing it to you and *only* you.

And *then* what?

I cross my arms in front of me and stare at the wall, making like I'm at the Guggenheim trying to interpret what I'm seeing. *What I'm seeing is my life flash before my eyes.* A glance at Curtis reassures me he's buying it, at least for now; all I have to do to stay alive is act *real* interested, like *this is the best goddamn exhibit I've ever seen,* this is what he wants from me right now, some *art* appreciation. I emit a long "Hmmmm." It keeps me from retching.

"I did some of the drawings, from memory," he brags,

brazenly looking me over, taking in flank, ribs, rump like the butcher he's proven himself to be. The body parts adhered to the drawings are just framework; he's not paying attention to them. "What do you think?"

"I...I don't know what to say," I choke. "I'm at a loss for words." His glowering stare tips me off that I better say something. "Wha...what gave you the idea of doing *all* your work around a central theme, um, *subject?*"

"My subjects seem to *demand* attention," he retorts, "and *lots of* it. They comport themselves in a way they know will guarantee it. I'm only giving them their due. A one-woman show." His stare makes me feel like bugs are crawling all over me. "I put my subjects on a pedestal."

And then he literally rams it *right through* them.

My tongue flickers over my lips. It feels like sandpaper. "Where's the work from some of your *other* shows? I'd like to see that too."

"You can't. I locked up that body of work in a trunk." *With a body.* "Use your head, Delilah. Surely you of *all* people should understand. Are you going to show your *Greek*-influenced work along with your *Roman* show?"

"No, but I *have* them, they're all mixed up in my studio."

"Take a look around. Where do you think I'd *put* them? This is a new studio. Every new exhibit demands new space to show it in. I don't want reminders of past failures. Every artist sacrifices. Even *you*, Delilah. Remember," he pulls the wire on the armatures taut, "I've *been* in your studio."

And my apartment. And everywhere *else* I've been. *Where can he go from here?*

On to another victim and another studio. Once he's finished with me.

"You know, as an artist, I...I'm always curious what draws other artists to their subjects. Just as a matter of professional curiosity," I confess. "L..like, for example, why did Leonardo choose Mona Lisa, wha...what was the attraction?"

Why me?

"You want to know why I chose *you*? Why should it even *surprise* you? That's what you do for a living on the side, isn't it, pose bare-assed for anyone who asks, who's willing to pay? Is *that* what's got you so worked up, that you're not reaping anything out of it? Christ, you're beginning to sound like the first one..."

"The first one..."

"The stripper, the *whore* in that goddamn bar I went to who said I assaulted her. Dancing up there on the fucking bar with nothing on except a smile, sits on my goddamn lap, *ain't I just so cute*, officer? She's rip roaring drunk, not even a professional dancer, just a wannabe. She even modeled in that same art school *you* worked in Wednesday night, Delilah, started doing her bit right in front of that window, knowing everyone in the Academy's standing on tiptoe on the drilling pad, looking down at her, doesn't care. Now she dumps her girlfriend who gets pissed and leaves, wants all the fucking attention of everyone in the bar and all of a sudden gets *too much* of it, she's scared. Are *you* scared?" He looks me over and, guessing the answer, he laughs. "The guys all eating it up, sticking money in that lacy ass floss she's wearing, and she goes for me, thinking I'm gonna dole out the bucks too and anyway I'm better than them, I'm in uniform, I'm gonna *protect* her, right? I push her off. *Put some clothes on*, I'm telling her, you're going to get raped. Not that you're not *asking* for it. I wait for her and follow her out and insist, I'm gonna walk you home or you're gonna get raped; something *awful*'s going to happen to you. I walked her as far as the subway stop and I grabbed her like *this*." He lunges and his powerful hand wrench makes me scream. "What the hell's the matter with you, acting like that anyway? *You're sweet*, she tells me, then starts pressing up on me, reaching at me." He reaches for my hand, presses it against his pants. I jerk it away. "I ought to *give* you what you want so bad, I said to her. You want it so bad, baby, you're going to *get* it."

I don't want *any part* of this.

"*After*wards she starts to scream that she's going to go back there, get those guys in the bar to take care of me. The guys who were shoving money up your ass? How much did you make anyway? Look, I tell her, d'you have any idea what you were *doing* back there? You go back there, you're gonna get gang banged. She's crying now, making like she's a *victim* all of a sudden. *Pooor thing*," he sputters in my face. "Do you have *any* idea what *you* just did to me, she whines. Yeah, I tell her, I got you away from there. Next thing I know, the sniveling little bitch has Internal Affairs on my tail and I'm lucky I can get fucking *security* work after that. Working as a bouncer in a bar in Queens one night last winter, you'll never guess who walks in."

I can guess.

"That twat, that piece of art herself, with a *gentleman* friend. She didn't recognize me because I'd gained a lot of weight since our *last* meeting and besides, let's face it, she was *very* drunk when the *alleged incident* took place and she's not doing too bad right now either; she don't know her limitations. I'm watching her from the doorway. The guy she's with waves off the bartender; she's had enough, he tells him, but I know she hasn't. Next thing you know he's slapping her and I gotta step in and make sure he don't bust up the place. She still doesn't make like she recognizes me, she's *that* plastered. Bleeding besides. The guy she's with, he gave her a good smack before I told him to get out. It's one of those places that has a jukebox, and I put some coins in. I know it's only gonna be a matter of time before off come the clothes. Then I can get the One-One-Four down there, get her busted, but then I get a *better* idea." He leans in so close I can practically count the fillings in his mouth. "You'll never guess what I decide to do."

I don't want to guess.

"It wasn't planned, what I did. She just walked into it. I didn't think I was gonna see her again. I've gotten better at this. Like with Majesty. *She* didn't just walk into it. She'd be in the store window setting up all those mannequins and I'd rap at the window and wave. She starts posing like the dummies she's got dolled up in there. I knew I was going to see *her* again. I got it down to a science. The uniform helped me get as close as I wanted to be. I was wearing my security guard uniform the first time I saw *you*, Delilah. Around the same time. Didn't it make you feel safe to know there was a guard on duty while you were *hard at work?*"

I shrug. I don't remember.

"Time for *me* to get to work *now*. You're going to be impressed," he says, walking over to a row of paint containers covered with a sheet of plywood. I spin on my heels, ready to run. Curtis grabs a handful of hair and reels me back where he wants me. Every follicle on my head hurts. He slaps me for good measure. "You oughta be *used* to that. Didn't your asshole stockbroker slap you around? Didn't you like it? *All* you exhibitionist bitches like the rough stuff, *don't* you? Her. You. Majesty." He slaps me again and laughs. "Bet you like your sex rough too. Can't picture *that* tight-ass giving you what you wanted in *that* department though."

I put my hand up to my stinging cheek to ward off any more blows.

"Yes, he *did* hit me and I *didn't* like it. I stopped seeing him, *that's* how much I didn't like it."

"Well, I don't know about *that*, but *I* didn't like it and you're right about *one* thing, you're not seeing him any more because *no one* is."

He would know.

"No one saw Majesty's boyfriend again either. He disappeared just like *that.*" He snaps his fingers. "You'd think she would have appreciated it after what he did to her. You're *not* gonna tell me *you're* sorry, *are* you, Delilah? You don't *seem* very sorry. How sorry can you be when you're already spending your nights with someone *else?* Did the *cop* give you the kind of fuck you *wanted,* Delilah? You think I got rid of the competition just so you could fuck some *cop?* No, precious, that wasn't in my game plan. Only one way to keep you to myself now, and that brings us back to the subject of performance art." He puts his hands on my shoulders. "Move and you're dead."

If I *don't* move, I'm *still* dead. I still don't move.

"Why'd you kill Vittorio?" I gasp. "*He* never hurt anybody. He was *gay,* he was the sweetest, gentlest..."

"I *had* to get him. He was the man in that relationship. The way he was touching you, looked to me like he might swing the other way. Give *you* a sweet, gentle fuck. I was outside the restaurant the night you had dinner with your friends, *cara.* I saw *everything.* You know what you get if you fuck *gay* guys, Delilah? Even with condoms. They break. All those magazines you have in your apartment, you oughta know, all they got in them is articles about men, how to make yourself sexy to men, how to have sex with men. All the magazines *you* read, you oughta be a *pro,* Delilah."

Curtis takes off his wristwatch and places it on the floor within view, then he removes the plywood and kicks the containers toward me one after the other, not taking his eyes off me. Water sloshes over the side of them. He picks up another pail and dumps fine white powder in with the water, stirring it with a ruler. I shift my weight. He shoots up and grabs my wrists. "I think I'm going to have to tie you up while I do this," he says, grabbing a cord from the floor. "Hands

behind your back, like the good cop says," he orders, then
wrenches them back with a twist and coils the cord around
them. I cry out as he knots it at my ankles. "Not going anywhere *now, are* you?" He scoops his hands into something
white and gooey that drips down his sleeves all the way to his
elbows. As he comes toward me, I realize it's plaster. "This is
even more appropriate for *you* than it was for *her,* the one in
the bar," Curtis drones. "In *her* case, she was plastered to *begin*
with. You're a sculptor, you *work* with plaster, how appropriate that you become a *tool of your trade.*"

I think of Majesty Moore, the window display artist,
impaled with a mannequin stand, a *tool of her trade,* and look
warily in the direction of the armatures. "Oh, those. I'm not
going to resort to that unless I have to. That depends on
you, Delilah. Stand *real still* now." He approaches me with
palms outstretched. "I think you're gonna have to take off
your clothes for this to work. Come on, come on, what's the
matter? *Shy* all of a sudden? It's nothing you're not used to."

"I'm sorry," I twist back and forth. "I can't. My hands are
tied."

"I'm gonna untie you now long enough for you to undress.
Don't try anything you'll regret."

I concentrate on a distant siren, willing it to come closer.
I wonder if the police would use sirens if they were on their
way here. I wonder if they have any idea where I am. I was
sure I heard *some*one coming to my rescue before I was hus-
tled out into MacDougal Alley. *Where'd they go?* I close my
eyes as his gooey hands release me. I unbutton my dress and
feel the breeze as it falls to my feet. I don't want to watch
what comes next. Curtis slips his hand along the elastic band
of my bikini pants, yanks them down to my ankles. "You can
step out of them now." He pulls until I lift one foot, then the
other, then he deftly unhooks my bra and kicks the discard-
ed clothes to one side, then ducks down to get more plas-

ter. I bite my lip as he spreads his first gob over me, starting with my left shoulder up to the breast bone. The chill of the wet plaster, then Curtis' molding strokes make me cringe. After his fat fingers smooth the plaster down, he moves to the right. "Don't look so sad. You're about to become *living art*, Delilah."

So he's going to use me to make a life mask. Does this mean he's going to let me live?

"You didn't put cream on first," I protest. "You're not going to get it off without cracking it unless you put cream on first."

"Who said anything about it coming off?" I bite my lip as his touch gets more and more intimate. Making his hand like a spatula, he goes to work on my breasts, using one hand to apply, the other to smooth. "I can make them *bigger*," he mumbles, ladling it on thick. Excess plaster rolls off me in thick globs and spatters the floor around me like heavy wet snow. *He's not the first to enhance what isn't there.* He leaves huge dollops of plaster on my nipples, something that *doesn't need* enhancing, before moving around to the back. I cry out as Curtis rams a wad of plaster into my rear and spreads it over my buttocks. His wet hand goes over my mouth. "Doesn't taste too pleasant, *does* it?" he snarls. "You want a whole mouthful?" I shake my head from side to side. "Then shut up and let me work in peace. I'll *tell* you when you can talk, you *got that*?" I nod. "Good." I feel his hands cup my buttocks and I hold my breath, afraid of what *else* he might be thinking of ramming in there, then sigh as I feel his fingers work up my spine like a pianist, playing sticky scales up and down my vertebrae. The wet mix burns into my open wounds, bringing tears to my eyes.

"Gotta mix a new batch. You going to stand still for me?" He's not moving far enough away for me to go anywhere. He slakes the next mixture of plaster and immediately goes to work on my left arm, slathering plaster from shoulder to elbow and then down to my wrist in long, drawn-out strokes, indifferent to the white rivulets rolling down the crook of my elbow. My skin stings on contact, like I'm being stuck by needles, *lots* of them. When he finishes the left arm, he moves to my right side. "Hold it out," he commands. "Like *this*." He holds his arm straight out. "You're *not* gonna tell me you can't hold a pose, *are* you, Delilah?"

My arm buckles under the weight of the wet plaster almost the minute he starts applying it, and noticing my discomfort, he slaps on more. Most of it drips off. He's not using plaster gauze to hold it in place or doing any of the other things *normal* sculptors would do to cast from a live model; he has *no idea* how to make this work. "I'll tell you when you can let it drop." He looks down at his watch, then reaches in deep, laying it on even thicker now. "Okay, now, relax it. Just put it down by your side." He takes my fingers and swings my arm down where he wants it, making sure I don't make any unexpected moves. "Is that better?"

I nod.

"Hold out your fingers. Both hands. Like this." He splays his hand in my face. I bend and unbend my fingers before offering them, palm down, like I would to a manicurist. Like I would if I were to suddenly reach out and slap him. One by one my fingers get gloved in wet white plaster. He takes a step back, then another, takes a long appraising look.

"Can I see?"

"When I'm finished," he says, "I'll get you a mirror. Vain bitch. Move your legs apart." He crouches down, grabs my left ankle, and drags it across the wood floor. A splinter slides under my skin. "*Don't move*," he commands, not letting go of my ankle. I bite hard on my lip as I feel fingers encase one foot, then the other, then work up from the ankles to my knees, stroking my calves lasciviously, then crawling up over my knees, over my thighs. I involuntarily jerk away when I feel him approach the area I shave for-bikini-wear-only. *It's not beach season.* He takes a handful of hair and pulls. I scream.

"I gotta *finish*," he says. I don't try to hold back the tears as I feel Curtis pack the plaster down there. He rubs some of it back and forth. "Feel good?" I want to spit the gravely plaster on my lips in his face. Just as I'm again expecting him to do something *else* down there, he draws his hands away and holds them up to my face.

This is it, I'm going to die.

Death by suffocation. *Every* pore sealed. *Every part* of me. I'm beginning to feel like I've been wrapped with an electric blanket set on low with the heat rising by degrees every second. He smoothes the plaster over my cheeks caressingly, salon-gentle now, tracing it over my lips, my eyelids, my ears with strokes that tickle, like a lover's first hesitant kisses. His hands roam up and down my neck, over my chin, smooth out the worry lines in my forehead. *I'm beyond worry now.* "Put your hair up," he commands.

"I have nothing to hold it up with."

"I do." He reaches in his pocket and pulls out a couple of dark blond bobby pins. *The color of my hair even. He really does come prepared.* He steps behind me and yanks my hair up, like it *needs* any help at this point to be standing on end. I feel metal scratch my scalp as he secures my hair where he wants it with the bobby pins. *He could have gotten coated ones at least.* The wet plaster going on my head feels almost but not quite like shampoo. I wonder how I'm ever going to be able to get all this plaster off me. *I wonder if I'm going to live long enough to get this plaster off me.* I feel Curtis' fingers knead the stuff right down into the roots. He ends with flourishing strokes down the nape of my neck.

He steps back and looks at his finished product and *very* unprofessionally says, "Wow."

"Can I see?"

"Of *course* you can see. I *want* you to see. You're the main part of the exhibit. The *pièce de resistance*." If I had put up some *resistance*, would I be here now? Would I have been rescued? Or would I be dead? He reaches behind one of the barrels against the wall and grabs a hand mirror. "I had a floor-length mirror," he says almost apologetically, "but it broke."

"Well, you know what they say. Seven years bad luck." Too lenient a penalty for him. *Life in prison with no hope of parole.* He scans me with the mirror like it's a Geiger counter checking for radiation. I see white arms, white torso, white legs. My head looks like a blanched version of my clay Vestal Virgin. I wonder if I'd glow in the dark.

"I don't know *how* I'm going to improve on *this*," Curtis muses. "Have to take pictures to remember this by. Seen enough?"

I nod. More than enough.

He sets the mirror down where he got it and picks up a cheap-looking plastic camera and aims it at me. The unexpected flash blinds me. The plaster makes me not want to close my eyes. *I may never open them again.* Even *blinking* is risky business. I begin to see green spots floating in front of me as another, then *another* flash explodes in my face, then Curtis moves around for some rear views. My skin burns under the thick coat of caking plaster. I want to dig my nails in, gouge, claw my way through to flesh. And claw Curtis' flesh for good measure.

"It's starting to set," Curtis says, prodding my midriff, the spot the plaster has been for the longest, with a fingertip, the way I do when I'm testing cookie dough. He checks his watch and smiles. "Time for this to bake."

You don't fire plaster. I don't see a kiln or anything resembling a kiln in this room. This was once a meat freezer. Nothing was *ever* cooked in *here*. He picks up his watch and pulls it back on his wrist, releasing it with an impatient snap, then looks at it again, in a big hurry to clear the area now. *He's rigged something to go off very soon to bake me.* I don't hear ticking. I wouldn't. He'd *make sure* I wouldn't. It's all part of *artist's ego,* which in artists sometimes borders on *super*ego and obliterates the *id.*

Take this, *ego!* "I've got to...scratch!" I cry out as he walks toward the heavy steel door. "It itches *so much.*" I bend my fingers. Shards of caking plaster pelt the floor like hail. I reach under my arm and scrape along the curve alongside my left breast, consciously scooping as much plaster as I can with my stubby fingernails.

"Look what you're doing!" he shrieks.

"I can't help it! I can't stand it! It itches so much!"''

Curtis comes closer. "Don't fuck it up," he warns.

Or else what? "It *itches,*" I protest. "This one too." I go to work on the other side. "It itches *all over!*" I claw at the plaster indiscriminately. Curtis runs over and slaps me. "Stop it, bitch!" he screams. "You're *ruining* it!" How much of *it* does he expect to survive an explosion? I'm ruining his perception of what he's done, that's all, turning his success into a last-minute failure he'll remember as long as he lives. I bite my lip as he puts his hands out to hastily smooth everything over the way it *was.* He doesn't see it coming, my sudden swipes across my nipples where he layered it on so thick, my swift jabs to his eyes, blinding him to his *objets d'art.* "*Bitch!*" he screams, flailing around the room, a shipwrecked pirate groping helplessly for a life raft, a way out. My tacky hands stick to the metal handle. I lurch backwards and wrench it open. Curtis staggers toward me, shrieking, "Don't close it... *don't close it..*.I'll be..."

Well done. I thrust my weight against it until I hear a reassuring *click,* like the snap of a camera. I don't know how much time I have left or what kind of sound is going to follow. I lumber up the stairs, leaving sticky white footprints, tripping on the uneven steps, scraping my knees, stubbing my toes. I hear desperate thuds echo from the gallery of horrors, Curtis pounding his fists on the steel door. Someone will be back to see him when he's done, but it won't be me. My feet skim across the damp floorboards. I stop in front of the glass-paned door and thrust it open as the floor rumbles under me. The force of the aftershock catapults me outside. I look around me, dazed. There are blue-and-whites and unmarked cars and fire emergency vans parked from corner-to-corner and wall-to-wall cops looking in doorways and windows. They suddenly stop what they're doing, turn in my direction, and stare as if they've just seen a ghost.

Which is what I must look like to them.

I take a few tentative steps toward them before they break position. My legs wobble. I fold my arms over me, a useless shield against the cold and all those eyes looking in my direction. I'm suddenly conscious of my nakedness under the wet plaster suit I'm wearing, aware of how aware *they* must be as they come closer. I spot Quick in the crowd. He intercepts me before anyone else can lay their hands on me. "Get a blanket over here," he barks, easing me down to the ground. "Is he still in there?"

I nod. "Downstairs," I murmur, trying to wipe some of the guck off my lips, only making matters worse. "The door's locked. He set something to go off. I think it already *has* gone off..." I watch as a contingent of cops approach the building, guns drawn. Quick waves them back and radios for the bomb squad. I overhear one of the uniforms say, "Thought she was Venus when she came out of there."

"She got arms, though."

"She got *all* her working parts. Lucky for her."

"Yeah, just needs to be treated for overexposure."

An EMS paramedic in an FDNY jacket brings over a blanket. Quick nods and backs off, giving the paramedic room to crouch next to me. He covers me while another hauls a stretcher out of the van. I keep staring up at Quick. His laser-like eyes burn right through me, diverting my attention from the paramedics busily poking around at my arm. I have no idea what they're doing to me until the sharp sting of an IV needle tips me off. Quick's stare doesn't give *anything* away. He exchanges a few words with the EMS crew out of my hearing range and nods. My heavy-with-plaster eyelids feel even heavier. I hear Quick promise "I'll be by to see you later," before the ambulance door slams shut and my lights go out.

35

THE GLARINGLY WHITE WALLS IN THE ROOM I WAKE UP IN MAKE ME HAVE to shield my eyes, adjust to the light slowly. As I draw my hand away, I see that it's flesh tone, marred only by the bullseye of a bruise where the IV needle stuck me. I don't remember any of the deplastering and wonder if and how it all came off. *I remember everything that came before.*

A nurse sticks her head in the door. "How are we doin' in here?" she coos in a soothing Jamaican accent. I nod, but before I can say anything, she ducks back out. I hear voices in the corridor, her soft voice lilting like a song, interrupted by a male voice that makes my heart beat so fast that its defibrillations would soar off the top of a cardiac monitor if I were hooked up to one. Quick steps into the room and gives the white curtain a yank even though the bed next to mine is unoccupied. The dark circles under his eyes look like bruises. He looks like *he* could use some emergency care. "You doing okay?"

I nod. "Was he...Curtis..."

"His name was actually Curtiz, Curtiz Szabo, and yes, he's dead," Quick affirms. "He planted a pipe bomb under the floorboards. When it blew, it took him down with it. Him and a *whole lot of* meat. That's how we traced his whereabouts, the lab tests we ran on some of our blood evidence was IDed as nonhuman, specifically beef blood. He gave it up to us some more the last time he left a voice mail message by calling you a piece of meat. But none of this should have happened, at least not the way it did, and I'm sorry about that." He clears his throat. "The Ten-Thirteen, it caught us off-guard."

"What was…oh, the injured officer?"

He nods. "Someone was supposed to stay in the building *no matter what,* but in the rush to get him to Bellevue while we thought he still had a chance…"

"How is he?"

Quick looks away from me, toward the drawn curtain. "He didn't make it."

I bite my lip. "I'm sorry."

Quick's left hand squeezes the side rail of the bed. When his knuckles stop showing white, I look up at him again. "The antigen testing wasn't the only thing that led us to his door. You left some clues for us," he says, his hand dipping into his pocket. He pulls out the pencil I picked up from the floor in the drawing studio *and* my zig zag saw *and* my cut-out tool. No fettling knife, no sabre saw; *they* must be lost forever. He holds them out to me.

"They must have fallen out when he lifted me out of the trunk," I say.

"This helped us close in on his location. This and some guys working in the meat plant down the street who said they thought they saw someone take a hooker into one of these buildings." *Thank God I did* decide *to wear a dress. Never* mind what *they thought I was.* The corners of Quick's eyes start twitching. "That didn't jibe. They were talking good-looking female hooker, and this isn't an area known for hookers any more and when it was, they were males in drag. You came out before we even had a chance to come in after you." He gazes at me in such a way that I feel I'm still that plaster goddess. "How'd you manage to get away from him?"

I feel blood rush to my cheeks and look down at the rumpled bedclothes piled high on my chest. "Things came to a head. The opportunity just presented itself. I...I don't remember exactly..."

"You did good. You're *alive*."

I nod. "Oh, uh, by the way, how's your sister?"

His jaw tightens, and I wonder if I've said the wrong thing. "Holding her own. I'm getting her checked into an inpatient facility," he says. "Right here in Manhattan. Better supervision and it'll be easy for me to stop by and see her. She'll be okay." I can tell by looking at him that he might as well add, *I hope.* "I'm sorry about how *that* worked out *too*."

"I guess it could have been worse."

"Yes, it could have." He turns to go, then stops. "Delilah," he says, wheeling around to face me, holding my sculpting tools up in front of me like he would if they were going to be Exhibit A and B in some criminal trial, "what the *hell* did you think you were going to be able to do with *these any*way?"

I shrug. It's a safe bet I'm not getting them back from him. *I don't need them any more.* "It's a *good* thing you didn't decide to get a *gun* to defend yourself with," he says. "You would have been in *big* trouble." *As if I weren't in trouble enough as it is.* I flush, recalling Heidi Obermeyer's after-hours target lessons. I *could* have shot Curtis; he *wasn't* a work of art. I would have done *any*thing to survive.

"You can't be upsetting her." The Jamaican nurse's singsong voice hits an off key as she brushes by Quick, carrying a draped tray. "I was just leaving," Quick says, backing away from my bed. He gives the side rail a pat. "Take good care of her." He watches as the nurse strips the towel from the tray with an abracadabra smoothness and swabs at the crook of my elbow with an alcohol pad. Watching his retreating back upsets me more than anything he said or could have said to me, hurts more than the prick of the needle piercing my skin. *I don't need him any more either.* I wonder if *he's* thinking this too.

36

"I DON'T BLAME YOU. IT WASN'T *YOUR* FAULT," MORGAN BLURTS OUT WHILE we're waiting in line in the West Broadway café he suggested we go to for a quick fix. In the week I've been out of the hospital, every minute of my life has been spent finishing up work on my sculptures and moving the pieces to the Soho loft in time for the exhibit. I don't know what I would have done without Morgan's help, and I've felt guilty because what happened to Morgan's life happened *because* of me. I'm relieved he brought it up first. "I didn't want to upset you with it," he says, "because you've been doing so good getting your shit together for the exhibit. I figured the last thing you needed was to be reminded of what you went through."

"I was afraid after what happened to Vittorio..."

"Curtiz killed Vittorio, *you* didn't. He would have killed you too, if you hadn't got away. I'm glad you got away."

"Thanks." I give his arm a squeeze. "*I'm* glad I got away *too*." I take a few tentative steps as the line moves. "Anyway, I certainly wasn't the first and I wouldn't have been the last. *You* read the stories in the *Daily News*. I saw them in your studio. Front page, two days running, nothing bigger bumped it. They found the name of his *next* intended with his remains, a runway grunge model *and* the names and addresses of all those near and dear to *her*."

"Snooping in my studio," Morgan tsk-tsks. "Shame on you." He frowns at the menu board behind the counter and decides on a latte and a heart-shaped shortbread cookie. "*They* didn't tell you everything?"

I know who *they* refers to, someone tall and dark and good-looking and close-mouthed.

I shrug. "Trying to protect me after the fact, I guess."

"To compensate for the half-assed job they did when it counted. What're you going to have?"

I order a triple cappuccino. Morgan does a double take. "Whew, you're going to be flying."

"I've got to get this work done," I sigh. "We're having an *opening* tomorrow." I take a slug of cappuccino the minute it's served to me. "And I got all this unexpected advance publicity...I'm not sure *what* to expect."

"I'll be there for you, *bella*." We sit at the counter facing the street within the frame of the triangular design featuring a roasting globe decaled on the window. "You don't have to worry about that." Morgan clears his throat between sips of his latte, "Okay if I bring somebody?"

I frown. "Somebody as in..."

"We're just friends. For now. I'm just lonely. I was living pretty dangerously for a few days there. Raoul and others...anyway, I'm going to get tested, Delilah. This afternoon. I'm going to be tested and retested until I know there's nothing wrong with me." The latte makes a foamy mustache on Morgan's lip, makes him look rabid. "I don't want to hurt anybody."

I put my hand over his. "I'll be there for *you too*. *Whatever* happens."

"You'll never guess who called me to see how you were." Morgan breaks off a piece of cookie and hands it to me. "Sachi."

I frown. "Let's see...hmmm, do I know someone named Sachi? Name rings a bell, but I can't remember the face." I stuff the morsel of cookie in my mouth. "*Either one* of them."

Morgan laps up the last of his latte and waits for me to finish my cappuccino. "You going back to work now? I'll be there to help you soon as I..."

"I'll manage." I squeeze his arm again before we head off in different directions. The chill makes me pull my anorak closer. It feels like winter already. If I manage to sell some pieces of sculpture, I'm going to invest in a heavier coat. I look to my left and right and behind me. Force of habit. *At least there's no one out here in the street responsible for giving me these chills.* A dark car suddenly stops short at the corner of West Broadway and Prince Street, the tires grazing against the curb with a loud rasp. I stand on the corner like a statue.

The driver shouts "Del*i*lah!" through the passenger window. I walk over to the car tentatively, recognizing its bad paint job, its stained, cracked upholstery, the driver's voice. "I stopped by Lafayette," Quick says. "They told me you went for coffee and where."

I smile nervously. *Detective Quick, are you stalking me?* "I was just on my way back."

"I have to swing back that way. I'll drop you off. Get in."

I settle in the seat next to him, avoiding the damp spot next to an empty coffee cup. "Royko," he grumbles, tossing the cup in the back seat. The interior of the car is nice and warm and I feel even warmer. "How're you doing?"

"Better than I was the *last* time you saw me."

"The people over at Downtown Hospital, are they doing a follow up on you for post-traumatic stress?"

"They talked to me about it and gave me some referrals."

"*Use* them."

"If I need to..."

"You *will*," he says adamantly. No ifs, buts, or maybes. He hangs a left on Spring Street. "When all the excitement of the exhibit blows over. When you stop being so busy."

I nod.

"It looks good," he says. "Your exhibit. What I saw of it."

"Thanks. Want to come up and see the rest?"

"I can't now. I'm on the job," he pats the steering wheel as if I need a reminder that this clunker doesn't belong to him. "Tomorrow," he says softly.

"You coming to the opening?"

"Tomorrow's my RDO," he says. I frown. "My day off. I should be able to make it." He pulls up to the curb, sparing the tires this time. "Before you go up, I've been meaning to warn you. I may call you if we need you to do a drawing for us some time."

I nod as I open the car door. "I could do that."

He smiles then, a rare top-hat-and-tuxedo smile that he dusted off just for this occasion. "I may call you even if we *don't*."

AUTHOR'S NOTE

I hope you enjoyed reading *Over My Live Body* as much as I enjoyed writing it. It's the first in a series of crime novels involving sculptor Delilah Price and Detective Patrick Quick as well as a motley crew of artist friends (and frenemies) and police personnel. At the beginning of my second novel, *Student Bodies*, Delilah has a lot on her mind; in order to survive as an artist in New York City, she applied for a job as a substitute teacher, which will leave her with less time to sculpt. Her first assignment is as a substitute for a substitute at a middle school in Brooklyn. The previous substitute failed to show up and is soon declared a missing person. On her way to the school the morning of her first day on the job, Delilah witnesses a teenage girl falling to her death from a subway platform. Several witnesses claim she was pushed. The girl turns out to be a student at the school where Delilah has been hired to teach. The environment there is anything but conducive to a positive learning experience. Delilah increasingly notices that female students seem intimidated by a tenured faculty member who seems to have a way with the ladies or at least acts like he thinks he does.

Her romantic interest, Detective Patrick Quick, is distracted. He's busy working a case, tracking down a serial rapist who had been attacking transient women on the Lower East

Side and Alphabet City. The most recent attacks, however, have been on young women in Greenwich Village and SoHo, and one of the victims is Delilah's fair weather friend Sachi. Quick and other detectives working the serial rapist case had been convinced that the suspect was a recidivist who was released from Riker's Island not long before the attacks began, but while there have been other cases matching the same M.O., some of the evidence in the Greenwich Village/ SoHo incidents doesn't match and Quick considers the possibility of a second rapist. That second rapist may be too close to Delilah for comfort.

I welcome comments from my readers, which can be sent to me at susanisraelbooks@gmail.com as well as on Facebook at:
https://www.facebook.com/pages/Susan-Israel-books/1422085928004817.

Be safe out there,

Susan

ABOUT THE AUTHOR

Susan Israel lives in Connecticut with her beloved dog, but New York City lives in her heart and mind. A graduate of Yale College, her fiction has been published in *Other Voices*, *Hawaii Review* and *Vignette* and she has written for magazines, websites and newspapers, including *Glamour*, *Girls Life*, *Ladies Home Journal* and *The Washington Post*. She's currently at work on the second book in the Delilah Price series, *Student Bodies*.